PRAISE FOR WE WERE HERE

"Daisy Prescott's *We Were Here* is a brilliant, nostalgic, emotional journey that takes you back to a time when all the firsts in life meant something—and set the course for journeys unknown. You'll have a 'book hangover' long after reading this funny, poignant story."—*New York Times* and *USA Today* bestselling author Julia Kent

"This story has it all! Just like a mix tape; we get a dose of steamy romance, angsty ballads and sweet love songs woven together in a compelling, heartwarming and sometimes heart-wrenching journey of self-exploration."—*New York Times* and *USA Today* bestselling author Helena Hunting

"*We Were Here* takes the characters we met in *Geoducks* and gives us their individual backstories in such a clever, engaging, emotional way. Set in the early 90's, Prescott shares with us the tender, driven, hilarious, heart filled and hard college experiences."—Erika, Goodreads Reviewer

WE WERE HERE

Adrienne's kickass mix

Daisy Prescott

A—

You are the
Salt to my
Pepa. xo Daisy Prescott

ebook ISBN: 978-0-9864177-4-0
Paperback ISBN: 978-0-9864177-1-9

Cover Design by ©Sarah Hansen
Front Cover Photo: ©DavidTB/Shutterstock
Editing: Melissa Ringsted at There for You Editing
Proofreading: Marla Esposito at Proofing with Style
Interior Design and Formatting: Christine Borgford at Perfectly Publishable

To Neil Diamond:
Thanks for all the memories.

"The past is never dead. It's not even past."
~ William Faulkner

PROLOGUE

"Don't You Forget About Me"
Simple Minds

LIZZY

"DID OWEN INVITE you to the screening?" Quinn drops his backpack next to Maggie's chair.

We're sitting around our table in the dining hall in Evergreen's student union, aka the college activities building everyone simply calls the CAB. Thursdays are the only day our schedules align for lunch this quarter. Typically, we take advantage of the time to catch up and plan for the weekend.

Before I can protest, Quinn steals half of my sandwich and has most of it stuffed in his mouth in a single bite.

"He did. I think he got us all." Maggie swats his hand away from her Diet Coke.

"Are we going?" Jo leans in front of Ben to see the rest of the group, but he barely notices because his head's stuck in a finance book. He's studying for business school non-stop these days even though he's already been accepted to Harvard.

"Do we have to? I'm not sure I'm ready to see my freshman self again. It's too soon." Selah's hair has changed more than anything else over the past four years. Currently, it's in a shaggy, punk rock pixie cut.

"We promised when we signed up we'd see it through to the bitter, bitter end." Quinn grins at her scowl.

"We were freshmen when we agreed to be filmed every year for his documentary. I was barely eighteen and hadn't voted in a presidential election yet. I believe that means I wasn't an adult, and therefore incapable of giving consent." Maggie picks at her salad.

"Come on, guys, think of how fun this will be. Our lives and friendships captured on VHS for eternity. Owen could become the next Spielberg and we'll all end up in the Smithsonian." Quinn's blue eyes dance with dreams of fame and notoriety.

"What's going to be fun?" Gil sits down at the far end of the table. Maggie's glance flicks over to him for a second, then returns to her salad plate.

"Owen's documentary is showing tonight," Jo explains.

"The one we started as freshmen?" Gil shakes his head. "No way. Lived it. Don't need to watch it."

"Really?" Maggie focuses her attention on him.

"Don't you remember my glasses?" He draws large circles around his eyes.

"Didn't you have a mullet, too?" Selah runs her hand over his dark shoulder-length hair. He's the poster boy for grunge music in his thrift store cardigan and faded Levis. Today's shirt is one of those old golf shirts with the little penguin over his heart. I remember my dad wearing them.

He leans away to escape her petting. "It was an awkward period all around. You try growing out your hair and not have a mullet at some point."

"I'm not taking no for an answer. We're all going. We're almost done with college. The time for nostalgia and reminiscing is upon us. These are the days . . ." Quinn sings the last sentence, and we all groan.

"I'll go." Ben finally joins the conversation. "We all should go. Quinn's right. It's the end of an era. We'll never be this young and stupid again. We might as well enjoy it while we can."

"Ben speaks." Quinn pats him on the back. "Okay, we'll meet

outside the theater at seven-thirty sharp."

"The documentary doesn't start until eight." Selah pulls the invitation out of her satchel and points at the time.

"I know, dear, but some of us are always late." He nods toward Maggie.

Maggie glares at him. "I'm not always late."

"Okay, Caterpillar."

"You mean the White Rabbit. Quit mixing your metaphors." Selah corrects him.

I smile at the use of her nickname from our first year.

It's highly probable I might be the only one looking forward to seeing our friendships and lives as they evolved over the past four years. The same good-hearted bickering that's seen us through countless dramas, failed love affairs, growing pains, and endless nights talking continues around the table.

With graduation a few weeks away, I'm trying to capture every moment and save them away for later. Who knows where our lives will take us or what fate has in store for us in the future. I want to stay in the present for as long as possible.

"I say we go to Lucky's before the screening for reinforcements." My suggestion is met with semi-enthusiastic agreement around the table. Jo volunteers Ben to buy a round to make up for always being boring lately. This earns her a high five from Quinn, and a grumble from Ben.

Lucky's is really a bar in Olympia called The Four Leaf Clover. Quinn renamed it freshman year when they stopped carding on a regular basis.

After wrapping the remainder of my giant chocolate chip cookie in my napkin, I stuff it in my bag. "Lucky's at seven. Nostalgia at eight."

MOST OF THE senior class mills around outside the theater. After grabbing snacks, we find a row of seats in the center. Quinn sits in the middle, hogging his huge bucket of popcorn with extra butter.

Owen stands at the front of the theater in a green corduroy jacket and Buddy Holly style glasses. "Four years ago, we began our journey of self-discovery at college."

"Is this going to be the feel good version of the Gettysburg Address? Four score and—"

Jo cuts off Quinn by placing her hand over his mouth. "Shh."

"Every quarter, I interviewed a handful of my fellow students. I asked them the same set of questions. These are our stories. Yours. Ours. Our collective history. These are our lives."

"Like sands through—" This time Selah stuffs a handful of popcorn in Quinn's mouth to silence him.

"Of course I had to edit this film down from its original six hours . . ." Owen drones on.

"Six hours?" Ben moves to stand, but Jo holds him back with her hand on his arm.

" . . . I think you'll find the final ninety-minute version captures the universal human coming of age journey into adulthood."

"Is he for real?" Maggie asks.

"Shh," we all shush her.

"Enjoy!" Owen finally finishes his speech to a smattering of applause.

"Why didn't we bring a flask?" Jo mumbles and eats some of Quinn's popcorn.

"Who said we didn't?" Quinn holds out his large soda. "Careful. It's a little strong."

We pass the spiked soda down the row and back as the lights dim and our lives flash before us on the big screen.

MAGGIE

Maggie Marrion, 18

French Literature
Freshman (Freshwoman? Freshperson? First year?)

What's your first memory of college?

Feeling anything was possible.
Freedom.

Oh, you mean literally?

Meeting the people who would become my closest friends. I can't imagine college or life without them.

ONE

"We Belong"
Pat Benatar

MY FIRST WEEK of college at Evergreen was a blur. Parental drop-off. Meeting my new roommate Jennifer. Getting used to co-ed dorms. Adjusting to having classes at random times and not a straight schedule through from morning to afternoon. Since I had three hours between classes on Tuesdays and Thursdays, I decided I should find a job to fill the time.

Which was how I found myself spending an afternoon at the library, interviewing with the circulation desk manager. He wore a tie with a cardigan. Most of my professors so far hadn't even worn ties.

After being quizzed about the Dewey Decimal system, and failing, I returned to my room in shame. At this rate, if I wanted to work on campus, I'd be washing dishes in the dining hall. Nothing could be grosser than the used food and unclean dishes of thousands of college students. I gagged at the thought as I opened our door.

Inside, Jennifer—my perfectly nice and perfectly normal roommate—was straddling a guy on my desk chair, making out.

She might have been trying to eat his face. I couldn't really tell in the two seconds I stared at them before clamping my eyes shut. I know I spied her tongue. Outside of her mouth. All I could see of him were his dark hair, long legs, and brown Wallabee boots.

Panicked about interrupting something, and simultaneously feeling like a prude, I backed my way through the open door. After it quietly clicked close, I pressed my head against the cool metal.

I could go back to the library, except I left there ten minutes ago. The dorm lounge was an option, but this time of day meant it would be filled with some random club. I couldn't remember if Thursday's meeting was German Lovers or Save the Geoducks—our school mascot. Neither appealed to me.

I stared harder at the painted metal, wishing the make-out session on the other side would end sooner rather than later.

"Are you locked out?" The blond guy from down the hall rested his head on the bulletin board next to my room. "Or are you praying?"

Pressing my cheek on the door, I twisted to see him more clearly.

"It's okay if you are. Pray if you've got to."

"I'm not. Just thinking."

A loud moan sounded from inside the room. "Oh, oh, oh God."

"Sounds like someone in there is praying." His lips curled into a smile. "You might want to step away, lest someone think you're a pervert for eavesdropping."

I jumped away from the door. "I wasn't listening!"

Chuckling, he held up his hands in defense. "Not judging you. Praying and voyeurism both have their places, usually in Madonna videos."

Another not so soft groan carried from my room. I took a step farther away. My favorite black on black Swatch showed the time as four o'clock. Too early to go to dinner. *Looks like I'll be going to the lounge after all.*

"You want to come hang out in my room until they finish whatever they're doing in there?" His offer sounded genuine and his smile was more than friendly. He gestured over his shoulder to the open door across the hall and down a few rooms. "I can promise you my roommate isn't in there making out with anyone. We should be safe."

"Okay." I followed him into his room. Weird, abstract, colorful art prints decorated one wall above a messy bed with black and white graphic sheets. The other side had a big poster of skiing in Colorado; Star Wars sheets covered the bed. Both sides were cluttered, but not bio-hazard boy gross.

"Guess which side is mine." My new friend leaned against one of the matching desks.

I studied him. He wore faded Levis and a Depeche Mode concert T-shirt. His blond hair was shaggy and wild. Paint splatters covered his well-worn Vans and his jeans. And his arms. Paint dotted everything.

"You're the colorful side." I pointed to his bed. "Not the nerd."

"The girl wins a prize. I'm Quinn Dayton, by the way."

I realized we skipped introductions and went right to discussing his bed. "I'm Maggie Marrion, the praying pervert."

"Hi, Maggie. Have a seat." He gestured around the room with a sweeping motion. "Probably best not to sit on that bed."

I sat in the same desk chair being occupied in my room. Unlike Quinn's desk, this one had neatly stacked books, a new Macintosh computer, a pile of floppy discs, and pens lined up in a row.

"Don't let the nerdy sheets and computer fool you, Gil's a cool guy."

"Your roommate's name is Will?" I must have misheard him.

"No, Gil like the fish."

I furrowed my brows. "He's named after a fish gill?"

"No, it's Gilliam."

"Gilliam." I nodded as if in agreement. Okay. He seemed like a nice, normal enough guy who probably liked to ski, loved Star Wars, had his own computer, and was neat about his pens.

"So, Maggie, tell me your life story."

I blinked, trying to think of something clever to say about myself. "Well, um, I . . . hmm."

"Sounds fascinating so far. You want a soda?" He moved toward the little dorm fridge tucked in the corner.

"Sure."

"Pepsi, Coke, or Blue Soda?"

"What's blue soda?"

"It's a soda that's blue. Flavor is under discussion." He held up a short glass bottle of bright blue, fizzy liquid.

"I'll have a Coke. Diet if you have it."

"Regular okay? Or I can get you a Tab out of the vending machine. Although I'm not sure how long it's been in there. Probably from the seventies, because who really drinks Tab anymore?"

I took the can from him.

"Let's get back to the fascinating life of Maggie." He sat on his bed, tucking a pillow behind himself. "I believe you were about to tell me about your first boyfriend."

I sputtered and almost spit out my sip of soda. "I was not!"

Shrugging, he grinned like the Cheshire Cat. "I figured you could skip to the good part, but by all means begin at infancy."

"There's not much to tell. I grew up in Washington."

"Child of divorce?"

"No, parents still married."

"Arrested at thirteen for organizing a shoplifting ring, but had the records sealed by juvie?"

"Never stolen anything." I sipped my Coke, trying not to laugh at this odd guy and his strange questions.

"You must have done something interesting by now. Otherwise, why would you end up at this weird school? If you were boring, you'd be at Washington State or UW, pledging a sorority and crimping your hair."

"I wanted something different."

"Or to be someone different?" His clever eyes studied me.

"Something like that. I want to see the world outside of Washington, go to Paris, eat bread and cheese by the Seine . . ."

"Ah, now we're getting somewhere. You're a romantic. Do these life goals involve a beret wearing, bicycle riding Frenchman?"

My cheeks heated. "In high school I bought a poster of a couple kissing on the street in Paris. It's an old black and white photograph— the most romantic thing. Like an old movie."

He picked up a pad of paper from a stack on his desk, then scribbled something with a nub of a pencil while I talked about romance and Paris. "Is this it?"

A loose sketch of the kiss I described filled the page, including the

Hôtel de Ville in the background.

"How did you know?" I asked, stunned. It was a beautiful drawing, almost prettier than the photograph. "Can I keep it?"

"It's yours. My friend had the same poster."

"You're an artist?"

"I want to be. Most of the stuff I make is garbage."

I studied the lines of his drawing. "This isn't garbage."

"It's only a copy of someone else's talent. Unless I want to become a forger or commercial sell-out, I need something original that's all mine. There's nothing wrong with an arts and crafts fair landscape painter whose work is destined to hang above plaid couches in suburban tract homes, but it's not my calling. I need to be original."

"You seem pretty original to me. I can't even finger paint."

"You are still a little caterpillar."

"I am?"

"You're not ready to be a butterfly, but someday you will. Now let's talk about your clothes."

I screwed up my face in confusion. "My clothes?" This was the weirdest conversation ever.

"What kind of statement are you going for with the flower skirt and baggy sweater? With your long red hair, I'm guessing a slightly more modern Anne of Green Gables."

I tugged at my favorite oatmeal colored sweater. Small pink roses decorated my black skirt. "Statement?"

"With the black tights, I thought you might've been the kind of girl who prays at her door."

"I had an interview this afternoon."

"And you wore that?" His face and his voice held nothing but disapproval. "What were you interviewing for? Spinster?"

"A part time job at the library. For the circulation desk."

"Librarian was my second guess. Well, you should get the job since you dressed the part perfectly."

"What's wrong with it?" I smoothed out the full skirt.

"You look like you're thirty and driving a mini-van with a 'baby on board' sign." He narrowed his eyes at me. "You're too pretty for such nonsense."

"You're very opinionated." Feeling defensive, I set down the can and stood up. "Thanks for the Coke and your thoughts on my outfit."

"Don't go away mad. I'm being mean. I'm not really a mean guy. I apologize. I did say you were pretty."

Flattered but still confused, I didn't know what to do. I didn't want to talk about myself anymore. I couldn't go back to my room. Sighing, I sat down again.

"What's your deal, besides art?" I turned the tables on him.

"My dad is a retired Marine. We moved around a lot when I was little before settling in Oceanside, north of San Diego. That's where I went to high school and discovered I enjoyed rebelling against all things conformity. My dad wasn't thrilled. Especially when I pierced my ear with a safety pin and an ice cube, then passed out and hit my head. I needed ten stitches." He lifted his hair, revealing a line near his temple.

"You pierced your own ear? That's so punk rock."

He beamed with pride. "That's exactly what I was going for. Unfortunately, unless I wanted to be on restriction for all of high school, I had to lose the earring."

"You could get it pierced now. What's stopping you?"

"I like your thinking, Maggie. Nothing's stopping me. Or you. Besides dressing as a church lady and shushing people in libraries, what do you like to do?"

Unlike sharing my boring life up to this point, I knew the answer to that question. "I like to dance."

"Do you go to clubs?"

"I would. My town didn't really have any underage clubs. Mostly we went to school dances or parties."

"Can you do the running man?"

I stood up and showed him my best running man moves. "Easy."

"Moonwalk?" He joined me and slid backward across the floor.

My own version wasn't as smooth, but I mirrored him.

"Hold on, we need music for this." He put a cassette in his boombox.

I laughed at the B-52s song immediately.

He began bouncing around and nodding his head. By the time he acted out the lobster claws, I could hardly breathe.

I jumped on his bed and shimmied to "Rock Lobster." When the moment came, I jumped down and sang, "Down, down . . ."

We ended up on our backs on the floor, laughing too hard to sing or dance anymore. The song finished and Blondie's "One Way or Another" started.

I turned my head to see his face. "You're strange."

He grinned up at the ceiling. "More weird than you can imagine."

His reaction surprised me, but I trusted he meant it. "I like weird."

He stared at me. "Good. 'Cause I like you."

My eyes widened. We lay on his floor, our arms resting against each other. He'd rescued me from an awkward moment, made me laugh, and drew me an amazing picture. Then again, he'd also insulted me and basically said I was a boring prude. Still, I wondered if he wanted to kiss me.

Our chests lifted and dropped as we tried to catch our breaths from the impromptu dance party. Neither of us moved.

He could have easily made a move.

I waited.

Did I want him to kiss me?

I thought about it while he stared at me. His focus flicked to my lips and then down to my chest. I waited for a crackle or spark of tension between us—the subtle shift in energy right before a guy leaned in for a kiss, but I didn't feel it.

He did lean closer, focus still zeroed in on mine. "I'm not going to kiss you."

His words struck me and I shook my head at the sting of rejection.

Wait, I didn't even know if I wanted him to kiss me.

"I didn't think you were." I huffed and sat up.

"It's not you, it's me." Rising, he held out his hand.

"I've heard that before." We'd gone from meeting to breaking up in the span of an hour. This had to be one of the weirdest afternoons of my life.

"You're not really my type."

"I get it. Your type isn't librarian prude."

"Not at all. In fact, it's probably the exact opposite of you." His smile told me he meant it. He practically grinned.

Ouch.

"I like boys, Maggie."

I sat down on his roommate's bed with a thump.

"Surprise!" He threw his arms open and spread his fingers wide.

I processed the past hour in a new light. "Now it all makes sense."

"The bitchy comments about your sweater? The B-52s? The *artistic nature?*"

"Pretty much." I gave him a small smile. "We can still be friends, though, right? I could use some."

"Definitely. Every great gay man needs a fabulous woman as his friend. Plus, your roommate might be, how should I say this? Slutty? No offense. In fact, more power to her."

I laughed. "I have a feeling today isn't a one off thing. We'll need a signal."

"Mi casa es tu casa."

"What about your roommate?"

"He's cool. He likes Star Wars, so we should be good."

No Gils came to mind. "I don't think I've met him yet."

"You'd probably remember. Tall, dark hair. Totally cute. Why? Are you interested? He's a little *Revenge of the Nerds*, but it might be the glasses. I'm one-hundred-percent sure he's hetero."

Unable to remember seeing a guy fitting his description in the halls, I shook my head. "No idea, except you described most of the guys around campus."

"Next time you're stuck outside your room, come over. I'll introduce you. For now, let's go grab dinner. If we don't get there early enough, the only thing left will be the mystery meatloaf. No one should be forced to eat that."

"I usually have cereal."

"For dinner?"

I shrugged. "I can be wild and rebellious, too."

"Wild Child." He bowed and pointed to the door. "Lead the way to cereal for dinner."

TWO

"Closer to Fine"
Indigo Girls

"ROOMMATE KICK YOU out again?" Quinn joined me on the sofa in the lounge. Turned out, nine o'clock on a Friday night, the lounge emptied out completely, leaving me in peace with Mr. Voltaire and *Candide*.

Quinn snatched my book and dog-eared the corner to mark my place.

"You did not just desecrate my book by folding the page, did you?"

"It's a used paperback. It's probably seen a lot worse." He flipped open to the page and smoothed out the corner. "Remember forty-two."

I scowled at him.

He stuck out his tongue. "Listen, Caterpillar, no one studies on Friday nights in college."

"I am. Therefore, someone does."

"Let me rephrase. No one should ever study on a Friday night. You physically could, but shouldn't. Like doing heroin."

"Did you compare studying to shooting up drugs?"

Pushing himself off the couch, he tucked my book under his arm. "I did and I stand by it."

"Give me back my book."

"Not until tomorrow morning. We're going out."

"Out?"

"Out out. Luckily, you are wearing appropriate clothes tonight."

I glanced down at my ripped overalls and old thermal shirt. "This is okay for going out? Are we chopping wood?"

"No, it's an apartment party with lots of cute guys." He tossed a leather jacket at me. "You can borrow this."

I stood and slipped on the leather jacket. It hung past my hips, and I had to cuff the sleeves. "Your jacket?"

"No, my roommate's, but he won't mind. Let's go." Quinn's own outfit consisted of old Vans, jeans, and a paisley patterned button down over a gray T-shirt.

After leaving my book in my mailbox by the front door, he led me outside. The cold, damp night made me grateful for the borrowed jacket.

"Where is your roommate all the time? I never see him. Does he really exist?"

"He's trying out for the crew team. Gets up at some unholy hour when it's dark out. I think he hides in the library and sleeps the rest of the day."

"Maybe he's a vampire. I read *Interview with a Vampire* over the summer. Totally made me believe they could really exist."

"I'm getting the sense everything you know is from books. Less reading, more living, Caterpillar."

"Why do you keep calling me that?"

"You're the caterpillar before she becomes the butterfly. You merely have to get your nose out of your books long enough to see the world is waiting for you."

AT THE PARTY, blaring music made it too difficult to talk, but was good enough to dance to. Fine by me. Quinn was a fantastic dancer and had me laughing most of the evening.

Plus, he had been right about all the cute guys.

I wished I'd changed into something less warm. Lifting my hair, I twisted it into a knot at the nape of my neck. Not sure sweaty was the most attractive look. When a song came on I didn't know, I pantomimed being hot and needing water to let Quinn know my plan.

Random students packed the kitchen. Following people with full cups of beer outside, I found the keg. *Bingo.*

"Hi, I'm Roger," a cute guy manning the tap said. "Beer?"

"Sure." I took the red cup from him and introduced myself. The flat beer tasted the way old socks smelled.

"It's pretty terrible stuff, but still does the trick." Roger smiled at me, lifting his own cup before draining it. Definitely cute. With dimples in his round cheeks and his brown, curly hair, he reminded me of a Disney version of a chipmunk.

Because speed seemed to be the key in drinking bad beer, I imitated him, finishing mine in one long chug.

He refilled my cup. "Want to dance, Margie?" Loud music poured out the door when he opened it again.

"It's Maggie," I shouted over the noise. It didn't matter. Given the choice between swallowing more bad beer and dancing, I would've always chosen dancing.

I followed him to the crowded dance floor. Unlike Quinn, who was fun and a little silly to dance with, Roger was all about the close dancing. I felt his breath sweep over my face.

He placed his hands on me and swayed my hips in time to his own rhythm, moving farther and farther into my personal space.

The beer must have gone to my head because when his tongue invaded my mouth, I didn't immediately shove him away. He moved his thigh between mine and pulled out a full on Swayze style dip move.

Okay, that was different. And impressive, given his tongue was doing its own dirty dancing with mine.

I'd gone from reading a book to making out in the middle of a party in less than two hours. I wasn't sure which was the better option. Not that Roger was a bad kisser. He seemed really into it and knew all sorts of tricks, but I'd only met him five minutes ago.

When his hand grabbed my butt, warning sirens sounded in my head like the sounds European police cars make. *Wee woo. Wee woo. Wee woo.*

Too much. Too fast. Too grabby.

Pulling away, I returned his hand to my waist. He leaned forward to suction his mouth back to mine, but I dodged him. I was unable to spot Quinn's blond head through the mass of people.

Someone tapped me on my shoulder. I glanced at the guy attached to the fingers. He wasn't familiar, but he was cute—tall, big glasses, dark hair, kind of skinny.

"May I cut in?" he asked.

"Yes!" I replied without hesitation, squirming my way out of Roger's grasp.

"Hey, where are you going? We had a thing going on."

"Sorry. My boyfriend showed up!" I shouted over the music as I walked away from Roger.

Cute stranger grabbed my hand. "Quinn sent me over, but I'd still like to dance."

"Quinn?" I craned my neck to find him.

"He's over in the corner arguing about Warhol with a bunch of artsy girls who all look like Wednesday Addams."

Of course Quinn had found a group of cool girls. Not sure why, but the thought made me feel insecure.

"I'm Gil, by the way. If knowing my name makes you more likely to dance with me." He gave me a funny little wave. "Hi."

"I guess you know I'm Maggie."

"Maggie. Quinn only said I had to go rescue the hot redhead from the overly sexualized woodland creature."

The music picked up again with a new song.

"Did you say woodland creature?" I shouted.

"What?" He leaned down so I could speak into his ear. He smelled of soap and boy.

"Overly sexualized woodland creature?"

Smiling, he nodded. "Quinn's words not mine."

We danced together for the rest of the song. It wasn't as silly as when I danced with Quinn, nor was it an invasion of the body snatchers like with Roger.

When the song ended, he gestured over his shoulder off the dance floor. I led the way and he placed his hand on my shoulder protectively.

Quinn clapped his hands when he spotted us. "You rescued fair Maggie from the soul sucking!"

I furrowed my brow. "Soul sucking?"

"From this vantage point, it looked like he tried to suck out your soul via your mouth. I sent Gil in to save you, and your soul."

"Then I owe you a big thank you, Gil." I smiled at him.

He grinned back. "You do owe me."

Quinn interrupted our goofy staring contest. "Let's go. I think we've had enough fun for the evening."

I glanced at my watch. "It's barely midnight, Quinn."

"And I'm going to turn into a pumpkin. Plus, Gil has to be up at the ass crack of dawn to row a boat."

I studied Gil. "On a Saturday?"

"Six days a week."

"You're crazy. No way could you get me up in the dark to exercise." Nope. I shook my head and crossed my arms as if he would force me to join him.

"That's what I've been saying." Quinn slapped him on the back. "After he explained what a coxswain really does, and let me tell you, the name is misleading, I said no thank you."

Gil shrugged and gave me a shy smile, then pushed his glasses up his nose. "I obviously have a thing for self-flagellation."

"I should have guessed you were into weird stuff." Quinn handed me the leather jacket. "It's always the quiet ones." He winked at me.

"Are you wearing my jacket?" Gil asked.

"Sorry." I paused with my arm stuck inside one of the sleeves. "Quinn loaned it to me."

"It's fine." He pulled it over my shoulders. "Looks good on you."

The leather smelled the same as him—soapy and a little spicy like cloves.

We walked back to our dorm discussing music we liked. As we passed the mail cubbies, Quinn grabbed my book. Gil stopped walking, then closed his eyes for a couple of beats.

"Just my luck," he whispered before opening his lids again.

"What?" Quinn asked.

"Nothing." Gil shook his head.

I paused to say goodnight outside my door. It swung open to reveal a disheveled Jennifer, who clearly wasn't wearing a bra under her big T-shirt. Or pants.

"I thought I heard voices." She focused on me then the guys behind me. "Gil, what are you doing with Maggie?"

"You two know each other?" I glanced between them as an image flashed in my head. Dark hair. Long legs. Brown Wallabee boots. "Ohmygod. You're the tongue masher!"

"What's a tongue masher?" Quinn asked.

"He's the reason I've been kicked out of my room!"

"Oh, that makes things interesting, doesn't it?" Quinn's Cheshire grin returned. Facing Jennifer, he introduced himself.

She tugged her shirt farther down her legs. "Hi."

"You're dating Gil?" Quinn continued to be the only one speaking.

Gil shuffled his feet. "We hang out."

"Geez, Gil. Make it sound serious." Jennifer flipped her long, blond hair over her shoulder.

Quinn slung his arm around my neck and backed us down the hall. "Darling, we don't want to get involved in their lovers' quarrel, do we?"

"It's not a lovers' quarrel." Gil stared at me.

"Can you settle this tomorrow? I'm tired and want to go to sleep." I ducked under Quinn's arm and squeezed behind Jennifer. "Or in the hall? Either works for me."

"Goodnight, Caterpillar!" Quinn waved from the other side of Gil.

I didn't know Gil well enough to read his expressions, but the likelihood of any roommate tongue action tonight seemed the last thing on his mind. Meeting my eyes, he gave me a small wave and a shy smile as he stepped away. "Nice meeting you, Maggie."

Jennifer glared at him. "No goodnight kiss?"

He obliged her with a soft peck on the cheek and a promise to hang out tomorrow.

Her interrogation began the second the door closed. Why was I hanging out with him? Where did we go? How long were we together? Did he try to make a move on me? What was the story with Quinn?

Then she told me how she let Gil touch her special flower. I didn't ask for clarification. If my suspicion was right, I didn't want to know.

On and on she droned until I escaped the room to brush my teeth. Leaving the bathroom, I ran into Gil again in the hall.

"Hey. About Jennifer." He stopped and leaned against the wall.

"No need to explain anything." I rested my back on the opposite wall.

"Are you sure?" His voice cracked into a chuckle. "For some reason I feel like I need to explain myself or apologize for something."

"Why? You're both single and adults."

"I know, but we've kicked you out of your space a lot recently. Quinn said you've been hanging out in our room or the lounge. That's not fair."

"No, it's fine."

"The lounge couch smells like urine. No one should have to have to hang out on the urine couch."

"No, really. Most of the time I'm in the library."

"Still. We'll give you back your room."

"Okay." I felt awkward and embarrassed, and I wasn't sure why. It was sweet he apologized. It didn't really make sense, but I wasn't going to make him feel bad for trying to make it right.

"Can I ask you a question?" He rubbed his hand over his hair and adjusted his glasses.

"Sure."

"Is that your Roxy Music poster?"

Above my bed hung a huge poster of Roxy Music's *Avalon* cover. "It is."

"That's cool. They're one of my favorite bands."

"Really? Mine too."

We started talking about songs and albums, both slumping down the walls to sit. His long legs extended across the carpet and I criss-crossed mine. A few fellow residents stepped over us on their way in or out of the bathrooms.

I recognized Lizzy, another freshman in my world views' lecture. She wore a pink fluffy robe and carried a coordinating pink bathroom caddy. A pony-tail pulled her dark hair away from her face, drawing attention to her perky nose and rosy skin.

"Hi, can I join you? Or is this a private pow-wow?"

Gil and I shrugged. "Sure."

I made the introductions. "Sit with us."

After setting down her caddy, she joined me on my side of the hall. "What are you talking about?"

"Music and bands," Gil answered. "Our mutual love of Roxy Music."

"Really? I have a huge crush on Bryan Ferry." Her voice became animated. "Did you know he's playing a concert at the Greek in Berkeley next month? I'm trying to talk my roommate into driving down with me."

"I could be up for a road trip." Gil rubbed his hands together.

I'd never traveled anywhere on my own without my family or school chaperones. The idea excited me. "You mean get in the car and drive from Washington down to California? For a concert?"

"Sure. Why not?" Lizzy sat up on her knees. "It would be so much fun. If we split the gas and find a place to stay for free, we'd only have the cost of tickets and food."

"Let's do this. I bet Quinn would be up for an adventure."

I nodded in agreement with Gil. "He seems the type who is always up for trouble."

"I swear I heard my name." A short brunette with green eyes stuck her head around the corner.

Dressed all in black and wearing unlaced, knee high Doc Marten boots, she reminded me of Winona Ryder. With smudged lipstick. A guy with curly brown hair followed behind her, sporting his own version of lipstick smudged lips.

"Selah!" Lizzy jumped up. "We're going on a road trip to Bryan Ferry!"

Selah didn't look sure. "We are?"

"Yes, Maggie, Gil, and Gil's roommate are going to join us."

"They are?"

Lizzy nodded. "Come on, it'll be fun."

"What? When? Where? Who?"

I like Selah already. No nonsense, cut to the chase.

"We're the who. I'm Gil and that's Maggie."

She eyed us. "Are you a couple?"

I laughed, maybe a little too hard. "No, he's dating my roommate."

"Is your roommate coming on this trip, too?"

I waited for Gil to answer. "I don't think so. We're already five people. Six would be too many. Unless one of us had a VW bus."

For someone who had spent hours making out with Jennifer, Gil didn't seem too committed. From my last conversation with Jennifer, she was far more invested.

"Quinn has a hatchback. We could take that. Plenty of room in the back for our stuff."

"Come with us," Lizzy pleaded. "Berkeley, end of the month, concert at the Greek."

"My brother goes to Berkeley."

Lizzy's dark eyes sparkled. "Can we stay with him? We only need floor space for sleeping bags."

Sleeping bags? Floor? I didn't remember signing up for camping.

"I'm not sleeping on the floor." Selah protested.

I knew I liked her.

"Okay. I'm in." Next to Lizzy's enthusiasm, Selah came off as monotone and as dry as a cracker. "You want to join us, Ben? We could take two cars."

I made eye contact with Ben and gestured to my mouth.

He mirrored my actions and swiped at the lipstick. "No, that's okay. I'm more into rap and hip-hop these days."

He looked like the last person on the planet you'd expect to love rap, except maybe Tipper Gore. Why? He wore a tie, although it looked like it had been loosened and maybe even removed, then hastily put back on over his head. In fact, his shirt was untucked, too.

After saying goodnight to Ben, plans were made to make plans as we returned to our rooms.

TURNED OUT JENNIFER going or being upset about going was never an issue. Her boyfriend from home showed up to surprise her the next day. At first she asked me to swear I wouldn't tell Gil, but that ended up being a moot point when he bumped into them in the lobby.

I knew Gil would be fine.

If anyone suffered, it was me having to listen to Jennifer moan about him then ask me a hundred questions whenever I hung out in his room.

Maybe I should've introduced her to Roger. No way. I didn't need to walk in on their battle of world tongue domination every day. A battle to the death. Death by tongue. No, thank you.

THREE

"Interstate Love Song"
Stone Temple Pilots

"WHO ARE YOU going to put in your sex hut?" Quinn asked as we sped south on the 5. The hills of northern California were parched and bleached golden by the sun. I already missed the forests around campus back in Olympia.

We'd been playing Quinn's stranded on a desert island game for what felt like hours. Three huts. A different person in each hut. The rules were more complicated, but honestly, I couldn't keep track. All I knew was I had to give the name of a celebrity I'd have sex with.

"Johnny Depp."

"Nice, I approve." Quinn held up his hand for a high five. "Which one? Current hobo, put a dollar in his cup 'cause he's down on his luck Depp?"

"21 Jump Street."

"Good cop, bad boy! Nice combination."

Dark hair and warm brown eyes combination was more like it. I turned my head slightly to peer in the backseat where the guy fitting that description rested his head on the door frame. Wind from the open window lifted his hair and sun dappled his skin. When a sigh escaped me, I quickly clamped my lips shut, hoping Quinn hadn't noticed.

His focus flicked up to the rearview mirror and then back to me. A single blond eyebrow arched in question.

I didn't want to admit what was obvious. Instead, I turned my head to gaze out at flat fields of late summer corn. Gil had made out with my roommate. Probably more girls. Embarrassingly, it didn't stop my crush on him.

"You know what word you probably don't hear around here very often?" Selah leaned forward between the seats.

"What?" I twisted my upper body to face her.

"Moist."

Lizzy's groan from the back seat echoed mine. Squeezed in the middle between Gil and Selah, she'd been riding the hump for the better part of the trip because she was the most petite. And the nicest.

Gil snorted and opened one eye. "What is it with girls and that word?"

Sleep-faker. I'd have to remember that.

"It's not only moist. There are a lot of words we don't like," I explained the crazy world of girls and words.

"Such as?" He leaned forward. "Educate me."

Lizzy squirmed to lean her back against Selah. "Crutch, clutch, munch, crotch . . ."

"It's the *uch* sound that bothers you?" Gill furrowed his brows together until I could easily imagine him with a unibrow. It wasn't his best look.

"I'm fine with bunch." Lizzy tucked a lock of her dark hair behind her ear. "And girls love brunch."

"I hate the word pantyhose." Selah stuck out her tongue. "Or panty. And hanky."

"Crutch, munch, hanky, panty, clutch . . . crotch. This sounds like a Dr. Seuss book gone horribly wrong." Quinn glanced at me with a sly smile. "You couldn't make me clutch a moist crotch. I shan't munch a panty, or pantyhose. No hanky or panky, not even with Glenn Close."

"Glenn Close?" I gave him a dubious look.

"Rhymes with pantyhose. Plus, *Fatal Attraction* ruined me for all women."

"That's it?" Selah leaned forward again, shifting Lizzy toward Gil.

"Actually, it was Han Solo. Sitting in the movie theater with all my friends going wild for Princess Leia in her gold bikini, all I could think about was Han Solo. So gruff, so sarcastic."

"Makes complete sense." Gil agreed. "If you were going to be gay in space, he'd be a much better choice than Starbuck in *Battlestar Galactica*."

After he came out to everyone, Quinn being gay didn't feel like a big deal to any of us. Most of the time he and I had similar taste in guys.

"How much longer until we get to Berkeley? I need to pee." Selah had the smallest bladder ever. Or maybe it was the giant sixty-four ounce cup of Diet Coke she bought every time we made a stop.

"I don't know. You're the one from Northern California."

Selah glanced out her window at the flat, gold fields in the evening sunlight. "At least four hours. Too long. Next exit please."

"Remind me what the plan is?" Gil stretched, and I stared.

Quinn's little hatchback didn't have a lot of space. When a tall guy like Gil squeezed himself into the backseat, stretching became a contortion exercise. His long arms grabbed the back of Quinn's seat. He rolled his neck side to side, his hair barely brushing his shoulders. There wasn't room enough for him to stretch his legs, unless . . .

He twisted and threw a leg over Lizzy and Selah, then the other one.

"Listen, dude. If you're going to lie across me with your stinky feet in my face, you could ask first." Selah batted at his feet.

To escape her assault, he stuck his feet out the opposite window. "Better?"

"Barely. Don't press on my bladder. Or I'll ruin this Ford's lovely upholstery."

We found a gas station with a dubious convenience store and even more questionable bathrooms—the kind requiring a key and located on the outside of the building near an overfilled dumpster. Never a good sign. When Selah opened the door and a strong odor of public urine hit us, Lizzy swore she could hold it for a couple more hours.

"Don't be a priss, Liz. Breathe through your mouth and hover."

Lizzy and I made eye contact. Our expressions mirrored fear and disgust.

"I have an idea. Stay here and guard the door for Selah." I slow jogged around the corner toward the store and found what I needed at the counter.

Returning from my mission, I handed Lizzy the yellow container of Carmex. "Here."

"Soft lips are your biggest concern when we die from asphyxiation in there?" She picked up the lip balm with her fingertips.

"No, it's super strong smelling. Put it on your upper lip and around your nose."

"This is weird." Frowning, she opened it up and dabbed a little on her finger, then sniffed.

"No, you need a lot." I swiped a dollop and applied it liberally over my lips and under my nose. The spicy scent of Carmex filtered out dumpster and lingering bathroom odors. "See?"

"You look like you were slimed." She copied my actions.

"So do you."

"What is taking Selah forever in there?" I banged on the door. "Did you fall in? Selah?"

"I'm changing my tampon! Give a woman a second of privacy."

"I didn't need to know that. I never heard that." Gil stood behind us, his hands covering his ears.

"What do you two have all over your faces?" He gestured in a circle near my face.

"It was Maggie's idea." Lizzy dabbed at the goop.

"Why?" He leaned against the cinder block of the gas station, crossing his arms in the nonchalant, cool guy way.

Selah burst out of the door. The bathroom smell followed her out like a toxic cloud.

"That's why." The answer was obvious, but I told him anyway.

He pushed himself off the wall and away from the stink. "What died in there?"

Lizzy gave me her wallet. "I'm going in. Send word to my parents if I don't make it out. Their address is on my driver's license."

"Good luck!" I called out as the door closed.

"I need a Diet Coke." Selah disappeared around the corner to the entrance.

"What's with the goop?"

I forgot lip balm covered my lower face. "Trick I learned from my dad when we went fishing."

"You fish?"

"Not really. But my dad made me a few times. With fishing comes cleaning the fish."

"I know. All those guts and gore squishing out everywhere." His mouth fought a smile.

I shuddered. "Exactly. He taught me the trick of putting lip balm by my nose. Totally helps block the smell."

"That's kind of brilliant. Is your dad a commercial fisherman?"

"No, he fishes for fun. My grandparents have a cabin on Whidbey. Lots of summers there meant lots of salmon fishing."

"That's cool. I grew up in landlocked Colorado, but my dad would take my brothers and me fly fishing."

"You have brothers?"

"Two. One older and one younger. You?"

"Only child. I'd always wanted siblings. Instead, I had Cabbage Patch dolls."

"Everything makes sense."

I pouted out my bottom lip. "It does?"

"I'm teasing you. I've noticed you don't like to be teased. That's a sure sign you didn't have to deal with it growing up."

"Oh."

He bumped my shoulder with his. Or more like his bicep to my shoulder. He stood much taller than me. His long arms and legs were thin, almost gangly, like he'd had a huge growth spurt but his muscles hadn't caught up yet.

Spurt. Another word to add to the word list.

Lizzy exited the hell portal. "Your turn."

"Wish me luck." I handed her the wallet. "Don't leave without me."

"We'd never leave you behind, Maggie May."

I scrunched up my nose. "Like the Rod Stewart song?"

Gil sang a few lyrics as he walked backward to the car.

Inside the dim bathroom, I wished there were a mirror on the wall. Not to ask it who was the fairest of them all, but to see how pink my face looked. My cheeks felt hot.

I wondered how obvious my crush was to everyone else. After he stopped sucking face with my roommate, we started spending more and more time together. We were in the same lecture with Lizzy and I hadn't even noticed him for the first month.

Most of all, did Gil realize I had a crush on him? He asked me all those questions about my family. That indicated interest, right? Or maybe he was waiting on Lizzy. They seemed kind of close. I could ask her about Gil, but if she liked him, I didn't know what I would do.

I was the last person back to the car. The others stood around talking and laughing.

"Shotgun!" Lizzy shouted.

"Same!" Selah and Gil said simultaneously.

"You want to hump or drive?" Quinn asked me.

I slowly blinked at him.

"Hump or drive? It's a simple question." Selah prodded.

I wished they'd stop saying hump. "I'd feel bad for making Quinn sit in the middle, but I can drive."

Sitting next to Gil right now would be too much.

"Nah, I'm good." Quinn cracked and rolled his neck. "I'll get us to Sacramento. Then Selah can take over since she knows the area and it's her brother's apartment we're going to."

"You're stuck next to me." Gil gave me a small grin.

After we settled in the car, Selah passed me her giant cup of soda. "You still have lip balm around your nose," she whispered.

I sighed and stole the napkin from around her soda to rub off the balm. There was no way he had been flirting with me. Not when I had a face full of goop. He'd been polite. Probably waiting for Lizzy and making random conversation.

His thigh pressed into mine in the small backseat. I scooted closer to Selah.

"Sorry," he said and returned to staring out the window, shifting his legs closer to the door.

I don't remember much of the rest of the drive. I focused too much on the heat from Gil next to me while trying to keep my breath even and normal. Luckily, Selah and Quinn took over the conversation.

Resuming their list of hated words, they devolved into a conversation about their favorite swear words.

"When I was in third grade, my older brother Steve taught me how to flip people off." Quinn shared. "Being four years older and in junior high, he was basically an adult in my eyes."

"Wait, you have a brother named Steve and you got the name Quinn?" Selah asked.

"My mother was in a hippie phase when she was pregnant with me. Steven is named for my dad. I guess she picked up a baby book and found Quinn. It works for either a girl or a boy—it's perfect for me."

"I wish my parents were hippies. Selah was my grandmother's name. It sounds like a grandmother." She sighed.

"Try going through life as a Gilliam. Not William. No, spelled the same way but with a G instead of a W."

"Where'd that name come from?" Lizzy asked.

"My father says it's because of my mother's fascination with maps and place names. I guess I'm lucky I'm not named Denver or Roswell."

Lizzy glanced at me over her shoulder. "Elizabeth."

"Margaret." I smiled. We were sisters of the boring names. Whatever competition or insecurity I'd felt toward her over Gil disappeared. I wasn't going to be one of those girls who put guys before their friends. Or allowed guys to come between friendships. Ever.

"Being born in the seventies, we're lucky we weren't named Goldenflower or Astronaut." Secretly, I'd always wished for a weird name.

"No one would ever name their kids those names," Gil scoffed.

"I went to elementary school with a boy named Apollo. After the spacecraft, not the deity. Or so he told us." Lizzy laughed.

"Um . . ." Gil joined her laughter.

"Exactly." She shook her head.

"Snatch," Selah said out of nowhere.

Gil leaned around me and his back pressed against my shoulder. I was hyperaware of every point of contact between us.

"Excuse me? Is that someone's name?" His eyes cut to mine.

I realized how close together our faces were. Too close. I sank into my seat.

"No, it's another word people tend to dislike." Selah sipped on her straw.

"Non sequitur, much," Quinn said.

"We were talking about words and names, reminded me of the earlier conversation."

"Speaking of earlier, we never finished my game. Selah, your turn. Who would you put in your sex hut?"

"Don't I have to do the talking and listening huts first?"

"Let's cut to the good stuff. Sex hut. And—go . . ."

FOUR

"More than This"
Roxy Music

WHEN WE ARRIVED at Selah's brother's apartment, it became clear there hadn't been much communication between siblings. The tiny two-bedroom apartment had one bathroom and a futon in the living room. Each bedroom had a mattress on the floor.

Except her brother's roommate was home. That hadn't been the plan. We knew we'd be cramped. Instead of five of us, six including Gabe, the roommate and his girlfriend made it eight. With one bathroom.

Awkward conversation followed as we plotted out sleeping arrangements. Girls in one bedroom and boys in the other was no longer an option. Gabe offered to share his room with Gil and Quinn, leaving Selah, Lizzy, and I the one futon in the living room.

"I'll take the floor," I offered, tossing a sleeping bag on the questionable brown carpet. I wondered about the last time it had been vacuumed. Never was my guess. I moved my bag away from a constellation of crumbs.

"We can switch tomorrow night. Make the guys sleep out here."

Lizzy sniffed a throw pillow and dropped it back on the futon.

"Only if Gabe has fresh sheets. I grew up with the guy. Trust me, you don't want to sleep in his bed. Or borrow his towel."

I gave her a blank stare.

"Think about what teenage boys do when they're alone." She stared back.

Oh! "Oh." Right. "Ew."

"Exactly."

Despite it being almost midnight, Gabe joined us in the living room, even offered us beer.

"Wow, you have Super Mario Bros? I kicked ass at this." Gil held up the game cartridge. "Can we play?"

The guys played a few rounds on Gabe's Nintendo. Selah set up Roxy Music's Avalon on the stereo and we talked about the concert the next night, teasing Lizzy about her old man crush on Bryan Ferry.

"What's the guy version of Mrs. Robinson?" Quinn set down his controller after he lost to Gil.

"Dirty old man?" I asked. "Pervert?"

"Chester the molester?" Selah quipped.

"Hugh Heffner," Gil stated.

"Gross. Blech." Lizzy shook her head in disgust.

"Hey, you're the one with the older guy fetish." Selah reminded her. "He's got money, a huge house—"

"And a grotto, don't forget the grotto," Gabe interrupted.

Selah shot him a sidelong look. "Right, a grotto. Because everyone wants one of those. I wonder how often they have to adjust the chemicals in that water."

"I hope they drain it weekly." I shuddered. "Think of all the body fluids."

"What are we even talking about?" Gil's position as grand champion had been cemented after he defeated Gabe in their final match up. "Who else wants to play?" He scanned the room, his focus finally settling on me. "Maggie May? You haven't played yet."

"For good reason. I suck."

"You can't be that bad. Come on," he patted the spot next to him on the carpet, "I'll go easy on you."

"I don't need your pity. Play like you would anyone else." I plopped down as delicately as I could, realizing the beer had gone to my head. "I'll be Luigi."

The game was a bloodbath. I went through all three of my lives in record time. And set a new bar for sucking, according to Gabe.

"See?" I tossed Gil my controller. My throw even sucked.

He tipped over to catch it behind him. "Okay, you were right. You are the worst player ever." He laughed from his new reclined position. "Really, really terrible."

He put his hand on my knee to right himself, giving it a squeeze. My breath caught in my throat as the heat from his palm pulsed under my skin.

"I'm sure you have other talents. We'll have to discover them."

Teasing or flirting, I wasn't sure, but one thing I knew for certain, I was confused.

"*Je parle français*," I declared.

"Well, that'll be helpful if you ever go to France. Or Quebec." He grinned at me, his hand still on my knee.

"Or I want to major in French Literature."

"You do?" He sat up straighter.

I nodded. "Ever since I read *Madame Bovary* in high school."

"Isn't that the one where she killed herself with arsenic? Not very happy. Or uplifting."

"Not everything ends with a happily ever after. Not even the fairy tales."

"Who knew you were such a dark soul, Maggie May?"

"You keep calling me that."

"It's your new nickname. You like?" His warm eyes glinted with amusement.

I shrugged, covering my delight over him giving me a nickname. "I guess."

The quiet of the room finally clicked. I glanced around. "Where'd everyone go?"

He kept his eyes trained on me. "Quinn and Gabe suggested a beer run before the store closed. Selah and Lizzy went with them. You missed all that?"

"I was concentrating on losing at video games, I guess."

We sat quietly for a minute, kind of staring at each other, kind of not, before it began to feel awkward. There were a million things we could have talked about—more books, whatever Gil wanted to major in, video games, music—but nothing came to mind. The record ended and the soft sound of the needle circling the vinyl echoed in the room. A scratch would break up the white noise every few seconds as it spun under the needle.

The tension became too much. I jumped up at the same time Gil did, our heads knocking together.

"Ouch!" I rubbed my forehead.

"I was going to change the record."

"Me too." I peered up at him. He rubbed a small circle on the bridge of his nose.

"Who even has vinyl anymore? He should at least have this album on tape."

"I think it's cool. I have this one back on campus. On vinyl."

"We're going to need to make you a mixtape. You can't travel with your record collection." He flipped the album over and reset the needle.

"Like Quinn's tapes for the road trip?"

"I'm thinking less Cher and more music made in this decade."

"There was a lot of Cher and disco on the mix."

"I need guitars and bass, fewer synthesizers."

"Do you play?"

"I play bass. I was in a band with a couple of friends in high school."

"Did you have gigs?"

"If playing in each other's garages and at the rec club counts, then yes. We were rock stars." He pushed his glasses up his nose.

I didn't say anything. I couldn't tell if he was being serious.

"We weren't rock stars. Furthest thing from it, actually."

"Why?"

"Besides being teenage boys? We sucked. We thought volume could cover up a lack of skill."

"Turned your amps up to eleven?"

He didn't move. Didn't breathe. Just stared at me.

"What?" I rubbed my nose, thinking some old lip balm lingered on my skin.

"You quoted *This is Spinal Tap.*"

"I love that movie."

"Marry me." His words were hushed, reverent.

My turn to hold my breath.

He shifted to bend one knee. In his hand he held his game controller, presenting it to me as an offering.

Boisterous voices carried through the door, getting louder as our friends entered the apartment.

"And that's when the alien tentacle—" Quinn stopped speaking abruptly. "Hey, what's going on here? We leave you two alone for ten minutes and Gil's showing off his joystick?"

I stared down at the controller in Gil's hand. A hundred thoughts raced through my mind, most of them dirty, heating my cheeks again. When I peeked up at his face, his own skin appeared redder than it had been a few minutes ago. He quickly shifted and sat down farther away.

"Nothing. Maggie quoted *Spinal Tap.* Things got a little crazy."

"*Right.*" Selah's voice held zero belief. "*Spinal Tap.*"

"It's a cult classic." I defended our love of the same movie.

"Oh, I know it is. Funny, I don't remember a proposal scene or any joysticks in the movie."

"Who's proposing?" Lizzy handed me a can and sat on the futon.

"No one. Nothing to see here." Gil chugged the beer Gabe gave him.

Quinn's focus bounced between us, doubt and judgment clearly evident in his squinty eyes. "Okay. We need a few rules. No one is getting together on this road trip. Certainly not with each other. Imagine the awkward drive back to campus. There'd either be groping and making out, and honestly, my car's too small. Or the odor of regret and self-loathing would be worse than the gas station bathroom from hell. Deal?"

"I assume you are speaking to me, Quinn, since I'm the only hetero man here." Gil scowled at his roommate. "Unless you are talking about the girls making out. Ladies?"

Selah sneered at him, jokingly of course. "You'd like that wouldn't you? Girls kissing is the white whale for hetero boys."

Quinn laughed. "Someone make a *Moby Dick* joke for me! Come on, she lobbed one up there for us."

"Every guy thinks his dick is bigger than it is." Selah looked up at the ceiling.

"Can we not talk about dicks around my sister?" Gabe changed the record to The Cure.

I'd completely forgotten about him. Had he ever met his sister and her lack of filter?

Quinn pointed out the obvious before I could. "Your sister is the one who brought it up. I think she's well aware of dicks."

"Gross." Gabe made a sour face.

"Let's change the subject before this gets all incestuous like *Flowers in the Attic*. Or *Blue Lagoon*," Quinn said with all seriousness, except his blue eyes glimmered with provocation.

Gagging and retching sounds came from both Gabe and Selah.

"That's my sign to call it a night." He shoved himself off the futon and set his beer on the kitchen counter.

"Don't go, dear brother," Selah said half-heartedly. "This is what Quinn does. He provokes. He sees a line and then runs toward it with glee. It must be a Southern Californian thing."

"It's true. It's something in the water. I think they put in extra glee with the chlorine and fluoride." Quinn nodded happily, not taking Selah's baited insult.

Gabe appeared unsure and unsettled as he said goodnight. After he'd gone, Selah curled up on the futon next to Lizzy.

"That's your brother?" Lizzy asked the question that didn't need asking.

"He's a charmer, isn't he? You wouldn't believe how much less up-tight he is now that he's getting laid and not in high school."

"I heard you! I'm not discussing my sex life with my sister!" Gabe called out from down the hall.

"No one wants to discuss your sex life! Trust me!" Selah shouted back at him.

WE SPENT THE next day wandering around Berkeley's streets. Quinn wanted to photograph People's Park. Selah hunted for the naked student wearing only his backpack and sneakers. Quinn offered to be Evergreen's own version of naked student. We rejected him as quickly and strongly as possible. Gil shopped music at Rasputin's. Lizzy and I bought long, flowy hippy skirts smelling of patchouli and lost dreams of peace, love, and understanding. I hoped the patchouli smell would come out in the laundry.

Selah never did find the naked guy, but she got us invites to two frat parties and a house party on the north side of campus after the concert. The girl had charms.

Gil and I seemed fine after his fake proposal last night. Quinn was right about getting together on this trip. Or any time. We were creating a posse of friends.

What if we got together and it didn't work out? Or worse, he was a terrible kisser? Or even worse, was terrible in bed? Or worst of all, not interested?

It might be a far better world to be in if those questions went unanswered. I could still fantasize about him and he'd be the best possible kisser, and probably the best possible lover, without a doubt. Not knowing the truth meant our friendship could remain intact.

Of course everything might change. Maybe next year he wouldn't room with Quinn. Or maybe they wouldn't even be friends. Maybe we'd have new cliques. Then all bets would be off.

"What's the name of the cat in the box Professor Roberts talked about in class last week?" I asked the group as we walked to the Greek Theater for the concert.

"Random question, Maggie." Quinn stopped and stared at me.

Gil kept walking, but faced backward to answer me. "Schrödinger. Cat in the box. Alive or dead. Both are possible until you open the box."

"That's it! Schrödinger." I matched my pace to his.

"Any reason why you're asking about this?" Selah walked a few feet behind us.

"Just thinking how we're only weeks into college and everything's possible at this point. We could study anything, create our own majors, meet people, meet more people, make new friends . . ."

"Fall in love," Lizzy added, walking next to me.

"Fall out of love," Selah snarked.

"Have sex," Quinn said. The rest of us laughed. "What? Isn't that the point? Kiss girls. Kiss boys. Experiment?"

"It is the time to learn new things, expand our minds, and gain new experiences." Gil smiled down at me. "What's your point?"

"Nothing really. The whole world is at our feet." I made the mistake of looking down. "Or at least a lot of gum and cigarette butts."

"Is this where I quote the puckish optimism of the opening credits of *St. Elmo's Fire*?" Quinn asked.

"Ugh, no. Too depressing," Selah said.

"Even the soundtrack is sad." Lizzy frowned.

"That'll never be us. Please swear none of us will become those people." I stared pleadingly at my friends.

"The eighties are over. Thank God. No more shoulder-pads." Lizzy adjusted her jean jacket and patted her shoulders.

"It would seem the eighties aren't over for everyone." Quinn pointed at a couple of women ahead of us, their hair in full spiral perm and spiked bangs mode.

Or at least I assumed they were women. One turned and I caught a five o'clock shadow. And guyliner.

My eyes bugged out. Selah whistled.

Our laughter burst out of us, simultaneous and in sync.

"Hot," she mouthed at me. "Hot pirates."

GIL SAT AT the end of our row, on the other side of Quinn. Lizzy screamed her declaration of love for Mr. Ferry in my ear for the first two songs. Selah bummed a hit off of the guys next to her, and got invited to another party. One of them looked like he probably dressed up like Robert Smith and went to dance clubs. His friend tried to pass me the joint, but I waved him off. "I'm trying to quit."

He gave me a raised eyebrow and a shoulder shrug.

Quinn leaned closer. "Have you ever smoked pot before?"

I shook my head no.

"Didn't think so." He slung his arm over my shoulder. "We'll add it to your list of things to do at college."

"I have a list?"

"You should. This is your chance to explore. Kiss boys. Kiss girls. Have lots of wild sex before your boobies droop."

I instinctively covered my chest.

"Ha, ha. You have nothing to worry about. My dear roommate seems fascinated with them." His arm tightened, pulling me into a one armed hug.

I wasn't sure if I should apologize for my breasts or beam over them having an admirer.

When the opening notes of "More than This" started, I thought Lizzy would pass out from too much joy. We all knew the words and belted them out like old crooners, but mostly off key and pitchy. The exception was Gil. His deep, smooth voice did something funny to my skin, making it all tingly and warm.

Off limits, I reluctantly reminded myself.

Quinn was right.

Friendship before hormones.

Selah

Selah Elmore, 19

I'm majoring in men.

That's not a major?
Fine.
Art history and aesthetics.
First year.

If you could change one thing about college so far, what would it be?

I'd skip to senior year. I'm tired of being too young. Sure, I can vote now, but I still can't drink . . . legally. I can join the military, but most places won't rent me a car. I can get birth control, get married, have kids, but I'm still a teenager. I'm bored of people reminding me how young I am. I know who I am and what I want.

FIVE

"You Got It (The Right Stuff)"
New Kids on the Block

WE RETURNED FROM winter break and fell back into the same habits we'd established in the fall quarter. Maggie's roommate, Jennifer, continued to pine over both Gil and her boyfriend at home. As a result, Maggie spent a lot of time in our room with Lizzy and me.

Thankfully, Gil hadn't succumbed to the weekly brownie bribes left at his door. Instead, he saved them for movie night after having his friend in the chem lab test them for drugs and scan them for shards of metal. A guy couldn't be too careful.

I liked Lizzy. She was the light to my dark, which didn't even really make sense because we both had dark hair. Her optimism and enthusiasm could've been extremely annoying. She always hoped for the best and saw the good in people. At times, it was like living with Jeannie in her bottle. So much optimism. So much sunshine. I doubted she had a weird side.

At least until I discovered her secret.

I'd ditched lunch and found her in our room singing that right stuff song by New Kids on the Block at the top of her lungs. Not my taste, but I couldn't turn on the radio without hearing one of their songs.

It wouldn't have been that bad. Annoying, but not even a big deal . . . if she weren't holding a Donnie Wahlberg doll as a microphone.

I screamed, "Busted!"

A hard plastic man body hurt when flung at someone's head. The someone being me.

"I'm blind," I screamed, covering my temple where Donnie had beaned me.

She turned off the music, then clutched her chest as her eyes filled with tears that clung to her ridiculously long lashes. "Are you okay? Are you really blind? Did Donnie take out your eye? I'll never forgive myself if I blinded you."

I moved my hand and slowly blinked. It stung, but I could see a blurry her. Closing my good eye, I focused on clearing my vision. "I don't think I'll need an eye patch."

"Oh, thank God!" She wrapped her thin arms around me in a claustrophobic hug.

"I'm fine, really. If I lost an eye and had to get an eye patch, I could rock it like a pirate."

Her exhale brushed against my cheek. "I'm so sorry, but you would make an awesome pirate."

Our laughter moved the moment past the pain and awkwardness to a place where I could ask the question I really needed to know the answer for.

"Why Donnie?"

"Why Donnie what?"

"Isn't he the lesser cute guy of the New Kids? I mean, why not have the Jordan Knight doll or the other cute one?"

"Joe? They're all cute. That's the point of a boy band."

"Like Menudo? I couldn't tell you a single one of those guys' names except Ricky Martin. In fact, I couldn't pick them out if there were six guys in our room and five of them were the other guys from Menudo."

"Charlie, Ray, Robi, Roy, Raymand, and Ricky."

I stared at her, stunned. I had no words.

"I also like Milli Vanilli."

Still stunned. She had appalling taste in music, but I couldn't say anything because it would make me a bitch. Then again . . ."You have terrible taste in music."

Her bottom lip pouted out and she nervously tucked her hair behind both ears, making herself resemble a little brown mouse. Or a baby hedgehog. "I do not. Just because I don't like all the dark, never see daylight, brood in an unlit corner music like you."

I laughed. "Yeah, pretty much describes me in high school. I like other kinds of music now, too."

"Name one pop singer or song you like." I swore her foot tapped as she waited.

"George Michael."

"Let me guess. 'I Want Your Sex?'"

Obviously. "I like some of his other songs, too. Like the one about the daddy issues. Very hot."

"We'll have to agree we like different music. Like we like different . . ." She paused and looked up, thinking. "We like pretty much different everything, but we still get along."

Of course she was right. I shouldn't have judged her. "You can listen to New Kids. Maybe I'm missing out." Leaning over, I picked up the Donnie doll. "I mean, look at his abs. Does he always go around shirtless?" I tucked his faux leather flag jacket back on his shoulders.

Her voice lowered to a whisper. "Uh . . . no, he came with a shirt."

"You pervert! Where's his shirt?" I ran my nail down the sculpted ridges of his little six squares of plastic ab muscles.

"I thought he looked better without it." She grabbed the doll out of my hand and tossed him in her bottom drawer.

"You know most of us keep our porn in that drawer."

Her hair whipped around her shoulder as she spun to gape at me. "You have porn in our room?"

I shrugged. "I'm calling it research for my biology of human sexuality section this spring."

"Your professor assigned porn? I know this is a liberal arts school, but honestly? Couldn't he get in trouble?"

"Lizzy, our mascot looks like a penis."

"It's a regional shellfish!" A blush climbed up her cheeks.

"Plus, they have huts in the thousand acre woods where students go to have sex or do drugs. Sometimes at the same time."

"That's not the point of the tree houses."

"It might not be the intended use, but the administration looks the other way. Plus, pot is illegal. Porn isn't. We're all adults here."

"What kind of porn are we talking about? Magazines, right? Or do you have a stack of VHS tapes in there?"

"You sound curious. Want to see?" She would be disappointed if she were hoping for videos. Opening my bottom drawer, I pulled out the one magazine I had.

"You have *Playgirl*?" She delicately plucked it from my hands like it might be dirty or germy.

"You're about to be sadly disappointed." I sat on my bed and patted the bedspread. "It's not as sexy as I'd hoped."

She flipped to a random page of a naked guy on a horse. Bareback. His mostly limp penis peeked out behind his thigh like a scared turtle. Another flip of the page revealed the centerfold. More life existed in that penis, but it was a weird purple color.

"This is supposed to turn us on?" Her voice held nothing but confusion.

"I think so."

"Do you, uh, get turned on by this?" She flipped more pages.

I reclined against the wall. "Are you excited?"

"Not really. I haven't really seen more than penises in art."

"Not in person?"

She shook her head. "Not really."

"Have you touched one?"

"Oh sure, but it was dark. I didn't really get a good look." She held the magazine up to her nose. "I don't think I realized they'd be different colors, like mauve and purple."

"Or puce," I added, helpfully.

"Green?" She shrieked.

"No, puce is a shade of purple."

"Sounds like puke." Another dimly lit and softly focused picture of a naked man in front of a fire caught her attention. "What's the point of *Playgirl*?"

"I think it's a man's idea of what women want."

"Maybe they should have asked us."

"If you want real porn for inspiration, you should read erotica." I pulled the bottom drawer open again. "Erica Jong. Or Anaïs Nin. She's the queen of sexy lit."

Lizzy picked up my worn copy of *Delta of Venus*. Turning the pages, she opened her eyes wide. "Oh, wow."

"Much better than the Purple Trouser Snake."

"Knock, knock." Quinn spoke the words, rather than actually knocked. He stood on the threshold. "What are you two up to? Want to grab some food in the . . ." His words trailed off.

I followed his gaze to the Playgirl sitting on my bed.

"You two were looking at boy porn without me?"

I quirked my eyebrow at him. "I believe the title clearly states it's for girls."

"Shh, semantics." He picked up the magazine and sprawled on my bed. "I found my mother's stash in high school."

"You can take it. Keep it, please," Lizzy pleaded. "Honestly, those things kind of freak me out."

"Why do you have it then?" Quinn asked.

"It's not mine!" She waved her hands as if trying to shoo it farther away from herself. "It's Selah's. For biology of human sexuality."

"Uh, huh. With Professor Driscoll?"

I nodded.

"He assigned you porn?"

"I asked the same thing!" Lizzy grinned at me.

"Not really, but the class is super boring. I decided I'd do my own research."

"The man is a hundred and two. He probably invited women back to look at naughty etchings when he was younger." Quinn rolled up the magazine and tucked it under his arm.

"I'm worried he'll keel over when we get to the part of the class where we discuss actual fucking." I shooed them out of the room ahead of me. "That might make things interesting."

SIX

"This Charming Man"
The Smiths

PROFESSOR DRISCOLL DIDN'T keel over. More like fell. He slipped on some ice and tumbled down his driveway, breaking his leg the last week of January. He would be out of the classroom for the rest of the winter quarter. Instead of canceling our section, the department brought in a doctoral grad student from University of Washington to finish out the term.

The day Jason Vincent, soon to be Dr. Vincent, walked into class was a blessing and a curse.

Blessing: no biology grad student should have ever been that hot.

Curse: no biology grad student, who was also my professor, should have ever been that hot.

He had curly . . . no, wavy brown hair hanging over his glasses. Pale skin, probably from spending all his time in biology labs. Broad shoulders and long legs. His torso made the perfect V shape, obvious even under his boring professor garb. He appeared to have perfect proportions according to Da Vinci's calculations. Jason Vincent was a perfect specimen of a man.

Making everything worse—for me at least—he continued Professor Driscoll's routine of starting off each class with a dirty limerick correlating with the day's subject.

About sex.

Most of them were goofy and embarrassing like someone's uncle telling off-colored jokes at the family table during Christmas dinner after too much spiked eggnog. We could tell Driscoll wrote them ahead of time.

A week into his tenure, the poems changed. Shorter, and dirtier, I knew without a doubt they came from Jason Vincent, who had a very dirty mind.

There once was a girl named Simone
Who spent most of her time alone . . .

Pretending to take notes, I wrote down "seduce Dr. Vincent" in my calendar. Then drew a row of stars next to it, prioritizing it.

When he finished his lecture about the anatomy of testicles, I waited until everyone left to approach his lectern where he stuffed his notes into a well-worn leather satchel.

Noticing me, he gave me a small smile. "Can I help you, Miss Elmore?" He wiped off the drawing of a side view of balls from the white board behind him, leaving a faint pink ghost outline of scrotum for the next class.

"I was wondering if you offer private tutoring?"

"Are you having trouble keeping up with the material?" He opened his grade book. "You seem to be right in the middle of the curve on the quizzes."

Of course Driscoll graded on a curve.

"I want to do better than average."

"Are you thinking of majoring in biology?"

Anatomy maybe, particularly his. "No, I'm more of a visual person."

"Aesthetics?"

"Something like that. Maybe art history? We don't really have majors here, more like concentrations."

"Sorry. I'm not really used to how things work around here."

"I could show you." Mine. Then he would show me his. If I

remembered kindergarten, that was how things progressed.

He studied me, his blue eyes calculating behind his glasses. Astute was the word for his expression. Shrewd.

"You could show me where I can get coffee on campus. Someone said something about a red square."

I smiled at his confusion. "That's the center of campus. The big red plaza near the clock tower? It's not a communist nod to Mother Russia in case you were worried. The pavers are red."

"I wasn't worried, but thanks for the clarification." He slung his bag over his shoulder. "Lead the way, and we'll talk as we walk."

During our five-minute trip across campus from LAB II to the quad, I dissuaded him from the idea of a group study session twice. "I think meeting in your office, one on one, would work better. At least before the research project outlines are due."

He choked and coughed. "Research projects?"

"No research? I figured there would be because this is a science section. Won't there be a lab, or experiments, or some sort of team project?"

His eyes focused on something above my head. "Experiments?"

"With a lab partner, I assumed."

He let his gaze settle on my face, but still didn't quite meet my eyes. "Experiments and lab partners? In a class about sex?"

"Am I totally wrong?" I knew this was preposterous. I'd read the syllabus. There wasn't a lab associated with this class. Or a research paper. In fact, the whole class was pass or fail. Come on, biology of human sexuality in college? Clearly, most of the experimenting would be done as independent study. I batted my lashes at him.

His eyes drifted down to my chest for a brief instant. He fought it, but I'd piqued his curiosity. Maybe his libido, too.

"You're kidding, right? I know this is a liberal school, but Professor Driscoll said nothing about any of this. Hell, the limericks are even crossing the line for most colleges."

"The limericks are my favorite part."

"Of course they are," he mumbled.

"Are you okay, Dr. Vincent?"

"I'm not a doctor. Yet. I have to finish my research and dissertation."

"Then what should I call you?"

"Mr. Vincent sounds like my dad, but Jason feels too informal inside the classroom."

"We're not in class now." I stepped closer to him. Close enough I could smell his cologne. He wore Polo. How preppy of him. "A lot of faculty go by their first names around here. Something about breaking down the hierarchy of learning and knowledge."

"Okay."

"Okay what?"

"You can call me Jason."

"And you can call me Selah." Before I lost my nerve, I handed him the folded paper with my phone number. I pointed at the doors in front of us. "Coffee's in there. It's not great, but it's hot."

I strolled in the other direction. "See you in class next week," I called out, not turning around. Not waiting to see what he did with the paper.

SEVEN

"So Alive"
Love and Rockets

NOT THE KIND of girl to sit home and wait for the phone to ring, I dragged Lizzy and Maggie out to a party that weekend. At the party, I ran into Ben from last quarter again. We'd gotten together a few times, but never clicked. Despite him being at this ultra laid back college, he was way too uptight for me. Plus, he wore a tie. A lot.

Unlike Jason Vincent, who never wore a tie, preferring instead to roll up the sleeves of his button-down shirts above his elbows. For a science geek, he had amazing forearms. Maybe he played racket ball or squash or something. He didn't seem the type for tennis.

"Selah?" Ben's expression told me he was waiting for an answer to a question I hadn't heard.

"Sorry, couldn't hear you over the music." The CD had stopped and my voice sounded too loud for the room.

Cocking his head to the side, he raised a single eyebrow. "I asked if you wanted to go check out a bar downtown. Rumor has it they rarely card, and if there is a bouncer, you slip him a five to get in on the weekends."

A quick glance around the room confirmed the party had faded. Most people were gone, with the exception of my friends sitting around the kitchen table and a couple making out in a recliner.

"Sure." I clapped my hands to get everyone's attention. "Guys? Let's blow this football team's popsicles and go check out a bar."

"I don't think that's the expression, Selah," Quinn shouted back. "Although I like the phallic imagery you inserted there. Nice touch."

"Thank you. Ben, you know everyone? Everyone, this is Ben."

Gil and Quinn said their hellos with guy nods and a mutual "hey."

Our little band of misfits piled into Ben's car, with Lizzy lying across the three of us in the backseat.

Up front, Gil checked out Ben's cases of tapes and CDs.

"You're really into hip hop. NWA, Public Enemy, Run DMC, and Naughty by Nature? Seriously?" Gil held up a tape. "No kidding." He popped the last one into the player and hit fast forward.

LL Cool J's "Goin Back to Cali" blasted from the Audi's speakers.

Yes, Ben drove an Audi sedan.

I wondered what kind of car Jason drove. Probably something not so yuppie.

Ben had been right about the bar. No bouncer and the bartender, while gruff and snarly, didn't card us either. Staring at us blankly, he waited for our orders.

The decor of The Four Leaf Clover combined all the charm of a Irish family pub and the seventies style of the Brady Bunch with lots of dark wood, avocado green booths and orange vinyl chair cushions.

"Pitcher of beer?" Ben asked the group. "Or do you want cocktails?"

"Vodka and something for me." I'd had my fill of beer at the party. I scanned the room for a table for the six of us. A group of men chugged the last of their beers, slammed the glasses on the table, and uttered a guttural shout. I didn't recognize any of the huge burly guys in construction boots. They definitely weren't college students.

A corner booth in the front opened up. It would be tight, but we could fit. Bonus, it sat next to an old fashioned jukebox—the kind with actual 45 records and a turntable inside. I stood in front of it, pushing the buttons to peruse the selection of classic rock and country singles. A few eighties hits were scattered through the catalog, among them

Whitney Houston, Bon Jovi, The Police, and strangely enough, Soft Cell.

"Ooh, play 'Tainted Love.'" Quinn excitedly jabbed at the glass.

"I don't have any quarters," I complained. I'd left for the night with my standard going out kit: room key, ID and a twenty-dollar bill in case I needed a taxi.

"Quarters! For the love of British Boys, we need quarters!" He held out his hand in the direction of our booth.

Returning with enough change for hours of music, he took over the selection process. Eclectic didn't begin to cover it. Dolly Parton's "Nine to Five" followed Soft Cell. Gil and Ben both groaned. Maggie and Lizzy strangely knew all the words and danced along to the song while remaining seated. Sitting next to them, I silently judged their taste in music.

Ben rested his hand on my knee. He was nice enough, but nothing would be happening again. I excused myself for the bathroom. Luckily he didn't take it as a subtle invitation to make out in a stall and follow me.

Even luckier for me, on the way back through the bar I spied a certain professor sitting at a table for two with a man I didn't recognize. Jason stared at me, watching me make my way toward his table.

"Miss Elmore."

Great. Despite most definitely being outside of class and off campus, he'd reverted to formal names.

"Mr. Vincent."

"I'm surprised to see you here." He ignored introductions to his friend.

"I could say the same. I didn't realize you lived in Olympia."

"I don't."

Geez, this conversation couldn't be more boring. Maybe his companion was friendly. I stuck out my hand. "Hi, I'm Selah, one of Mr. Vincent's students at Evergreen."

"Pleased to meet you. I'm Kevin." If someone could be described as beige, he was that person. Nothing remarkable about him except how unremarkable he looked. "Are you taking Jason's sex class?"

Thankfully, I remained composed enough not to swallow my

tongue. "Is that how he's describing it? Professor?" I held my gaze steady on Jason's face. I swore I saw his cheeks color with pink.

"Kevin." His voice lowered, stern and threatening.

Kevin's grin told me he enjoyed teasing Jason. They must have been old friends. "Fine, are you in Professor Vincent's biology class?"

"I am. I'm hoping for an A."

Kevin's clever eyes swept over me. "What year are you?"

"First."

Jason groaned while Kevin nodded and asked, "Tell me, Selah, has anyone ever called you Lolita before?"

Now my own cheeks heated. My skirt suddenly felt too short—the gap between it and my boots exposing a lot of fishnet covered skin. Or it could have been my short pigtails. I realized all I needed was a lollipop.

"Can't say it's happened before, Kevin."

Clearly, Kevin knew my game. Or maybe Jason's. I'd never thought he could be the type to seduce his students. As far as I knew, this class was his first teaching job.

"How did you get in here?" Jason changed the subject. "Fake ID?"

Busted. "No one carded us."

"Doesn't make you legal."

"Are you going to call the police? Have us arrested and handcuffed?" It might have been the vodka, but I decided to be bold and push him. "Are you into handcuffs, Professor?"

Jason choked on his beer, coughing to clear his throat.

After making sure his friend wasn't dying, Kevin laughed. "This is more entertaining than I imagined a college dive bar could be."

I focused my attention on the non-choking friend. "What brings you to Olympia, Kevin?"

"I'm in politics."

Jason found his voice again. "He's an assistant to an assistant to a state senator."

"Then you know all about impropriety." I gave him a sweet smile.

"It's been a political tradition since the Founding Fathers." Kevin raised his glass. "I like you. Care to join us?"

Jason set his beer on the table. "I can't be seen drinking with students. Kevin, shut up." He pointed at me. "You return to your booth and your friends, and we'll pretend we never ran into each other."

"Yes, sir." I saluted him. "Can I ask one question first?"

"If he doesn't answer, I will." Kevin gave me a wicked grin like a wolf in beige clothing.

"Stop." He directed the word at Kevin, not me. "One question only."

"How old are you anyway?" It didn't matter to me, but he appeared young, not much older than us.

"He's twenty-six," Kevin answered for him.

I nodded. Seven years. Nothing overly scandalous.

"That's it?" Jason asked. He attempted to remain stern, but the corners of his eyes crinkled, betraying his amusement.

I smiled at him. "All set. Thanks."

I turned away, not looking back as I returned to my friends. I pretended not to see them when they walked by our table on their way out.

"Bye, Lolita." Kevin waved at me before the door closed behind them.

"Lolita?" Maggie asked. "Wasn't that Driscoll's sub?" She swiveled in the booth, craning her neck to see out the window.

"It was."

"What did he mean by Lolita?" Quinn elbowed me.

"Nothing. It rhymes with Selah."

"It does?" Lizzy tilted her head in thought. "Lolita. Selah. It's not even the same number of syllables."

"He's a terrible poet." To myself I noted he made up for a lack of rhyming skills with amazing forearms and his super smart science brain.

EIGHT

"The Tide is High"
Blondie

TUESDAY'S BIOLOGY LIMERICK mentioned Lolita.

I tripped over my feet when I read it on the whiteboard, catching myself at the last moment before I smashed my face into a desk. Maggie picked up my bag from the floor.

"I wondered about today's limerick." She sipped a big cup of tea, nonchalant and seemingly disinterested.

"It's probably a coincidence. Or one of Driscoll's." I plopped down in the seat next to her.

Her voice repeated the words out loud:
"There once was a girl from Alameda,
Whose friends all called her Lolita.
Ever since puberty
She teased men with cruelty
Discovering her charms she'd shouted, eureka!"

"I can read it myself. Thank you very much." I slouched farther down in my chair, hoping to make myself invisible for the duration of class. I grew up near Alameda, but Maggie knew that. There was no way Jason could.

Jason flipped on the slide projector at the back of the room. "We're going to discuss puberty today. I have slides. I know how exciting this is, but please try to remain awake. Miss Elmore, can you please dim the lights?"

I twisted to see him. He waved me toward the door.

With a small huff, I extracted myself from my slouch and dimmed the lights.

The projector's fan hummed as he clicked the first slide. Droning on about the pituitary gland, he wandered up the aisle closest to Maggie and me.

"Hormones begin to take over at the approach of menses in girls."

Menses. Not even sexy Jason Vincent could make the word hot. He paused next to my chair at the end of our row. A crumpled piece of paper fell to the ground, but he kept walking. In the dark, I don't think anyone else noticed. Maggie focused on taking notes.

I kicked the note under my feet and brushed my pen off the desk, accidentally of course. Picking up the paper along with my pen, I tucked the ball into my bag.

The class dragged on forever. I wanted to create a drinking game over the word gland. Everyone would've been drunk by the end of class

Jason flipped on the lights, blinding us all. "Quiz on Thursday. Be sure to review the section on the role of the pituitary gland (drink). Yes, that's a hint."

While Maggie put away her notebook, I pulled out Jason's note. His drop move was about as smooth as a high school student.

"Come to office hours today. 4:00 p.m. Sharp."

Delightfully bossy.

I liked it . . . I disliked I liked it. What would my women's studies professor have to say about all of this? She'd probably have made me burn my bra and stop shaving my armpits. Or write a letter of apology to Gloria Steinem herself. I'd heard a rumor they had been friends back at Smith.

Never had I ever been excited for office hours before. I wasted the afternoon lost in fantasies of him locking his door and doing naughty things to me. My still life in drawing class included a big phallic shape in the center, despite no bananas in the bowl of fruit.

At promptly four o'clock I stood outside Dr. Driscoll's office. Quiet echoed in the hallway and the rest of the doors were closed. I lifted my hand to knock, but the door swung open before my knuckles made contact with the door.

Jason pulled me into the room by my wrist and closed the door behind me.

I didn't hear the click of the lock. Too bad.

"So, Professor Vincent, you wanted to see me?" I felt breathless and dizzy.

"I think we're beyond the professor formality." His gruff voice scraped along my skin like sandpaper. Everything felt too much all at once.

Tall shelves lined three of the walls, books and files formed precarious stacks on the crowded desk and one of the chairs, leaving only one place to sit. I stood still, toying with a loose thread on my bag's strap. My bravado faded away as realization swarmed over me.

Jason Vincent wasn't any other cute guy, a slightly older cute guy. He really was a professor and an authority figure. He could fail me and throw off my GPA. Although, I wasn't even sure how a fail in a pass/fail class would affect my transcript.

He brushed past me in the cramped room and flopped in his chair, sending it into a slow spin. "You asked about private tutoring last week."

I nodded.

"You don't really need extra help in this class, do you?"

I shook my head.

He ducked his chin and spun the chair to stare out the window. Outside, rain pelted the glass, washing the room in shadows.

I cleared my dry throat. "Was the limerick about me?"

He nodded.

"Why?"

With his fingers intertwined behind his head, he faced me again. "Because you're driving me crazy. Kevin's nickname for you is perfect."

"I'm hardly twelve." I felt like a kid in the principal's office. "And you aren't a dirty old married man. Wait, you aren't married, are you?"

"No."

"Engaged?"

"No."

"Girlfriend?"

"Not at the moment, no."

I exhaled with relief.

"But I can't go out with you, Selah."

"Why not?"

"The whole faculty student thing?"

"You're not even a real professor."

He flinched.

"Sorry. I mean, you're almost a doctor, but you aren't a professor here. What does it matter?"

"I need this class as a future reference for my CV."

I stared at him.

"Curriculum vitae?"

"You should speak Latin more often."

"Thank you, but that's not the point."

"I'm not going to go around broadcasting anything. I can be discreet."

His gaze lowered to my outfit. "Hmm . . ." He let his eyes scan down my legs to my boots. "To clarify, this outfit wasn't in reference to our conversation at the bar?"

I looked down. Okay, the low V-neck of my T-shirt showed off a lot of boob, and maybe the length of my skirt wouldn't pass inspection at a Catholic school even though it was plaid.

"Probably not the best outfit for this conversation, is it?"

Again he shook his head no, but this time, his lips lifted in amusement. "It's more than a little naughty school girl."

"I'm not looking to be deflowered. The HMS Virginity sailed ages ago. Nor am I looking for a boyfriend. The whole going steady business isn't really my thing." I needed to stop talking and oversharing about things he probably wasn't interested in hearing.

He ran his finger over his lips, contemplating me like he studied a strange animal out in the wild. "What is your thing, Miss Elmore?"

"I thought we were beyond the whole last name thing." I mimicked his earlier words.

"Fine, Selah. Better?" He shifted in his chair, resting his ankle on the other knee.

I'd never had a guy be this direct with me. Usually we played the game of not interested unless the other person indicated they were interested. Or the other game of *I like hanging out with you, but we're just friends*. Friends who have sex. Never had a boy, or in this case a man, asked me what I wanted like I had some control over the situation.

Yes, I instigated this, but I didn't think my flirting would lead anywhere. Yet here we were in a dimly lit office, with the door closed.

"Cat got your tongue?" he whispered. The energy in the room shifted.

"I hadn't really thought all this through."

"Did you have a plan?"

"No. Not really." My entire plan had consisted of three words: seduce Jason Vincent.

"Maybe if we met under different circumstances. And you weren't my student."

"That's a no then?"

"I'm afraid so. Listen, it's not a judgment on your looks. Or intelligence. Nor do I think any less of you."

I stared at a ceiling tile in the corner and counted to five before exhaling. "Okay, got it."

"You're doing fine in the class. As far as I'm concerned, you'll pass with no problem. In fact, you seem to have a knack for this subject."

"You're not going to fail me?"

He blinked up at me. "No."

"You think I have a knack for biology?" I'd never done well in a science class in high school. Numbers and calculations always made me want to pull out my hair.

"No, I suspect you have a knack for the sexuality part."

I snickered.

"Am I wrong?" His hands returned to the back of head, his biceps curving out to tighten his pale blue oxford distracted me.

"I'd say your hypothesis is correct."

"Thought so. If I'm being honest with you, I'm flattered."

"To be put in the awkward position of having a student try to seduce you?"

"Not the awkward part as much as my ego thanks you. Biology

geeks who spend all their time in the lab and with their noses stuck in books aren't usually the guys girls fall over themselves for."

"Are you kidding me?" I gaped at him. "Do you own a mirror?"

He chuckled and his cheeks pinked a little.

"Every girl in the class has a crush on you and is thanking God, the Goddess, and probably Vishnu for Driscoll's poor choice of footwear."

He held up his hands in defense. "Okay, I get it. Thank you."

"No problem. Can I ask you one more thing?"

"Sure. As long as it doesn't cross our new professor-student diplomacy line."

"What are you doing in April?"

His head jerked back a little in surprise. "That's over a month from now. Probably spending it at UW doing research for my dissertation. Why?"

My hand wrapped around the door handle. "You said you thought I was pretty. And after March, you won't be my professor anymore."

His laughter followed me down the quiet hall. I resisted skipping like a promiscuous Red Riding Hood who wanted to do naughty things with the wolf.

I may have lost this battle, but I hadn't surrendered the war.

NINE

"The Perfect Girl"
The Cure

"REMIND ME AGAIN why I'm here?" Gil shifted on the floor, angling his legs to the left of Maggie.

"Experiencing new things?" I pulled out my drawing pad, pastels, charcoal, and several pencils.

"I wonder how much the models get paid?" Quinn stole one of my pencils, then taped several pieces of paper to his oversized masonite clipboard.

"I hope a lot." Maggie crossed her legs. "Imagine standing there while a bunch of people draw you naked."

"Would you do it?" Gil sounded interested in the idea of naked Maggie.

I swore the two of them were going to get together on our road trip last year before Quinn turned all chaperone and shut them down. Maybe she was over him, because of the whole roommate thing, but I didn't think he was over her. He sat next to her whenever possible and watched her every move.

"No way!" Her blush extended down her neck.

"I'd do it," Quinn replied, even though the question wasn't asked of him.

"No one doubts you would, Q." I settled myself and got ready for the session to begin.

A portly man in a blue terrycloth bathrobe entered the large room, walked to the center, and dropped his robe.

"Okay, one minute poses. Ready?" Tina, our hostess for this life drawing class at the art center, asked the group.

"I can't even see his dick," Quinn complained next to me.

"Are you seriously complaining about that?" My pastel flew over the page, outlining curves and more curves.

After a minute, Tina called for a new pose.

"Oh, there it is!"

"Quinn," I muttered. "This isn't a game of I Spy. You don't win a prize."

Tina called time again and the model shifted into a new pose.

"It's more like hide and sneak." Quinn gestured with his charcoal. "Now you see it, now you don't."

Maggie giggled and ducked her face behind her hair.

"Settle down you two. This is serious." I refused to give into their immaturity.

Our model leaned back over his chair in a pose straight out of Flashdance.

"Oh, come on." Gil put down his pencil.

Directly in front of us, we had a view of everything. Every little thing.

"Nope. I'm out of here." Standing, Gil gathered his stuff.

"I'm with you." Maggie pushed herself up off the floor.

"Shh," Tina shushed from across the room. "Please wait until we break to leave."

Trapped, Gil and Maggie shuffled around people to stand against the closest wall.

Another pose change and I nearly dropped my pencil.

"Is that an open sore?" Quinn leaned forward.

My morning coffee threatened a return. "Focus on his face for this one."

I didn't want to quit.

I wanted to be the cool girl who drew nudes and was all about the beauty of the human form, no matter the shape or size. But if I were being honest with myself, I signed up for the class hoping the model would be male and hot. Or even a hot woman.

"I think he has a cold sore, too." Quinn squinted, his pencil hovering over a detailed sketch of a lower face. He had talent. "I'm adding a cold sore."

When Tina called for a break, I admitted defeat. "I think I've had enough."

Gil and Maggie waved from the door.

"Let's go for brunch instead." I gathered up my things. I tried. I really did. I gave myself permission to give up. I'd had the experience and could check it off my list.

Quinn remained seated. "I'm going to stay."

"Whatever floats your boat, Q."

AT AN OLD diner near the waterfront, Gil deconstructed his experience in class. He sounded like a vet returning from war.

"I know, we were all there, too." Maggie poured a lake of syrup on her pancakes.

"I don't know what I expected, but it wasn't him." He stuffed a big bite of home fries in his mouth.

"I'm guessing you were thinking the model would be a naked woman." I stabbed one of his potatoes with my fork. "Young, hot, and naked."

His shrug told me he didn't deny it.

"Typical." Maggie sighed.

"I'm not going to apologize for liking naked women. I'm a healthy, all-American boy. It's in my DNA."

"He wasn't who I expected, either." Maggie swirled her bacon through the pool of syrup. "I wonder why he signed up for nude modeling."

"Exhibitionist," I guessed.

"Money. The reason anyone does anything."

"You sound so cynical, Gil."

"Maybe the plasma clinic was closed." Gil stuffed eggs in his mouth.

"Speaking of clinics, did you see—"

Gil cut me off. "I'm eating here!"

"He should get examined. That's all I'm saying." I pushed a huckleberry around on my plate.

"Hey, isn't Professor Vincent sitting at the counter?" Maggie pointed behind me.

My head spun around faster than *The Exorcist* girl's did in the movie.

Jason sat at the counter reading the newspaper. Apparently alone.

"I'll be right back."

I sat on the empty stool next to him. "Morning, Professor."

His face appeared from around the paper. "Ah, Miss Elmore."

"What brings you to Olympia this fine Saturday morning?" I swiveled back and forth on my seat.

"The girlfriend of one of my roommates is in town for the weekend. I'm giving them some privacy."

"You have roommates?" This fact surprised me.

"Two of them. Poor grad students, remember?"

"The sex professor is hiding out in Olympia to avoid all the sex going on in his own apartment?"

"He is. Plus, I need to grade your quizzes, which I left in the office last week."

"Distracted?"

"A little." He gave me a secret smile from behind his paper before folding it and resting it on the counter. "What about you?"

"Distracted?"

"No. What are you doing today?"

"We ditched a life drawing drop-in at the art center."

"Life drawing as in . . ." He left me an opening, not wanting or willing to say the word.

"Naked. Life drawing is drawing naked people. Well, really only one naked guy. One really big, really naked guy." I scrunched up my nose.

"Is this part of your degree?" I noticed how long his lashes were as he stared at me.

"I guess."

"Or you wanted to look at naked men on a Saturday morning?" He rolled his lips together.

"There are better places to see naked men on Saturday mornings." I met his eyes, unabashedly.

He studied the sugar shaker near the metal napkin dispenser. "I'm going to ignore that comment."

My lips curved into an evil grin. Something about seeing him uncomfortable made me happy. He marked himself as forbidden fruit, which only made me desire him more. "What brings you to this fine establishment?"

"The excellent coffee?" He picked up his nearly empty cup.

I frowned. "The coffee tastes like bilge-water with fake creamer."

"At least they have free refills."

"If you want good coffee, go to the Heron Bakery. Excellent bread, too."

"Are you on their payroll?"

"Me? Bake? Or serve people?" I stared at him in disbelief. "Are you kidding me?"

"You don't seem the type." He laughed before finishing his coffee. "Your friends are watching us."

I realized I'd completely invaded his personal space as we talked. He'd turned his stool and his legs framed mine. We leaned close to each other.

I jumped off my stool and practically landed on his lap.

"Guess that's my cue to leave. Bye, Professor." I walked backward away from him, taking in his amused expression.

"Good-bye, Miss Elmore."

I'd hated the formality of him using my last name, but now that we had a wall of propriety between us, I liked it. It felt like an inside joke. Plus, he hadn't said no to seeing me after the quarter ended. March was only a few days away.

TEN

"Principles of Lust"
Enigma

INSIDE MY ORGANIZER with the cats on the cover, I crossed off another day with a red X. Only one more week until the quarter ended and Jason Vincent would no longer be my professor.

I flipped back to the beginning of my planner. There in all its permanent black ink glory was the goal I'd set for myself: seduce Jason Vincent.

I said a prayer of thanks to whatever saint or deity created academic quarters instead of semesters. Ten weeks of torture beat months of waiting.

Spring break followed the end of the quarter. Gil had plans to go skiing at home in Colorado. Quinn talked about another road trip. Lizzy wanted to go someplace sunny and warm. San Diego or Arizona—it didn't matter as long as wherever they went a bright ball of sunshine illuminated the sky. Maggie agreed, and the three of them started plotting their route to sun.

I was on the fence about joining them. Jason hadn't given me a sign the truce would start immediately after he turned in grades. I'd taken his silence as agreement and worried I'd been wrong.

Returning from a long, hot shower, I padded down the hall in my flip-flops and robe, my hair wrapped in a towel. As I got closer to our room, I could hear the phone ringing inside. Our answering machine had stopped working two weeks ago. It probably needed a new mini-cassette, but with finals, we hadn't bothered to get one. Our bulletin board outside the door had become an ink and paper answering machine like in the dark ages of telegrams and carrier pigeons.

I dropped my caddy trying to get the key in the door. Then slid out of my wet flip-flops, nearly tripping as I lunged for the phone. The cord tangled around the base and I dropped the whole thing.

"Hello?" a male voice echoed from the receiver on the floor.

"Hello?" My voice took on a breathless quality after the effort of simply answering the call.

"Hi, I'm calling for Selah." The voice sounded familiar, but remained a mystery.

I lifted the phone off the floor, untangling the curled cord. "This is me."

"Hi, it's Jason."

He hadn't lost my number. He kept my little scrap of paper for weeks.

"How'd you get this number?" I wanted him to say it. I needed confirmation.

"You gave it to me. Then I lost it. Luckily, being faculty allowed me access to your contact information."

He'd looked up my number. Even better. I did a Bender at the end of *The Breakfast Club* style fist pump.

"Hello?"

I'd forgotten to speak.

"I'm still here."

"I turned in my grades this afternoon. You passed."

"Thanks for letting me know. Most of my professors don't call me personally. I appreciate the extra step."

"That's not why I called."

Twisting the cord around my finger, I waited for him to speak again.

"Do you have plans tonight?"

I contemplated ditching my friends. "I do."

He didn't respond, but I could hear him breathing.

"Quinn's been planning a seventies style disco party for ages to celebrate his birthday and spring break. It's in the dorm, otherwise I'd invite you."

"Oh. Thanks. Okay."

"Another time?" I crossed my fingers even though he couldn't see me.

"Maybe we could meet up at the Four Leaf Clover after?" He sounded exactly like a man trying not to sound simultaneously eager and disappointed.

"Are you suggesting for me to break the law?"

"I suspect this won't be the only time you've returned to that fine establishment."

He was right. We went there weekly, sometimes twice. "What time?"

"I'll be there after eleven." His confidence returned.

"I'll be the one in the Mrs. Roper style muumuu."

"Sounds oddly sexy." He lowered his voice to a whisper. "I'm looking forward to seeing you."

After saying good-bye and waiting for the dial tone, I hung up and did a small shimmy. On my bed. While jumping up and down. Screaming.

DONNA SUMMER BLASTED from Quinn and Gil's room. No way the RAs didn't know about the party, but they hadn't cared enough to break it up. Friday night before spring break meant they were probably gone or at their own party.

A trip to the local Salvation Army had reaped many fabulous outfits made of highly flammable polyester and its cousin, rayon. My muumuu had a cornucopia of flowers on it in dazzling day-glo colors. Gil sported a light blue leisure suit and neck scarf. Maggie wore a flowy dress in lilac—a seventies bridesmaid dress at the ugliest wedding ever.

The color made her skin glow against her red hair. Lizzy's micro mini barely passed her ass, but white tights covered her indecency.

Quinn looked like a disco ball in his sparkly, open-collared shirt and shiny silver bell bottoms. Round rose-tinted sunglasses partially hid his blue eyes.

I think Ben dressed as Bob Ross. His curly hair looked extra poofy above his denim suit. Yes, he wore a denim blazer and matching slacks. Leave it to Alex P. Keaton to find a denim suit.

All together, we looked like a bad mashup of seventies television shows.

"I can't believe anyone ever thought these clothes were cool." Gil ran his hand over the rough texture on his arm.

"Are you kidding? This is the best invention ever." I spun around. "If it had pockets, I'd live in these things. Stylish, yet airy and breathable."

"There's nothing breathable about these pants." Quinn's bell bottoms were the tightest fitting, leave-nothing-to-the-imagination man pants I'd ever seen.

"I've never understood guys and their need to let their penises *breathe*?" I used air-quotes to demonstrate my doubt. "Your lungs aren't attached to your genitals."

"It's more about containment and the ability for things to, um . . ." Gil paused.

"Listen, things move around and need their space," Ben explained for him.

"Didn't you learn this stuff in your biology class?" Quinn asked.

"She was too busy flirting with our professor." Maggie nudged me.

Quinn made a face. "Old Driscoll?"

"No, the hot, super young grad student who subbed for him. Where have you been?" I set him straight. Figuratively of course.

"Super hot, young grad student? And you didn't share?" Quinn mock glared at me.

I contemplated telling them about my plans after the party. I needed to get them to the bar, but didn't want the teasing that would ensue for the next couple of hours in between now and then.

"He's on our team, Quinn. Sorry."

"How do you know?" He raised his eyebrow at me.

Maggie huffed. "It may have been a biology class, but there was a lot of chemistry. All of it aimed at Selah."

Really? "There was?"

"You were too busy trying to play coy to catch him staring at you."

Hmm, news to me. I didn't think I could play coy.

Before everyone got too drunk for the second act of the night, I made my suggestion. They all agreed, with the caveat we kept our costumes on.

"We'll match the interior."

"It's not Halloween, Quinn." I really didn't need to show up wearing a muumuu. I was ninety-nine-point-nine-percent sure Jason had been joking about finding Mrs. Roper in any way hot, but I guess I would find out.

Fellow students as well as townies packed the bar. We definitely stood out like flamingos in our brightly colored polyester among all the jeans and plaid.

The booths were full and tables overcrowded. I scanned the room for Jason, but couldn't see more than a few feet ahead of us through the crowd. Being short sucked in these situations. My current view consisted mostly of Gil's back and the buttons of some random guy's flannel.

The crowd waiting at the bar counted five people deep around the stools. Dehydration while waiting for our drinks became a real probability. Sighing, I resigned myself I'd never find Jason.

A warm hand grabbed my wrist and then long fingers interwove with mine. I glanced around at my friends—all hands were accounted for. The fingers tugged me backward, into flannel guy.

I caught my balance and twisted to see Jason smiling at me over his shoulder as he pulled me through the crowd.

Before I could question where he was taking me, he shouldered the backdoor open into a dim alley. He spun me around and pushed me against the cold bricks of the building.

"I've been thinking about your mouth from the first day of class."

I gasped and his lips crashed into mine. Not hesitant. Not asking for permission. Claiming. Demanding. Owning.

His hands framed my face, angling it to go deeper. This wasn't bumbling exploration like high school. He used his tongue as a weapon to conquer me.

My fingers clenched in his soft hair, pulling, tugging, tethering me to him. I wanted to claw at his skin, leave behind marks. I needed to feel his flesh between my teeth. I had to touch all of him. If I didn't, I might have imploded from sexual frustration.

The door we'd exited opened, spilling noise from the bar into the quiet. A guy dumped a bag into the dumpster across the alley. If he saw us, we didn't shock him enough to comment.

Jason ducked his head into my neck, gently nipping the exposed skin. "I like this dress."

His kiss had disarmed me. I'd completely forgotten what I was wearing.

"Most guys had a thing for Chrissy or even Janet on Three's Company, but I find the one guy who had the hots for Mrs. Roper."

"Maybe she didn't wear anything else underneath for easy access." His hands drifted to my hips and bunched the fabric, slowly lifting it high enough so he could reach skin. "Are you naked underneath this?"

I didn't need to answer him when his fingertips skimmed along the edge of my underwear.

"Ah, too bad." He traced the border between skin and lace.

"They come off," I stated the obvious in a breathy plea.

"I imagine they do." The tip of his finger slipped underneath the material.

I stopped breathing for a moment, letting the sensation of his touch roll over my skin. I bit my lip to stop a moan from escaping my mouth when he pressed himself against me. That was no lip balm. Nor was it a pack of Lifesavers or quarters.

I trailed my hands down his arms, examining the biceps I'd been fascinated with for two months. They were as hard and sculpted as I'd imagined. I'd spent hours, days, and weeks fantasizing about them. Now I was touching him. I almost pinched myself to make sure it was real, but losing contact with him would've been a bad idea.

Leaving a trail of small, open kisses along my jaw, he found his way back to my mouth. His kisses became softer, longer. The pent up frustration left him. We fell into a rhythm. Our mouths, his hips, my hips, his fingers exploring me synched into a singular experience. My entire body hummed with building anticipation. My breasts ached to be touched. Everything clamored and screamed for attention from him. He was every boy band member rolled into one and my body acted like his adoring, screaming fan.

Instead of waiting for him to read my mind, I placed his hand over my nipple, pressing his flesh into mine so he could feel how he affected me. He responded by rolling the bud between his fingers, sending a fresh wave of electricity between my legs.

I sought out a new, faster beat with more friction, more pressure. More something. I closed my eyes to concentrate on his touch. I'd never been touched like this, with such self-assurance and deliberate focus.

"I will make you come right here, right now, if you ask nicely." He nipped my ear lobe as his breath warmed my neck. "Or if you're willing to delay your gratification, we could go back to my apartment."

Yes and yes, please? I could ask nicely. Or beg. I wasn't above begging at this point. If he asked me to purr like a kitten, I would have. Anything to make him finish what he started.

"Why not both?" I whispered, unable to focus on the thought of stopping the wave of pleasure about to crash over me. "I'm close."

"I know."

A shift of his fingers, a pinch of my nipple, and I fell into an abyss of sensation. Sweet goddess of orgasms and bliss. The man knew what he was doing.

ELEVEN

"Damn I Wish I Was Your Lover"
Sophie B. Hawkins

"HOW DID YOU know I was close back there?" I sat in the passenger seat of his VW Rabbit on the drive north to Seattle.

"Miss Elmore, you should be able to answer your own question. Did I teach you nothing about biology?"

I thought about it for a second. "Tell me. It'll be hotter coming from your mouth. I like it when you go all scientific."

He stretched his arm over the gearshift to rest his hand on my thigh. His fingers traced the pattern of my dress. "Your breath became shallow, your nipples engorged and extended, a flush bloomed on your chest and neck, and that's only what I saw with my eyes. My fingers told me more. Your vulva puffed and your clitoris swelled with excitement. I could feel how slick you became. How your body opened for my fingers, preparing itself for penetration."

I could have done without the terms engorged and vulva, but his frank, honest description of what he experienced and witnessed was all kinds of hot. Much hotter than slang terms guys in high school used. None of them could find a clitoris even using a map. Or had their finger placed directly on it. They were all about insertion and screwing. Literally.

I FELL BACK into the pillows on Jason's bed. His mouth on my sex was almost too much. He knew what he was doing.

This wasn't fumbling around in new territory. No random jabs or pokes. Nothing about his movements felt awkward.

Part of me wanted to find the woman, or women, who taught him how to do this. No man was born knowing a woman's body like he played mine right now. Most needed a beacon like a little pink lighthouse sitting at the apex, beaming its light into the darkness. Or tiny versions of those guys at the airport with their mini light sabers guiding the penis into the vagina.

Then again, Jason did teach biology. Maybe he lied when he said he'd never taught human sexuality before. He could be a natural. Or an amazingly quick learner.

His tongue pressed against me, sending sparks of pleasure firing throughout my body.

Or a damn genius.

His mouth began to gently suck while his fingers explored. No, not explored. Claimed me.

My hands curled into the pillows. I wanted to pull his hair. Hard. Some part of me wanted to inflict a little pain to balance out the pleasure he gave me.

From my center, energy crackled and snapped through my body out to my fingers and toes. My muscles coiled and tightened.

Oh. Oh. Oh.

"Vulva!" I yelled, clamping my thighs around his head.

Oh, oh, oh, no.

No. No. No.

Maybe he didn't hear me because of the thigh-muffs.

Who was I kidding?

Everyone in his building, and maybe out on the street probably heard me. Vulva echoed down the hall, the stairs, ringing off of the brick buildings along the parked cars, scaring flocks of birds from the trees. Children stopped playing in the park and looked around in confusion before their mother's hands covered their ears. Dogs howled out their own version of vulva. Ruh-ra, ruh-ra.

His hands pressed my legs apart and he sat up on his knees between them. "Did you shout out vulva?"

I covered my head with his pillow. He pulled and I held on tight, wishing for a quick, soft, down-filled death to claim me.

Unfortunately, he was stronger and the pillow went flying across the room.

"I'm pretty sure you said vulva."

"I don't think so." With my eyes closed, I shook my head against the mattress. If I couldn't see him, he couldn't see me. "Who would say such a word out loud? Ever."

"I said it in the car less than an hour ago." He tickled me and I peered at him through my lashes.

"Well, that makes one of us." I widened my eyes in faux innocence. "You're probably the only guy to ever say that word."

He crawled up my body and kissed my left nipple. "Don't be embarrassed."

"Why would I be embarrassed? I didn't say anything."

He dragged his teeth over the sensitive area, causing the nipple to rise in a salute. "Vulva."

"Stop!"

He lifted his mouth away from my skin. "You want me to stop kissing you?"

"No, keep doing that part. Stop speaking. No more words."

"Vulva?" He rubbed his nose over my ribcage to the other breast.

I scraped my nails over his scalp, and then yanked on his hair.

"Ouch. Okay, I'll stop." He sucked on a spot below my ear.

I sighed in relief.

"What are your feelings on labia?" he whispered, and then stifled my annoyed mumbling with a searing kiss.

WE SPENT ALL of my spring break at his apartment. Mostly naked, although we did drive back to Olympia to pick up some clothes from this decade. He might have loved to torture me with anatomically correct vocabulary, but he wasn't so cruel as to make me do a walk of shame in a caftan.

It poured rain every single day. Friday afternoon the sun peeked out and we literally ran outside to witness it like a rare comet. Blinking into the bright light, he suggested we go to Alkali Beach, west of the city. It wasn't a warm, sandy beach in San Diego where my friends had headed, but it worked.

We stopped for groceries and rented a movie at the video store on the way back to the apartment. As we passed through the lobby, he paused to get his mail. An envelope from Ohio State stuck out on top, his name typed in neat lines.

"What's that?" My curiosity got the better of me. I'd promised myself not to ask anything about the future after this week. I was a freshman. He was a grad student. No way would this thing between us have a chance of lasting.

"Oh, nothing." He tucked the letter under a copy of *Scientific American*.

"If it's nothing, then why are you hiding it?"

"It's not important. Come on, you promised me your famous Campbell's tomato soup if I made grilled cheese."

I narrowed my eyes at him, but wasn't going to let this come between me and grilled cheese with tomato soup.

I managed not to burn the soup and his grilled cheese skills impressed me. As we watched *Bull Durham*, the stack of mail on the chair by the front door kept calling to me. I didn't understand what needed to be secretive about a letter from Ohio. He attended grad school at UW already, why did it matter?

I half watched the TV and spent the rest of the time shooting dirty looks at the mail.

"Why are you staring at the door?" He stroked his hand down my hair where my head rested on the pillow in his lap. "Are you expecting someone? Or wanting to leave?"

I rolled over to face him. "What makes you think I want to leave?"

"Every time you look away from the TV, you move your head. Even with the pillow, it rubs across my lap like the world's slowest, worst attempt at stimulation."

"Sorry."

"Nothing to be sorry about. Unless you thought you were turning me on. In which case, I have better suggestions." He tapped my nose.

I sat up, then straddled him. "What did you have in mind?"

Instead of touching me, he laced his fingers behind his head. "What've you got?"

"You want me to take charge?"

Closing his eyes, he nodded. His Adam's apple bobbed in his throat as he swallowed. A week's worth of beard growth covered his jaw. The wave of hair over his forehead earlier this year now reached past his brows. I brushed it back.

A small group of freckles dotted his nose and cheeks. I removed his glasses and leaned back to set them on the coffee table, giving one more scowl at the mail before sitting up again. I traced his bone structure with my fingertips, running them along his cheekbones and down his jaw. He lowered his hands to my hips, but didn't open his lids. His only encouragement was a gentle squeeze.

My index finger outlined his lips and the faint smile lines in the corners of his eyes. Each action committed him to memory. I tugged his sweater over his head and the shirt underneath came off as well.

I read his skin and muscles with my fingertips. He had a small pox vaccine mark on his shoulder and another scar, maybe from the chicken pox under his left eye. A mole on his right pec blemished the smooth expanse of pale skin. A small patch of chest hair centered his chest. I scraped my fingers through it before moving lower to his ribs.

As I continued, the truth of us came to be.

He would be leaving. Ohio. Or someplace else would offer him a job, a future. He'd take it because that's what academics did. They followed the dream job, the promise of tenure, the perfect research position.

What was I going to do? Ask him to stay? Wait for me?

This wasn't a beginning.

This would be good-bye.

"You stopped."

I focused on his deep blue irises. "You're leaving."

"Where am I going? I can't even get up with you sitting on me."

"No, not right this minute. Or tonight. Or tomorrow. Or next week."

He furrowed his eyebrows together. "Eventually we'll have to leave the apartment again for food and condoms."

"I mean Seattle. That's why you won't tell me about Ohio."

He closed his eyes for a beat before he nodded. When he reopened them, his gaze was steady, but held regret. "I applied for post-doc programs months ago. I don't even know if I got accepted."

"It's a thick envelope."

"It could be filled with all the reasons why I suck and they'd never accept me."

"That's probably it. You'll be stuck teaching freshmen about sex forever."

"There are worse jobs in life." He tightened his arms around my lower back. "I'm sorry."

"For what?"

"I should have told you the truth. Instead, I made it about crossing some ethical line with you."

I rested my head on his shoulder. "Let me understand this. You're saying you have no morals, but you do have ambition?"

His laughter made me bounce on his chest. "Maybe I should give up biology and join Kevin in politics."

"You do have nice hair. Like a Kennedy."

He kissed the top of my head. "We can still hang out until summer. I'm not going anywhere before June, if not later."

Tears pricked behind my lashes. I couldn't invest more and have it end. As tough as I pretended to be, I still had a heart.

Rather than answer him with a lie, I stood up. Taking his hand, I led him to the bedroom.

We never did get our answering machine fixed. It made it easier to move on from Jason if I couldn't get messages from him. He thwarted me a few weeks later with a note left on my bulletin board. A sweet good-bye I didn't really deserve. I put it in my boxes being stored for the summer.

There once was a girl who shouted vulva
So loud it was heard from here to Russia
I've never met a girl like you
Now you're gone, I'm feeling blue
Something something something rhymes with vulva
(I suck at limericks. Even more so at good-byes.)

BEN

Benton Grant, 19

Economics and Finance major
Sophomore

What moment changed the course of your life?

Bombing in statistics.
Yes, I'm serious.
Having to get help. No, having to admit I wasn't perfect and maybe I did care a little bit changed everything. For the first time in my life, I cared.

TWELVE

"Peter Piper"
RUN DMC

I WANTED TO get stoned.

Punch something.

Listen to rap and curse.

Run.

Drive fast, with all the windows open. No destination or schedule in mind.

Why?

Somehow I was on the verge of failing the statistics section of my global economics and world markets course.

Two weeks into sophomore year and I'd already bombed two quizzes.

Unacceptable for many reasons.

I had to make an appointment with my professor according to his note on the last quiz.

How could I make my first million by thirty if I couldn't pass a lower level statistics section?

I found Roger in the student union, aka the CAB, hanging out with some chick with a thousand piercings in her ears. With a nod of understanding, he agreed to stop by my room in thirty.

Back in the dorm, I blasted *Licensed to Ill*, and lay on my bed, waiting for Roger to show up with a quarter. Old habits were habits for a reason.

He did the classic shave-and-a-haircut-two-bits knock. He thought he acted smooth and clever. In reality, he was neither. Because his older brother had a direct source for amazing BC bud, I put up with him.

I checked the bag for seeds and stems, then handed over the cash. The stuff was sticky and sweet. We hung out shooting the shit for ten minutes, while I loaded up my bong, stuffed a towel under the door, and opened the window.

"Where's your roommate?" Roger made himself at home on the empty bed.

"Don't have one. I have the whole double to myself."

"No way. How'd you swing that?"

"Amazing what money can do." I lit up and took a long drag. The water bubbled as smoke billowed up the glass, entering my lungs when I moved my finger. I held my breath, letting the heat burn. After a moment, I exhaled the smoke out my window.

Calm began to invade my bloodstream.

Roger took a hit and then checked his beeper. "Gotta go."

I wasn't going to ask him to stay. "Thanks, man."

He kicked the towel out the way. Half the dorm probably smoked pot, but old habits had also taught me to be smart about it.

After a couple more hits, I replaced the bong in the closet next to the box holding various pipes, and stuffed the baggie in my sock drawer.

The sense of panic and anxiety abated. Feeling like I could breathe again, I opened my statistics text book and started studying before dinner.

ACCORDING TO DONALD McDonald, statistician and Santa impersonator, I needed to attend a weekly study group with a tutor if I wanted to get through stats. Okay, he probably didn't impersonate Kris

Kringle, but he could rock the mall Santa gig if he wanted.

He suggested a guy who took his class last year. Joe was a Legal and Public Admin, aka pre-law, major, and some sort of statistics wizard. Whatever floated his boat as long as he could get stats to stick in my brain.

Old McDonald told me to show up in the library on Monday at noon for the weekly study session.

I arrived a couple minutes late after making a stop at my room for a quick smoke. There were only two other people in the room, besides Joe, who sat at the head of the table. He looked like one of those wan-nabe jocks who kept records of all his favorite baseball players' stats, but never played a game himself. Could've been the backwards Mariners' cap on his head.

Being late, I'd missed the introductions. The other two students under Joe's tutelage included a stunning blonde and another girl across the table from her. I didn't really pay attention to the other girl.

I sat next to the blonde. Her perfume reminded me of my mother's weekly flower arrangements, which cost a small fortune. She didn't even look at me; instead, she remained focused on Joe. He explained a problem from our homework, punching away on a giant calculator on the table in front of him.

"I think you missed something in your calculation," Blondie interrupted him.

Wow. That was bold of her. Telling our tutor he was wrong.

"I have a completely different answer, too." I finally gave the other girl a good look. She sported short hair and an old man cardigan in olive green. Not unattractive, just plain. Especially when Blondie occupied the same space.

"I don't think so." Joe shoved his notebook in our direction. "Check it."

Blondie studied his calculation, then stood up and walked over to the big white board behind him. After copying the formula and Joe's numbers onto the board, she paused.

"I see where he went wrong," other girl said.

Wrong? He was supposed to be teaching us this shit and he got the problem wrong? I stole a look at Blondie's notes. She'd already done all the work. I could see she had a different result for this problem.

"He missed the seven." I pointed at the error on the board.

Blondie smiled at me in thanks for taking her side.

I cocked my head in reply. I'd be on her team any day, especially if it was a doubles team.

Joe stared at the board. "You're right. Excellent catch."

I shot him a sidelong glance. Was he testing us by making mistakes and hoping we'd catch them? This being my first study group ever, I had no idea how these things worked. I'd never had to put much effort into studying or classes before. Somehow, I coasted. Smarter and more clever than was probably good for me.

Blondie resumed her seat, slid Joe his notebook, and then turned to me. "Did you bring your homework?"

Oh, right. I pulled everything out of my backpack. "I did."

"What are you stuck on?" Joe asked. "Let's have it."

I shuffled through papers, looking for the worksheet. Next to me Blondie sighed and tapped her pen on the table.

"Here it is. I had an issue with the population variance on the second question."

"Oh, that's an easy one." Blondie once again went up to the white board. Erasing the previous equation made her ass wiggle in her jeans. No baggy man cardigan for her. Her figure looked athletic and toned, not like a jock, though. She probably worked out in one of those thong leotards like on Jane Fonda's aerobics videos. A guy could hope.

She wrote everything down and then turned to me expectantly.

I stared at Joe, waiting for him to speak up and guide us.

"Wanna take a shot?" Blondie asked me directly.

I scratched behind my ear and squinted at the numbers. Everyone focused on me, waiting for me to solve it. If I could have figured it out, I wouldn't need this weird ass study group.

Sighing, Blondie began adding to the formula while explaining her work. I couldn't figure out if she were a kiss-ass or one of those know-it-all girls who had to always be right.

"If you're doing simple random sampling, use the sample standard deviation?" Joe's voice went up at the end like he didn't know the answer.

"That's the most basic approach." Other girl's voice held the same disbelief at this clown I felt. I gave her and her ugly sweater a mental high five.

"I understood that part. The calculation at the end throws me off." I pointed to the board.

Blondie explained her work, slowly and thoroughly. She was much better at this than Joe. Maybe he was some sort of savant. Like he could count cards at casinos, but didn't know to look both ways when crossing the street.

We worked through the rest of the questions. At the end of the session, I felt better about the equations. Maybe I wouldn't bomb this week's quiz.

As we packed up our stuff, we agreed to meet again on Wednesday after class.

I found myself following Joe out the door.

"Thanks for the session, Joe." Slinging my backpack over my shoulder, I caught up to him.

"I don't think she heard you."

I flinched. "She?" Whoa, what?

"I'm Curtis. She's Jo." He pointed down the hall at Blondie.

Ah, that made more sense. I snapped my jaw shut and followed her departure with my eyes. My stats tutor wasn't a doofus savant. She was a beautiful girl with a big brain and a sweet ass.

THIRTEEN

"Around the Way Girl"
LL Cool J

IMPRESSING MY TUTOR ended up being better motivation than the threat of not passing global economics.

I wasn't late on Wednesday. In fact, I arrived early and I had an extra to-go cup of coffee in front of me. Because I'd bet she took it sweet and milky, a bunch of creamers and a selection of real and fake sugar sat on a napkin next to the cup.

Cardigan showed up first and eyed my coffees. "Double-fisting?"

The old adage about bringing enough for the whole class flitted through my head. Shit. Obvious much?

My plan didn't really work out the way I'd hoped. Curtis took the seat closest to me, leaving the head of the table for Jo or the seat next to Cardigan.

Jo arrived and sat at the far end of the table.

Aborting the mission, I pushed the extra cup across the table. I didn't need two cups of coffee.

"That's sweet of you." Cardigan grinned at me.

I returned her thanks with a closed mouth smile. "No problem."

"I don't think you're supposed to have drinks in the library, but I'm going to pretend I didn't see those." Jo gestured at our cups.

This was not going as I'd planned.

Worse, she nailed me—and not in the good way—on two of the problems. Instead of letting us ask questions, she made each of us go to the white board and copy our own work for the group to figure out where we went wrong.

Every once in a while, I'd catch her checking me out. Her pert nose would wrinkle when one of us went off track with a problem. An adorable line appeared between her brows as she attempted to backtrack and find our errors.

Today, her long golden hair had been woven into a braid. She wore black leggings with sneakers and an oversized sweatshirt. Even casual, she looked beautiful.

She had no idea who I was, where I came from, or how much money my father made. To her, I was some schlub who couldn't master something she could do easily.

Nor could I charm my way out of these calculations or buy myself a better grade. This was uncharted water for me.

Her no-nonsense attitude turned me on. I felt out of her league, which had never happened to me before. In the past, even at both of my former boarding schools surrounded by household names, trust fund kids, and a few distant royals from smaller European countries, I'd never felt anything but among my own kind.

She intrigued me.

At the end of the hour, as we put out stuff away, an idea came to me.

"Do you offer private tutoring?" If I had to pay her to hang out with me to see how charming I could be, that was cool. It wasn't like I was paying for sex or anything. No *Risky Business* for me.

"Not getting what you need out of the group?" Genuine concern in her voice, she focused on me.

"No, it's great. I think you're doing a fantastic job."

"Thanks." She stood and came up to my shoulder. Next to me, she felt more petite, more delicate. "I guess I could meet with you one-on-one before the midterm if you think you need extra help."

I liked the sound of one-on-one.

"When were you thinking?"

"This weekend." A lightbulb flashed above my head. "I have a single where we could study there uninterrupted."

"I think we'd be better off meeting here or in the CAB."

Clearly, she saw through my attempt to make this more private. "CAB works for me. We could combine eating and studying. Kill two birds."

We made a plan to meet Friday afternoon.

She might not have thought of it as a date, but she didn't know everything.

FRIDAY AFTERNOON NONE of us had classes. Gil showed up to chill in my room with Maggie in tow.

"Anyone want to smoke?" My mother's over-the-top hostess skills had worn off on me. I had guests, I needed to offer them something. Although the idea of my uptight Yankee mother ever getting high was crazier than Nancy Reagan passing around pot brownies.

"Sure!" Maggie clapped her hand.

"Have you ever smoked pot before?" Gil gave her an incredulous look.

"Not really, but I did the inhale someone's exhale thing freshman year."

I shrugged my shoulders and grabbed the bong.

"It's very pretty." She stroked the tall glass cylinder.

"Thanks. I know a local guy who hand blows them."

Gandalf the Gray was my favorite bong. Probably bigger than needed, various grays and white swirled through its clear glass.

"He's got real talent. Does he make other stuff not related to drug paraphernalia?"

"Yeah, but the bongs and pipes are his best sellers."

Gil put in the CD of the Beastie Boys' *Paul's Boutique*. He and Maggie sprawled on the other bed. I leaned back on the pillows on mine. I couldn't figure out their deal. They always seemed to be around each other, but I'd never seen them actually together like kissing or anything. If they were a couple, they weren't into PDA. If they weren't a couple, they acted like one. Weird.

A knock sounded on my door. I jumped up to put the bong in the closet, then sprayed the room with aerosol room deodorizer.

"Yeah?" I moved closer to the door, but didn't open it.

"It's Selah."

Exhaling in relief, I let her in. Selah and I had a history, but that's what it was: history. I blamed freshman freedom syndrome. Poor decisions made because they could be. We both knew it was what it was, nothing more.

"I could smell pot down the hall, and I figured you guys were hanging out in here. Share the good stuff."

I'd forgotten to put the towel by the door. After remedying my oversight, I pulled the bong back out of the closet.

Maggie asked for snacks and I opened a drawer in the spare desk. I had cereal, Cracker Jacks, chips, peanut butter and pretzels—the perfect munchies emergency kit.

Maggie shoved a handful of Captain Crunch into her mouth and winced. "Ouch!"

"What's wrong?" Selah asked from her spot splayed on the floor.

"I think I cut the roof of my mouth." Maggie finished chewing with exaggerated carefulness. "Got any milk?" She eyed my mini fridge.

"I'm out."

Frowning, she set down the box. "Selah, share your caramel corn with me." She crawled off the bed and collapsed with her head in Selah's lap.

"Here, but give it back to me." Selah passed her the box.

"What's interesting about a box of Cracker Jacks?" Maggie asked with a full mouth.

"In my aesthetics of advertising class we had a guest lecture this week. She talked about all the subliminal messages snuck into ads and illustrations."

"Like what?" Gil shifted to stretch out on the bed.

"Mostly naked women to make things subconsciously more appealing to men."

"And are there naked men to make things more appealing for women?" Maggie asked, studying the box of caramel corn.

"There's a hidden man in the camel on Camel cigarettes. He has an erection," Gil added to the discussion.

Maggie threw back her head and laughed. "The things you know."

"Maybe I need to switch from Marlboro Lights to those," Selah mused. "If women found pictures of penises as stimulating as men find boobs, such thinking might work. But would a penis make you buy something?"

"Probably not. Wait, I see a penis!" Maggie pointed to the box. "See? Right there? With a pair of balls below it."

Selah peered at the box. "That's totally a dick. Ben, can I borrow a pen?'

Gil and I locked eyes. We'd smoked the same thing, but I wasn't hallucinating imaginary peckers.

He shrugged his shoulders and went back to reading the liner notes. "The Beastie Boys are geniuses."

I had to agree. We ignored the girls and their giggling on the floor while we had a very serious discussion over the sampling of the *Jaws* theme on "Egg Man."

Another knock pounded on my door. Over and over again.

"Hide the bong," I told Gil.

"Who is it?" I asked, scrambling up from my spot.

"It's Jo."

Oh, shit. I squinted at the radio alarm clock on my desk as its numbers flipped over to display 4:00. Shit. I'd completely forgotten about our tutoring date.

I mouthed the word fuck a few times at the door, then banged the back of my head on the wall for emphasis.

Maggie and Selah, oblivious to my personal struggle, continued laughing and shouting about subliminal dicks.

"Can you guys shut up for two seconds?" I whispered at them.

A thin haze of smoke lingered near the ceiling. If I opened the door, a cloud of smoke to rival a Grateful Dead show would probably fly into Jo's face. I didn't know her opinions on recreational pot smoking, but something told me now wasn't the time to find out.

"Sorry," I told both the people in the room and Jo on the other side of the door. "I fell asleep and got out of the shower a minute ago."

"You're almost an hour late. Must have been an amazing shower." Even through the door, I could tell she didn't believe me. Who knew if she could hear the raucous giggling before she knocked.

"I'm sorry. Let me get dressed and I'll meet you in the lobby in a couple of minutes."

"Never mind. I don't have time now to meet." Yep. She sounded annoyed.

"Then why did you come find my room?"

"To let you know I don't appreciate being stood up. Ever."

I closed my eyes again and rested my head on the door. There wasn't anything I could say. I'd already apologized. "Let's reschedule then. I'm free all weekend."

Silence greeted me for a few seconds.

"I'll see you in study group, Ben." There was no mistaking the disappointment and frustration in her voice.

"I'll make it up to you." I wanted to chase after her, but not when I was high.

She didn't respond and probably didn't even hear me.

FOURTEEN

"It's Tricky"
RUN DMC

ON MONDAY I wore a tie to study group to show I wasn't a pot smoking slacker.

It didn't seem to charm Jo at all.

"Nice tie." Other Girl complimented me. "When do the campus Young Republicans meet?"

"First Tuesday of the month at lunch," I responded without pause. She didn't seem the Republican type, more like Green party or whatever group would piss off her family the most.

Her laughter in response sounded like a seal barking. "Of course you knew that!"

I'd missed her sarcasm. Grumbling, I turned my chair to ignore her.

Instead of letting Jo walk away from me after class, I followed her. Not in some sort of creepy way. I matched my pace to hers as soon as we exited the library.

"Thanks for the tip on standard errors. It made some things click for me."

"You're welcome." She picked up her pace. I easily kept up. "How did you master statistics?"

"Surprised? Because I'm a girl and girls aren't good at math?" Her voice turned cold. The label "ice queen" came to mind.

I choked on my own spit. "No, that's not it at all. I'm good at math in general, never had an issue with it, but something about this class fries my brain."

"Maybe it's not the class," she mumbled.

"I'm sorry?" I said, thinking I didn't hear her right.

She faced me, annoyance clear in her expression. "Maybe it's not stats that's frying your brain."

Guess she smelled the pot.

"Hey, I'm sorry about Friday. I apologized already. My friends came over and we hung out. That's what college kids do."

"Not every college student gets stoned."

"Don't knock it until you try it. It might help you relax."

The line between her eyebrows deepened as she scowled. "Are you saying I'm uptight?"

Her chest bounced with her quick breath. I'd pissed her off again. "I was speaking in the universal sense of you."

"Right." She strode away.

"Hey—" I caught up with her in the middle of the quad. Grabbing her arm, I stopped her from storming away.

She stared at my hand on her arm until I removed it.

"Listen, we got off on a bad foot or something. I'm a nice guy. You seem nice. Let's start over." I made my eyes big and bit my bottom lip. The look had worked for years, because it made me look like a sad puppy. What I discovered as a kid typically worked on girls, too.

She sighed. "We don't have to be friends. Me liking, or not liking you, won't make a difference in you passing this class. That's the goal, right?"

Ouch. Her words stung.

I needed a different approach. "How about we make a bet?"

Doubt and a big dose of reluctance settled over her expression. "What kind of bet?"

I stared back at her. "I get a B or higher on the midterm in a couple of weeks, we hang out. As friends. No statistics talk. Get to know each other."

Her lips twisted to the left as she considered my offer. "What's in it for me?"

"Other than the pride of knowing you helped me master stats? What do you want?"

She started walking again. "I'd like to negotiate. Let's make it a bigger challenge."

My ego couldn't resist. "Okay, what are your terms?"

"You get an A and I'll hang out with you. Anything less, you forget you met me after the class ends."

Harsh. "How about an A–and I'll buy dinner?"

Negotiating with her had my adrenaline flowing.

Without pausing, she studied my face, searching for sincerity. "Okay. Deal."

She stuck her hand out to shake on it.

I pressed my palm to hers and clasped her delicate hand in mine. It fit perfectly. I hesitated to let go after a normal handshake period ended. She had to tug her hand back.

I let her walk away from me, again staring at her backside like a pervert standing in the openness of red square.

I needed a miracle to get an A–and direct divine intervention for a solid A. Unless I could negotiate my way into a better deal after mid-terms. I wondered if she'd be open to the idea.

MY EPISCOPALIAN GRANDMOTHER would've approved of my praying in the days leading up to mid-terms. However, she'd have clutched her pearls over all the swearing and deals I'd also tried to make with the devil. Playing both sides meant I'd win either way. I needed to work every angle on this bet with Jo.

I resisted taking a single hit first thing in the morning to ease my anxiety. Instead, I went for a long overdue run. All my smoking caused me to hack and cough before my lungs adjusted to the unfiltered oxygen I sucked into them.

Post run, I showered and dressed in a green and white rugby shirt over Levis. No tie today.

I half expected to see Jo outside the exam room or proctoring the test for McDonald.

Less than an hour later, I felt confident I'd nailed it. Instead of staring at a bunch of confusing questions and formulas, everything had clicked. I'd been one of the first to turn in my test and leave.

I wanted to find Jo to celebrate early. Then I realized I didn't know what dorm she lived in. I didn't even have her number to call her. The dorm I could find out easily in the class book, but I decided to play it cool until I got my grade.

Instead, I headed to the CAB to meet my friends for lunch. Inside, I saw a huge banner covered in weird drawings of green balls and the following words:

"Free the lettuce! Lettuce is slavery! Boycott salad!"

Taking over most of one wall of the dining hall, it couldn't be missed. I had no idea how the granola freaks even hung it without a major ladder.

"Ben!" Someone called my name and I glanced around.

Maggie waved from a table in the corner by the windows.

"What's up with the sign?" I set my bag down on an empty chair.

"What do you think?" Crazy Quinn appeared at my side. His hair touched his shoulders. In his overalls, he looked like a hippie lettuce farmer.

"About what?" The guy seemed nice enough, but kind of weird.

He gestured to the banner.

"Boycott salad? Comparing lettuce to slavery? What does it even mean?" I asked the group.

"It's a protest in support of Cesar Chavez and the migrant workers in California," Maggie explained it to me.

"Really?" I sat down. "What's the point?"

"We need to be aware of where our food comes from and the people who suffer to bring it to us!" Quinn's enthusiasm clued me in.

"Ah, you made the banner."

He beamed. "I did. Then I convinced the maintenance guys to help me hang it up. Turns out, most of them are from Mexico or Ecuador, and they're totally down with the cause."

I shook my head. How did I end up being friends with a hippie, tree hugger like him? More green near my feet caught my attention. A frog's face greeted me from its position on Maggie's foot.

"Are you wearing Kermit slippers? In the college activities building in the middle of the day?" Honestly, who were these people and how did they become my friends?

"I am." Lifting her leg, she rested a disgusting slipper on the table in front of her. "I've had them since junior high. They bring me good luck."

Age and dirt dimmed the once bright green. The sole had a hole on the heel and the beginning of a few more tears near the toes.

"Junior high? Those look like they're much older." I pointed at the hole, but didn't dare touch it. "You probably shouldn't wear them outside."

She bent her knee to inspect the bottom of the slipper. "Oh, bummer. I love these things."

Thankfully, she moved the fuzzy green petri dish to the floor.

"What are we doing this weekend?" I needed distraction from stewing over my mid-term grades. And Jo.

"My new band has a gig in downtown Olympia tomorrow night." Gil reached into his bag and showed me a neon orange flyer covered in thick black letters and a blurry, black and white photo of three guys.

"Inflammable Flannel?" I read the page. "Is that your band's name?"

"That's the worst name ever." Quinn gave his unsolicited opinion.

"Says the guy who loves Soft Cell." Gil glowered at him. "We wanted something to capture the local scene."

"Flannel definitely works. It's practically the school uniform." I glanced around and could've pointed out ten, no fifteen, people who were currently sporting flannel.

"I like it." Maggie smiled at him. "You guys will become big rock stars and we'll all say we knew you when."

A group of men in blue custodial uniforms marched a tall ladder through the dining hall.

I tapped Quinn's shoulder. "Looks like your banner's coming down."

He spun around and jumped out of his chair so quickly it tipped over. "Stop the man!" he shouted as he dashed across the room.

"Poor Quinn." Maggie sighed. "He means well."

"He's crazy." I wasn't judging. It was the truth.

From our table we watched Quinn block the ladder by climbing up it and sitting on the top. Once on his perch, he crossed his arms and refused to budge.

"Atticus! Atticus!" Quinn's voice carried over the room.

"Does he mean Atticus Finch? From *To Kill a Mockingbird*?" Maggie asked.

"I think he means Attica, like the prison riots. Or the Al Pacino movie quote." Of course Gil knew those random facts. He could tell you anything about US history. "How long do you think he can stay up there?"

"Wanna bet?" Maybe my lucky streak would continue.

"He'll be done by this afternoon. He has a critique in his sculpture class over in the Art Annex at three." Maggie smiled and waved at Quinn, who grinned and waved back, nearly falling off his perch.

"This might be the world's shortest sit in," Gil said.

"We're a much more apathetic generation than the real hippies." Maggie ate a french fry.

"It's because we have cable TV and video games." I knew I'd rather stay at home, watching movies and playing games than marching in a circle out in the elements.

"And MTV. Let's blame them while we're at it." Maggie poked a fry into her soft serve ice cream.

"The radio star and civil disobedience, both victims of the video." Gil wrote down his quote on a napkin. "I'm using that line in my history of unrest paper."

"Um, the guy sitting on the ladder is calling your name," a familiar voice said behind me.

I glanced over my shoulder to see Jo standing there. On the other side of the room, Quinn yelled, "Benjamin," and waved his arms over his head, causing the ladder to tilt precariously to the left before he found his balance again.

"Not me."

"Aren't you Ben?"

"I am, but it's short for Benton."

"He's Benton Grant, the fourth," Maggie said.

"The second." I corrected her.

"Figures." Jo sighed and crossed her arms.

"Want to join us?" I pointed to the chair next to me currently occupied by Kermit the Slipper.

"I . . ." Jo paused.

In the small silence I saw my opportunity. It wasn't a no. I introduced her to Maggie and Gil.

"Sit with us." Maggie took over for me like I knew she would. She moved her feet and Jo took the seat next to me.

We fell into easy conversation. Jo laughed as we explained Quinn's misguided attempt at social action.

By the end of the half hour, Jo felt like part of our group.

"Gil's band is playing downtown tomorrow night. You should join us." Again, Maggie played the role of hostess.

"What kind of music is it?" Jo asked.

"We don't really know yet. It's the three of us. Mark on guitar and vocals, me on bass and back up vocals, and Mike on drums. We play mostly covers."

"Mike Ramirez?" Jo crumpled up her napkin.

"Yeah, you know him?" Gil asked.

"I dated him a couple times last year."

Dated? Some punk wannabe drummer? He was the kind of guy she dated?

"He's totally cute." Maggie's compliment made me want to kick her, but she sat on the other side of Jo and I didn't want to miss. Whose side was she on?

"Yeah, but not really my type."

I exhaled with relief. I hadn't completely misjudged Jo.

I OFFERED TO drive to the club. We could fit all of us in the Audi since Quinn bailed after having to meet with the Dean of Students to discuss his stunt with the ladder.

Gil drove in the van with the equipment. Jo said she'd meet us there, which sounded like an out to me. I doubted she would show up at all.

Maggie and Selah rode with me.

The bar had a long line out front when we arrived. Two other bands were scheduled to play. The crowd buzzed about another three piece with some Zen Buddhist name.

"Gil added us to the list." Selah pushed her way toward the bouncer.

Inside, the crowd jostled for space near the bar. The long, narrow room ended with a stage in the back. Stickers from bands and previous shows decorated the black-painted ceiling and walls.

Most of the people there looked like Selah, wearing used clothes and flannel, with big boots and leather jackets. I stuck out in my navy and green striped rugby shirt. I worried someone would carjack the Audi even though we found a spot directly across from the bar.

Inflammable Flannel had the opening slot. They tuned up, squawking their amp and making the crowd cringe. Mark apologized and introduced each of the members. Selah and Maggie yelled so loud for Gil, I swore he blushed.

More than a few guys heckled them about the name. Ramirez flipped the bird at the crowd, which only incited more heckling. A fight brewed before they played their first song.

A brawl probably would've gone over better than their cover of "Like a Virgin." Not sure I would've led with Madonna in this place.

"Madonna sucks!" a drunk guy next to me with an anchor tattoo on his forearm screamed in my ear.

"Posers! Posers!" the crowd chanted.

"This is a bloodbath," I shouted in Maggie's ear.

"I have an idea," she said, then yelled, "Play 'Freebird'!"

"Freeeebird!" Anchor-man gave her a high five.

Gil strummed the first notes of "Another One Bites the Dust." He turned away from the crowd to say something to Mike, who picked up his sticks and played a different drum beat.

"What are they doing?" Selah asked over the grumbling crowd.

"Stalling for time?" Maggie guessed.

Finally, Mark followed Mike's lead on drums with his guitar and Gil shifted to follow.

The first lines of "Jesse's Girl" came out of Mark's mouth, and the tide shifted in the crowd.

Selah whistled. I recognized the look on her face. Officially on the prowl, Mark was Selah's new target. I gave the guy credit. He owned the lyrics.

"I fucking love this song." Some guy slapped me on the back. Hard enough I spilled my beer.

I turned to see who the asshole was, and spotted a familiar head of blond hair a few feet away. I told Maggie and Selah I'd be back, and elbowed my way in Jo's direction.

She smiled when she saw me. I gave her a goofy wave.

I squeezed in next to her, my shoulder brushing hers. "Can I get you a beer?"

"Thanks, I'm set." She held up a cup containing what looked like soda.

She leaned closer to me. "They don't suck."

I nodded and spoke directly in her ear. "You missed their first song then. I thought the crowd would start rioting."

She laughed and sipped her drink. Given the space and the music, we couldn't talk other than shout a few words at each other. It was enough to stand next to her. The same scent of flowers and summer created a bubble around us in the smoky bar. I dipped my head to inhale more of her.

Inflammable Flannel finished their set to a round of low key applause, with the exception of Selah and Maggie. They hollered their heads off and whooped like Julia Roberts in *Pretty Woman*. I wouldn't compare them to uncouth hookers, but if the dog woofs fit . . .

Selah stalked up to the stage like a panther on the prowl, and immediately chatted up Mark. Maggie stood to the side smiling at Gil. I couldn't hear either conversation, but from the way Selah kept touching Mark, I didn't need to know the exact words to know her intent.

My ears still ringing from the speakers, I overestimated my voice and shouted, "Want to go outside?" loud enough for the majority of the bar to hear me.

Jo gave me a soft smile. "Sure. I could use some fresh air."

Smoke hung in thick bands and the entire place reeked of old beer and spilled Jägermeister shots.

Outside, I steered us across the street and away from the cloud of smoke above the crowd by the door. I wanted to check on my car. Leaning on the hood, I patted a spot next to me.

"You're going to get in trouble for leaning on this car. I bet the owner is some uptight yuppie." She stood out of traffic, but didn't rest against the car.

I chuckled. "I'm the owner."

"Oops." She laughed it off.

"You called me an uptight yuppie."

"If the car fits . . ."

"I bought it used." Not sure why I felt the need to defend my car.

"With money you earned slaving away at a summer job?" She toyed with the sleeves of the sweater tied around her waist. I took in her outfit of black leggings and white T-shirt.

I could've lied, but instead I went with the truth. "My parents gave me the money. In fact, I bought it for less than they gave me, and banked the rest."

"I guess duping your parents for money is commendable." Her tone said it wasn't.

"Sarcasm suits you." Without thinking, I pulled out my one-hitter. Our bet hadn't included anything about me stopping smoking. Part of me wanted to test her. I offered it to her with my lighter. "You want some?"

She swiveled her head to look up the street. "You're going to smoke out here in the middle of the street?"

I shrugged. "Sure. Why? Do you think one of those guys by the club is a Narc?"

"Probably not. You're either really bold . . ."

I lit up and inhaled. "Or?" I asked, still holding the pot in my lungs.

"Completely crazy."

Exhaling, I blew the smoke away from her. "Probably both. No risk, no gain. Basic economics."

Her gaze flit around my face. "Probably both."

I held the pipe out to her.

"Okay." She rolled her shoulders back before taking it, and holding it up to her lips. After she inhaled, she coughed. And kept coughing. Handing me back the one-hit, her blue eyes watered as she waved her hand in front of her face.

"Smoke much?" I teased her, taking another toke.

Unable to speak through her coughs, she shook her head. "Not really."

"Ever?"

She glared at me. "I'm not a boring good girl."

I held up my hands. "No one ever said you were."

"Because I'm smart and good at math and don't want to marry my high school boyfriend, doesn't mean I'm not fun." She got the words out in between small coughs.

"Whoa. Pot's supposed to relax you. Not work you up into a rage."

She grabbed the one-hit back. The fire had gone out, so she didn't get any smoke when she inhaled. "Light me up."

"Okay." I followed her orders and refilled it.

She exhaled almost immediately, but didn't cough.

"Are you two smoking illegal drugs?" Selah called from across the street.

A couple guys in the crowd turned to stare at us. Jo dropped the one-hit at our feet.

"Really cool, Selah!" I shouted back at her, picking it up and tapping the tip on my bumper before stuffing it into my back pocket.

Selah gave me a ridiculous wave. I flipped her off.

"What's the deal between you two?" Jo stepped into the street to cross.

"We're friends."

She arched an eyebrow. "Just friends?"

"We tolerate each other, but to answer your unasked question, we did hook up last year."

"I see." Those words could mean a whole bunch of stuff in girl language.

None of them good.

FIFTEEN

"Don't Believe the Hype"
Public Enemy

WITH MY GRADED midterm in hand, I sprinted to the library as soon as economics finished.

Only Jo sat at our table when I arrived. I slapped the test in front of her and stood back to assess her reaction.

"Ninety-five-point-seven." She blinked several times and her lips pressed together before she nodded.

"Round it up and what do you get?" I grinned.

"An A. Congratulations."

"Where do you want to go celebrate? I thought we could drive up to Seattle. Maybe go to dinner."

"There are restaurants here in Olympia."

"Don't you want to get out of this backwater town?"

"It's the state capital."

"It still manages to feel like the middle of nowhere. Come on, I'll treat. You pick the day."

She gazed up at me.

I expected to see happy excitement in her eyes. Instead, they held trepidation. "What? What's going on? We had a deal. We made a bet."

"I know."

"What? You made the bet because you didn't think I'd get the grade. Is that it? Now you're welching?"

"We already hung out. On Saturday."

"Saturday didn't count. Shouting a few words at each other while terrible music played doesn't come close to hanging out."

"We stood around outside in between bands. There was drinking. That's hanging out."

"Why are you arguing semantics with me?"

Sighing, she wound a few long strands of hair around her fingers. "I don't want to be some sort of prize."

I sat down at the head of the table, confused. "We had a deal. We negotiated. We shook on it."

She got up to write something on the board, not making eye contact with me. "I showed up Saturday in good faith you'd get at least an A–. So we're even."

This wasn't the way things were supposed to work out. Saturday night had been a bonus, but not the real deal.

"We agreed on dinner for an A–. On me. Going to the diner with all my friends, and you paying for your own fries doesn't count."

She faced me. "It counts."

"What does a guy have to do to get you to go out with him?" I leaned back in my chair.

"Ask me."

Her two words changed everything.

I never had to work for anything in my life. Not even boarding school. When I got kicked out of one for breaking rules or smoking pot, my parents found another school willing to take my full tuition. Smart enough to coast, that's what I did. Good looking enough to have girls ask me out worked for me. I could've dated anyone I wanted. They knew it. I knew it. Everything had been too easy.

Then I arrived here on this rainy campus in a podunk city on the wrong coast. What mattered two years ago, meant nothing now. I was adrift and out of my element. Sure, I managed to cover it up with the same bravado and cocky attitude, but clearly Jo saw through my bullshit.

And happily called me out on it, without me having to mention a thing.

Ask her out?

How stupid was I?

I'd been playing it so cool, I didn't think to be direct.

Clearly, for the first time, how deeply I'd underestimated Jo hit me.

Before I could fix the mess I created, Curtis and Cardigan walked in holding hands. When they saw us, they quickly broke apart and took seats on opposite sides of the table.

Today had been full of revelations. I wonder what the odds were for their relationship.

"I INVITED JO to our Halloween party this weekend." Maggie dipped a crouton into ranch dressing and ate it. Her salad bowl contained tomatoes, cucumbers, a few black olives, and croutons, but no lettuce.

Evidently, Quinn had harangued her into guilt.

Somehow he'd managed to convince both the Dean of Students and his academic advisor the protest had been a performance piece. Even got his advisor to write a letter of support since nothing was damaged and no lettuce harmed. Or something. The tree-hugger had mad persuasion skills.

"And? Is she coming?" I focused on deconstructing and reassembling my turkey sandwich into the proper order of bread, meat, tomato, lettuce, cheese, and bread. The tomato should never touch the bread.

"She said she had other plans, but might stop by." She crunched on another crouton. "But I got the feeling she didn't really mean it."

I frowned at my tray. I could man up and ask her out, but every signal she sent me told me to back off.

No way was I going to stick out my neck and get rejected. Benton Grant didn't get rejected. Rejection wasn't something I'd experienced and I felt fine with avoiding it.

I jabbed my finger into the center of my sandwich. My appetite had disappeared.

Maggie prattled on about party plans. "Quinn's making something called jungle juice. He's buying the fruit today and will start marinating it in whatever liquor he can get a hold of. He mentioned a source for Everclear."

"With Everclear?" Basically pure alcohol, it packed a serious punch, and should've been illegal . . . and was in a couple of states

"It might be the one night I stick with beer." She wrinkled her nose.

"Sounds like it should be renamed hangover juice." I bit into my pickle. The sourness matched my mood. "We made something similar in boarding school with oranges and vodka. Soaked the orange wedges, then ate them. What looked like a healthy snack appropriate for a Saturday soccer or lacrosse match got us seriously messed up."

"You got drunk *at* the matches?" She sounded shocked.

"Not when I played. Well, not really drunk. More buzzed. I played better with a little buzz going. It made me more aggressive."

"Bet your coaches loved you."

"They did until I overdid it the night before State Finals."

"You showed up drunk?"

"No, with a major hangover. I threw up in the cooler."

"Ewww." She pushed her bowl away. "You lost the championship?"

"We shut them out." Pride colored my words.

"Teenage boys are weird." Wadding up her napkin, she tossed it on her tray.

"Speaking of boys, have you seen Gil around?" The two of them were typically joined at the hip. I figured she was the best person to ask.

"I think he's hanging out with Dawn."

"Who's Dawn?" I ran through a rolodex of names in my head.

"The girl he's been seeing this month?" Her tone told me I hadn't been paying close enough attention to my friends' dating lives.

"Wait, I thought you two were dating."

She snorted and the snort turned into an awkward laughter. "No!"

"It's not completely crazy. You're always hanging out together."

"He's like my brother."

"Lies. I have a sister and she has never once looked at me the way you two look at each other. Ever." I shuddered at the thought.

She blushed, but denied it. "No way. Girls and guys can be best friends."

Smirking, I lifted an eyebrow. "No, they can't. I saw *When Harry Met Sally.*"

"We're friends."

"Yeah, but we're not best friends. And before you say Quinn is your best friend, he doesn't count. He no more wants to get under your skirt than he wants to go to a strip club."

"I disagree. Gil and I have even slept in the same bed. He's never made a move."

I frowned, thinking about why any guy wouldn't make a move on Maggie. I knew I hadn't because she was also Selah's best friend. To avoid drama, unless Maggie would be "the one," she was off limits. Some sort of girl code.

"Doesn't mean he didn't want to." I took a bite of my sandwich, confident in being correct.

"You're crazy." She glanced down at her watch. "I'm going to be late for class."

I dropped the subject of Maggie and Gil. None of my business if they were playing the platonic game.

"Don't forget to get a costume for Thursday!" She left me alone at the table.

Costume?

SIXTEEN

"Sabotage"
Beastie Boys

LATE THURSDAY AFTERNOON I realized I forgot to buy a costume. Or even a mask. Opening my closet door, I studied the contents. I flipped through my clothes and ties, hoping for inspiration. Taking out Gandalf, I set it on my desk to reach the stuff I didn't wear often. In the back I found the garment bag with my favorite suit. The suit had a few wrinkles, but considering it had been in a bag for months, it wasn't too bad. I shook it out. It would do.

An idea came to mind. Rather than go scary this year, I'd play to character. Or who people saw me as.

Easiest costume ever.

AFTER I GOT dressed, I packed my pipe and tucked it in my suit pocket with a lighter. Eyeing my bong, I decided to take a quick, pre-party hit.

I didn't bother with the towel or my window. One hit. No harm.

Satisfied with my buzz and costume, I swung open my door right as Jeff the RA walked by. Nose in the air and sniffing audibly, he had clearly been looking for the source of the herbal smoke that followed me like my shadow.

"Grant."

"Hey there, Jeff. I'm headed out for the evening."

"Nice suit. We need to talk before you take off." He gestured behind me. I followed the direction of his finger and saw Gandalf sitting majestically on the desk in plain view.

"It's a sculpture."

"Don't bullshit me, Ben. I know what a bong looks like."

I held up my palms. "Okay, it's not only a sculpture. It has a water feature, too." I cracked up at my own joke.

He didn't even twitch a lip in amusement. "I'm going to have to write you up for an infraction."

"No way. Come on, Jeff. We're buddies. You know I'm a good guy." I searched my brain for something to bargain with, some angle I could work. "Aren't you from Denver? Broncos are doing really well this season. You going home for winter break? I know someone who could get you sweet seats for one of their home games."

"I hate football." He crossed his arms and planted his feet. "Nice try, though. Subtle, but still a bribe. It's campus policy. I need to write it up. Or I could lose my job."

"Is this going on my permanent record?" I tried to joke.

"It'll go in your file, yes."

I started to panic, my anxiety ratcheted up with my heart rate. "Like on my official transcript? What if I want to apply to grad school or run for office?"

"You want to run for office? Like politics? Maybe you should have thought about your future before you smoked ganja."

Who even said ganja anymore? "No, I want to get my MBA. I can't get the job I want without it."

"Again, you should have listened to Nancy and said no." He quoted Nancy Reagan's famous anti-drugs slogan.

Sighing, I shook my head and closed my eyes. "Fine. Do what you got to do. I'm late for a Halloween party."

"You're going to a party in a suit?"

"'It's a costume." I held up my briefcase.

"Yuppie asshole?"

"Close enough, but no prize for you."

"You'll have to attend a disciplinary hearing next week." He stood where I left him in front of my door.

"Fine. Let me know when and where."

"You won't need to wear the suit."

"Thanks."

The night went from mediocre to horrible in the span of five minutes. My mood followed.

AT THE PARTY I stood in the corner, drinking Quinn's version of spodie. Koolaid, fruit, alcohol—the combination worked its magic on me. After my fourth cup, I couldn't give a rat's ass about anything.

WHEN I WOKE up the next morning, my head pounded and my lip hurt. I ran my tongue over the tender skin, and tasted copper. If I moved my head, the room spun. I lay on my back, keeping as still as possible while I waited for details of the night to filter through my fuzzy brain.

Jeff spying Gandalf was crystal clear. Arriving and chugging a couple of cups of liquor out of a trashcan were less solid. Everything else fused together into loud static in my brain.

Drinking, smoking my pipe.

A room crowded with too many people. Dancing.

Loud music.

Women shrieking with screams of laughter.

Being called Alex P. Keaton by anyone who got my *Family Ties* costume.

Jo.

I shut my eyes to concentrate on the memory of Jo. What had she worn? Who did she show up with?

Her costume had something to do with feathers. Or wings. Maybe both. An angel? No, too trite for her. Swan?

Sitting up too quickly, I groaned.

Bile tickled the back of my throat as I remembered throwing up in some bushes outside a dorm. Somehow I knew it wasn't my own dorm.

I swallowed. A painful throbbing took over my left temple. I closed one eye.

A grainy video played in my brain. Me. Standing outside the un-known dorm, shouting and slurring my words.

Dread settled in my stomach.

I'd been shouting Jo's name.

Outside her dorm.

In the rain.

Like a drunk asshole.

With both my palms, I rubbed my eyelids, pressing into the sock-ets, trying to erase the memory while simultaneously filling in the gaps.

My fist making contact with a guy's face flashed clearly into focus. I touched my lip in memory of his knuckle busting my lip.

Who was the guy?

He wore clown makeup.

I hated clowns.

Maybe he was a mime.

I hated mimes even more.

Hobo? He might've had a stupid sack on a stick.

Reality broke through my haze. He'd come with Jo.

I'd asked if he was her date and she told me it was none of my busi-ness. That pissed me off. Then the clown dissed my costume. I threw a punch.

Probably not one of the smartest things I've done. And I've done a lot of dumb shit over the years.

Someone pounded on my door.

"Go away!"

They kept pounding.

The last person who assaulted my door had been Jo.

I leapt up. Bad idea. Being vertical made my head throb and spin. The bile rose again. I bent over to let the nausea pass for a minute while the pounding continued.

"Hold on. Give a guy a minute."

The knocking stopped.

The second I opened the door, Jo stormed into the room. I leaned against the wall to get out of her way.

"Welcome." I rubbed the scruff on my face and ran my tongue over my teeth. I should've brushed them before answering the door. My mouth tasted like something died in it while I slept.

"Your lip is cut." She gestured to her own mouth.

"Yeah, I think I remember how it happened."

"You think?"

"Last night's pretty fuzzy."

She stood in the middle of the room, arms crossed.

"You want to sit down?" I gestured around my room, pointing out options.

"No, I'm good. I don't plan to stay."

I pressed my lips together and nodded. "What can I do for you?"

"Last night is never going to happen again."

"You're going to need to be more specific. There are some gaps in my memory."

"You don't get to act possessive of me. Or punch guys who talk to me. No, you shouldn't be punching or fighting with anyone."

"Fighting isn't really a problem."

"None of that Lloyd Dobler in *Say Anything* stuff outside my dorm either."

"I had a boombox?" Wow, I really didn't remember much from last night.

"No, but you screamed my name loud enough that everyone on my floor who had been sleeping, because it was three in the morning, heard you, and woke up."

"I didn't know your room. If I did, I would've thrown rocks at your window."

"And probably broken a window."

"You heard me?"

"How do you think you made it home? My roommate and I helped lug your dead weight back here. You could have played Bernie in *Weekend at Bernie's*."

"You know that movie? I love Bernie."

"Not really the point, Ben." No question about it, she was mad.

Slumping to the floor, I exhaled a long puff of air. "The two of you carried me back here?"

"Three of us. My friend Trey helped."

The name sounded familiar. "Is he the asshole I punched?"

"He's not an asshole, but yes, that's the guy you gave a black eye to last night."

"Only assholes dress up as clowns. I hate clowns. They're fucking creepy, hiding behind their costume and makeup. But underneath the bright, cheerful exterior lurks evil. Trust me."

She let me prattle on for a minute before interrupting me. "The reason I stopped by this afternoon is to draw some boundaries."

I squinted at my clock. "It's three o'clock?"

"Boundaries?" She leaned against my desk.

"What? Right. Why?"

"To be blunt? You're a mess."

"But you like me. I know you do. You showed up at Gil's gig."

"Maggie invited me."

"But we hung out."

"With the group. Listen, I like you, but that's as far as this goes. You need to get your shit together."

I laughed, tilting my head to rest on the wall. "You sound like my parents."

"You should probably listen to them. You're not a stupid guy."

"Gee, thanks. Are you my guidance counselor now?" Defensiveness edged my voice. "Last time I checked, I'm an adult."

"Then start acting like one."

My head hurt too much for this nonsense. "You're pretty bossy for someone who doesn't know me."

"I know you well enough."

"Is this why you turned me down for the date?"

Staring out the window, she sighed. "Pot smoking slacker isn't exactly the kind of guy I'm interested in dating."

"I'm not some stoner, spoiled rich kid."

"Then prove it."

I banged my head on the wall. "I don't need to prove anything to you or anybody else. I don't owe you anything. You don't like me because you think you know me from hanging out once or twice? Fine. Your loss."

"Fine." She wouldn't make eye contact. "You do what you gotta do. Don't involve me in your train wreck." She stepped over me still sitting on the floor.

I reached up to grab her leg, but she moved too fast.

"See you in study group." Her voice held none of her usual warmth.

I knocked my head against the wall a couple more times before deciding to smoke away my hangover.

SEVENTEEN

"Better Man"
Pearl Jam

THE JUDICIAL COMMITTEE held weekly disciplinary hearings on Wednesday mornings in one of the meeting rooms in the CAB.

I managed to make it there with a minute to spare. Showing up late wouldn't buy me any points, and I needed more than my usual charms to get out of the mess I'd made.

All week Jo's disapproving frown and words from our last conversation echoed around in my head. Other than being a smart blonde, she was nobody and nothing to me.

I gave myself a pep talk, but when I walked in the room and saw her sitting at the long table at the front with the rest of the committee, my confidence disappeared. Of course my luck was such shit, she'd decide my fate. Pre-law major and everything.

After the stunt I pulled on Halloween, and how pissed off she had been when she showed up to my room the next day, I had no doubt she'd throw everything at me she could.

Maybe I'd be kicked out of the dorm. I didn't plan to live on campus after next spring anyway. An extra six months of rent? Nothing. I still had a few thousand in the bank from the beginning of this year. My parents would cover rent. With my money in the bank, I could even live comfortably without room and board paid for by them. If they cut me off. Which was always a possibility. Hell, I could get a roommate and make him pay most of the utilities and rent. Maybe even turn a profit.

I sat in the row of seats at the back and waited to be called. Some guy stated his defense for urinating in a library stairwell. Even I didn't believe his argument about the similar paint color in the men's room confusing him. The lack of urinals should have been his first clue.

After him, some girl had a long story about parking repeatedly in the fire zone. She had over two hundred dollars in unpaid parking tickets and wanted them forgiven.

Good luck, sister.

I zoned out as Jo and the other four on the council debated. Resting my head on the back of the seat, I shut my eyelids. In my head, I sang the lyrics to "Fight for Your Right" and drummed my fingers on the armrest. The warm room and the afternoon caught up with me. I felt my head loll and the voices in the room disappeared. I let sleep overtake me.

"Benton Grant."

"Benton Grant."

Why was someone shouting for my dad?

"Ben Grant!" Jo's raised voice snapped me out of the half-sleep I'd fallen into.

I snapped my head forward. "What? I'm here!" I scrambled out of my seat and dropped my bag.

Jo rolled her eyes and the woman next to her shook her head. One guy laughed, while the other two stared me down.

A bored looking older man sat at the end of the front row taking notes. He had to be the faculty advisor. He read Jeff's write-up out loud. "Benton Grant, for drug paraphernalia, suspected possession of a personal amount of marijuana, and evidence of drug use. No police report filed."

I stood in front of the panel.

"Do you have anything to say in your defense?"

Part of me wanted to joke about the bong being a water sculpture, but even I wasn't dumb enough to make a bad joke right then. "I promise it was a one time lapse in good judgment and I won't do it again?"

"Sounds like a question, not a statement," The woman who wasn't Jo said.

"It was a statement." I straightened my tie. "I realize I broke a campus rule. I promise not to do it again."

"I don't see a note if the bong was confiscated. Is it still in your possession?" The guy on the end of the row glowered at me. He sat too close to Jo. Way too close. He needed to scoot his chair about two feet to the left.

I nodded. I hadn't thought to get rid of it, or my pipes. "It'll be gone by the end of the day. I can give it to you if you want it."

He jerked back like I offered to gift him a snake. "It should be destroyed, not passed along to someone else."

The thought of Gandalf being destroyed bummed me out. I'd leave it with Roger if I had to. At least until the end of the year.

I looked to Jo for support. We'd smoked pot together, so I knew she wasn't a complete prude. I wouldn't implicate her or get her in trouble.

She took notes and focused on the papers in front of her.

"It's a first time offense. I think a warning is warranted." I recognized the guy who spoke as a friend of Roger's. We'd never been introduced, but I swore I'd seen him hanging around Roger's room. Or with him in the CAB. I knew I had an ally in him.

The group told me to take a seat while they deliberated. For the first time, Jo spoke to the group. Because she whispered, I couldn't hear what she said, but she gestured a lot to the paper in front of her.

The whole school was liberal and tended to look the other way about non-violent crime on campus. Sure, pot was illegal, but it wasn't like I damaged property or attacked anyone. Hell, people got high on LSD and mushrooms in the woods on campus.

My stomach roiled over the memory of Saturday night's fight. At least I hadn't been charged with assault.

"Benton?" Roger's friend called me to the front of the room.

"Yes, sir?" I straightened my back and stood up straighter.

"The judicial board has decided to give you a warning and require you to attend an all-day seminar about drug abuse at the health center

before the end of the quarter. You'll be on probation. No more infrac-
tions. Got it?"

I nodded. "Thank you." I directed the words to Jo.

She frowned and shook her head, disappointment clear in her
expression.

I'd gotten lucky this time.

As I left the room, I vowed to make some changes.

JO

Jo Asotin, 19

Legal and Public Admin
Sophomore

Have you ever been in love?

If you asked me in high school, I would have said yes. Without a doubt.

Now I don't know.

I had terrible taste in guys.

I wasn't one of those girls who liked bad boys or weirdos. No, I liked the normal guys. Great on paper. Nice to my parents. Then turned into jerks. Those kinds of guys.

My high school boyfriend had been beloved by my parents. Football player, track all-star, church youth group leader, lived in the right neighborhood, and had professional, white collar type parents. Everything they wanted in a boyfriend for me.

Also, one of the most boring humans on the planet.

No ambition. No drive to be more or do more with his life. He'd be happy to buy a house in the same neighborhood and send his kids to the same schools we went to.

Back then, I didn't know any better. He fit with every stereotype I'd been taught to want.

Not that there's anything wrong with that thinking.

Unless you wanted more.

I wanted more.

Did I love him? In a way, I guessed I did.

Before I knew what love—real love—felt like.

Love was a river that swept me away, pulling me under and

tossing me around rapids and rocks. Slowing down in quiet spots of peace before rushing on again, taking me with it. I resisted and clung to the safety of the bank. Worked against the current as hard as I could, thinking I could outpace it.

I was a fool.

The river changed how I saw the world. It's brought me to places I never imagined. Showed me what really could be possible when I gave in and allowed it to support me, carry me.

I thought I knew what love was before. I didn't know anything.

EIGHTEEN

I RETURNED FROM winter break to find an envelope with my name on it pinned to my bulletin board. After recognizing the scrawling handwriting as Ben's from statistics, I tossed it in the trash.

"SOME GUY NAMED Ben left you a message on the answering machine. I saved it for you." My sophomore roommate Jenni meant to be nice, but she was clueless.

"Is his the only message on the machine?"

"Should be."

The machine displayed a steady "1" which meant all the messages had been heard.

I hit "delete all" and listened while the tape rewound itself.

She gasped. "You're not even going to listen to it? He sounded really cute and nice. He asked if you'd call him back because he owes you a dinner in Seattle. He even said please."

I cut her off. "Not interested in hearing what he had to say. If I were, I would've played the message."

"Oh, wow. You're totally serious." She blinked her big brown eyes at me. Not the smartest doll in the house.

"I am. In fact, if he calls again, and you pick up, can you tell him to save his energy for someone who cares?

"That's really mean, Jo. What did he ever do to make you hate him?"

I couldn't tell her the truth. Or about the judicial hearing I had to sit through after his RA caught him with a giant bong in his room.

"Nothing. He's not a bad guy."

"Is he single?" Her brows lifted in excitement. "He sounded super cute on the message. Where's he from? What's his major? Is he tall? His voice sounded tall."

"How does a voice sound tall? Height has no correlation to vocal chords."

"You know what I mean."

"I guess he's cute. Not super tall, but above average." I kept my tone disinterested.

Cute? Understatement of the decade. Benton Grant wasn't cute—puppies and kittens and baby tigers were cute. Ben was handsome. Classic handsome with a straight nose and strong jaw. A drawing of Ben illustrated the dictionary entry for "good breeding."

Cocky as hell, too, but he had the looks to back up the attitude. And rich. Which meant he'd also been spoiled, arrogant, and entitled.

No way would I tell Jenni any of that. If I had, she would have sat by the phone waiting for him to call back.

Jenni dating Ben would've been a very bad idea. She was nice enough and pretty, if he liked big hair and big boobs.

No, there was one reason and one reason only it would've been the worst idea ever. Against my better sense, and my vow only to fall in love with the perfect man, I had fallen in love with him.

Ridiculously, stupidly in love.

My grandmother in Spokane always told me it was as easy to fall in love with a rich man as it was to fall in love with a poor one.

She left out the part about being rich didn't equal perfect.

Ben was far from perfect.

He was too busy rebelling and flipping the bird at some perceived authority oppressing him. An angry white boy who didn't want to take responsibility for his own actions.

He was a spoiled child.

He was the most beautiful man I'd ever seen.

The worst part? I saw glimpses of the amazing version of himself he tamped down with pot and bravado.

That man had my heart.

And he didn't even realize it.

NINETEEN

"Think of You"
Guns N' Roses

THE ONE GOOD thing to come out of knowing Ben had been meeting his friends. After going to Gil's gig, we'd met up for other parties and shows, and spent hours hanging out in each other's rooms. I felt closest to Maggie and Lizzy. Selah, less so. Knowing she and Ben had hooked up made things awkward for me.

Because I was jealous.

Not of her specifically. She didn't seem his type. At all. Too much of a man-eater. Although, I could see the appeal. She wasn't the kind of girl he could introduce to his parents. She fit perfectly in his whole rebellion phase.

No, I felt jealous because she knew what it was like to kiss him. I'd spent so much time wondering what it would be like to kiss him it was embarrassing. Or would be if anyone knew.

Maggie, Lizzy, and I strolled across the red square at the heart of campus in the middle of a rare sunny January day.

Up ahead I spied Jenni walking in our direction. I waved at her.

"Maggie!" a guy yelled from the other side of the quad, near the library. I froze.

Maggie stopped and waved behind me. From the corner of my eye I spied Ben jogging toward us. From the opposite direction, Jenni made a beeline for our group.

Wonderful. I stepped away, hesitating while I thought up an excuse. "I forgot something in the library."

I paused too long.

Ben stepped next to me, slightly out of breath. "Hey. I've been trying to get a hold of you for weeks."

I shrugged.

"Hi, I'm Jenni. With an 'i.'" She stuck out her hand to him. "I don't believe we've met, but we've spoken on the phone."

He gave her a perplexed look.

"I'm Jo's roommate."

"Oh, right." His grin caused her to sigh. "I appreciate you taking all my messages for Jo."

"You must be Ben." She grinned back at him, showing all her teeth like a shark. "Jo didn't tell me how cute you were."

If I were standing closer to her, instead of backing away from the group for the safety of the library, I would've elbowed her into next week.

Ben looked at me expectantly. I took another step away from him.

"Sorry I haven't called you back. I, um, I've been busy with . . ." I exhaled a long breath. "You know, classes and stuff. Beginning of the quarter is madness." My sentence ended with a high-pitched, awkward laugh.

A slow, sweet smile spread across his face. "Sure. I understand."

Maggie observed us with her head tilted slightly to the side. I'd never talked to her about Ben, but the way she nodded told me she knew something didn't add up.

Having had enough, I made a run for it. "Gottagobye!" I mumbled over my shoulder as I jogged away.

Inside the library, I stuffed my hat into my bag and realized I'd lost a glove. Through the glass doors, I saw Ben bend over and pick up something pink from the concrete. When he turned his head toward the library, I ducked behind a pillar.

This Cinderella didn't want to be found by Prince Slacker. No matter how charming he could be.

"BEN'S REALLY FUNNY. You didn't tell me he was so funny. Or how cute. I was right about him being cute. And tall. I could tell from his voice." Jenni babbled on and on about Ben while I tried to read the history of the Supreme Court for class. I should've stayed in the library.

"I didn't tell you anything about him. That's probably why I left out the funny part."

She scowled at me. "Honestly, something is wrong with you if you don't think he's cute and funny."

I rested my forehead on my book.

"If you aren't remotely interested, then you won't mind I asked him out for coffee. He's going to stop by and pick me up in five minutes."

A date explained the curling iron and the cloud of Jovan Musk perfume. She had enough Aqua Net in her hair to keep it up for a week.

"He's what?" I lifted my head from the desk. No, Ben wasn't coming to my room. I had to have heard her wrong.

Someone knocked on the door.

"Ooh, he's early. That's a good sign he likes me." She bounced out of her chair and skipped over to the door.

"Come on in. I need to run to the little girls' powder room. You can hang out with Jo until I get back."

I was alone with Ben in my room.

Not the way I'd envisioned my evening going. I contemplated leaving again, but he blocked the one exit, unless I leapt out the window. I imagined landing on the shrubs below and decided against it.

"I have your glove." He placed it on my desk beside my hand.

"Thanks," I mumbled, and tossed it in the direction of my bag.

"Do you want to tell me why you are completely avoiding me this year?"

"Am I?" I wrapped a lock of hair around my index finger and gently pulled. "We don't have any classes together or live in the same dorm."

With his warm brown eyes, he stared at me, seeing through me.

At least it felt like he could look inside me from the intensity of his focus.

"Yes, but we share a social group and have the same friends, yet somehow are never in the same place at the same time. Don't you find it odd?"

I frowned. "Not at all."

"You don't return my calls."

"Jenni is really bad about giving me messages."

"That's not what she said." Of course he'd quizzed her. "I left a note pinned to the board by the door."

"Huh. Never saw it." The role of ice queen served me well. I pointed at my textbook and pile of index cards. "You and Jenni have fun. If you don't mind I have a test tomorrow . . ." I focused on the book, trying not to listen to him a few feet behind me. I could hear him sigh.

"Jo, I'm sorry."

The door shut behind him.

An hour later, Jenni stomped back into the room.

"What a waste of hairspray." She tossed her bag on her bed.

"Not as funny and cute as you thought?" I didn't lift my attention from my notes, but was dying to know more.

"Oh, he's both. Totally."

"What happened?" I glanced at her without turning my head.

"All he could do was talk about you."

I twisted in my chair and glared at her. "No, he didn't."

"He did. Of course, I did most of the talking, but he kept bringing the conversation back to you. If I asked him something, he'd make it about you."

"Shut up."

"I think he's obsessed with you. I told him you weren't interested. In fact, I repeated the whole line about putting his energy elsewhere."

I gaped at her. "You didn't." I wouldn't admit to myself why her telling him what I told her to tell him upset me. It didn't even make sense to me.

"I did. You're welcome." She picked up the phone and dialed. "Chris? Hey, it's Jenni. With an 'i'. Want to hang out? Great. Be over in five."

"That was fast." She amazed me with her ability to bounce back.

"I told you. This hair is too good to waste." She reapplied her bright pink lipstick. "Don't wait up!"

Left alone, I had zero focus for recalling the names of justices from the sixties and seventies. Instead, I played Guns N' Roses on my boombox. Loud.

As Axl wailed, I wove my hair into two French braids.

Turning the music up louder, I sang along to "Sweet Child O' Mine" and attempted to deafen my thoughts about Ben.

In spite of yelling at him, calling him a loser, and ignoring him, he still asked about me.

Asking about me was bad. Very bad.

Or really, really good.

No, it was bad.

The next song came on, its beat fast and crazy. I danced around, trying to exorcise the unwanted feelings from my body.

Benton Grant was bad news.

I needed to stay away.

The song finished and I fell face first on my bed. Pulse racing and chest heaving with my breath, I admitted defeat.

He'd apologized.

Those two words could change everything.

TWENTY

"What Have You Done for Me Lately?"
Janet Jackson

"WE ALL WALKED down to Geoduck Beach and got stoned the other night." Maggie sprawled on her bed, her feet in the air as she pretended to read some depressing, existential French book. We'd been studying together all evening.

"Even Ben?" His name slipped out. My avoidance skills had improved and our paths hadn't crossed in over a week, but he still occupied a big part of my thoughts.

"It was weird. Gil offered him some and he turned him down. Even though Gil has his old pipe."

I sat up straighter. "That's odd. Was he sick?"

"No. He drank a couple of beers. Said he wanted a clear head this quarter."

"Very strange."

"Have you ever known him to turn down getting stoned before?"

"Why do you ask me?" My voice remained flat and nonchalant although my pulse quickened.

"You two used to hang out all the time last fall. Or so it seemed." I could see her hook dangling in the water. She was fishing and not being subtle about it.

Okay, I'd bite. "Not really. I tutored him in a study group. Then the few times we all hung out."

"Really? I thought you two dated. Or, you know, *hung out*." The real meaning behind her words sat down in the room like an elephant on a little stool.

"Hmm." I played with the ends of my braid. "Not really."

"Not really or not at all?"

"We've never gone on a date, or kissed." The words flew out of my mouth like a flock of tiny birds.

"Never? Selah swore you had. She said Ben always stared at you."

That was news to me. "Never."

"But he talked about you all the time."

"Did? Like in past tense?"

She tapped her feet together as she pondered her answer. "Now that you mention it, he doesn't really bring you up these days. Last fall everything was all Jo did this and Jo said that. I guess that's why I figured you two dated or had a thing, but you broke up with him."

"There was nothing to break up. Trust me."

"I probably shouldn't tell you this, but he's been pretty sullen lately. Quinn called him a sour bastard the other day."

I didn't know what to do with the new information. Or anything she'd said about Ben.

"Why didn't you go out with him?" She kept up her casual interrogation.

Truthfully, it felt good to unload it. I explained about how we'd met, the drugs and the cocky attitude. I left out the part about him getting written up, but included the fight and the mean words we'd said to each other. His uncaring, cold dismissal still stung.

"And that's it?" She closed her book

"No." I paused, debating whether to share all of it. "He reached out at the start of the quarter."

"What did he say?" She rolled over and sat up on her knees.

"I don't know." I slowly unraveled a thread from the seam of my T-shirt.

"You lost me."

I told her about the note I threw out and the unheard messages. How Jenni went out with him for coffee. I spilled every pitiful detail.

She listened, nodding and frowning where appropriate.

"This explains the fight on Halloween."

My cheeks heated. "Oh, God. I can't believe that happened. I've apologized to Quinn a dozen times for the fight ending his party. I still feel terrible."

"Quinn's fine about it. He was thrilled a real old fashioned brawl with strapping guys broke out at one of his parties. Don't you remember he kept shouting for a video camera?"

I chuckled at the memory. "It wasn't a brawl. Ben got in one punch and then fell over when Trey clocked him."

"If you weren't seeing Ben, is Trey your boyfriend?"

Giggling, I shook my head. "No! I'd brought him to introduce him to Quinn. He didn't say he was gay, but my gaydar and his Whitney Houston poster told me he might be."

"He had a hell of a right hook."

"He got bullied in school a lot until his dad took him for boxing lessons."

"You should still set him up with Quinn."

"Not happening. Turned out my gaydar and the poster belong to his roommate, Kyle. Unlike Ben, Trey actually made a move on me after the party. I had stupid white and red clown makeup all over my face."

"You made out with a clown?" Her laughter turned into a cackle.

"He made out with my face before I realized what was happening. It was completely unexpected and awful. Then Ben started screaming my name outside the dorm, ruining the moment. Thankfully."

Maggie nodded. "Bad kissers are the worst. It's like being licked by a dog."

"Or pecked by a tiny bird. Or sniffed."

"Sniffed?" Giggles overtook her until she wheezed. "You mean snorted? Like a pig?"

I couldn't breathe. "Exactly."

"I've never been sniffed. So many guys don't know what to do with their tongue. They're all in or nothing."

"Or the lizard tongue." I darted my tongue quickly in and out of my mouth.

"All teeth like a shark." She chomped her teeth together.

"Snake tongue." I gagged.

"Rabbit?" She scrunched up her nose and brushed it across the back of her hand.

We continued laughing until tears spilled from our eyes. I sprawled onto my roommate's bed, trying to catch my breath. "My side hurts. I think I have a cramp."

Maggie wiped her cheeks, still giggling. "I can't breathe."

Lizzy and Selah walked into the room, took one look at us, and declared we needed margaritas.

Large tumblers filled with tequila-laced slurpee concoctions in hand, we settled on the floor and beds. With Maggie's prompting, I summarized the earlier conversation.

"Speaking of nebulous relationships . . ." Lizzy took a big gulp of her drink, then cringed. "Ow. Frozen headache." She pressed her fingers against her temple. "Okay, I've wanted to ask this since last year. Margaret, my dear, what is the deal with you and young Gilliam?"

Maggie choked on the liquid in her mouth.

We waited for her to compose herself. She'd asked a question we all wanted the answer for. Yes, we had our theories, and Quinn had started a pool end of fall quarter last year, but no one knew for sure. Except Maggie and Gil.

Instead of answering us, Maggie took another sip of her drink.

"I told you mine, tell me yours." I prodded her leg with my foot.

"Come on, spill," Selah whined.

"There's nothing to spill. End of story. I need a refill." Stretching over to the dressers, Maggie grabbed the blender.

Lizzy and I made eye contact.

"If not Gil, anyone else?" Selah didn't let her off the hook.

"Not really."

"Because everyone thinks you and Gil are a couple?" Lizzy took a direct approach. Beneath her sweet demeanor and Electric Youth perfume, the girl had a hidden strength like a small, fluffy guard dog.

Maggie refilled our glasses. "Ben said the same thing. You know Gil hangs out with other women, right? Lots of them. They show up at his shows and loiter around like a flock of pigeons by the stage."

"Vultures is more like it." Selah grimaced into her cup.

"Best nickname for the groupies ever, Selah." Lizzy gave her a high five.

"Yeah, but they don't stick around for long." I tried to be optimistic.

"I'm not sure that's better or worse." Picking at her shirt's buttons, Maggie avoided eye contact. "I'm not surprised. He's been like this since freshman year. Bouncing between girls."

"That's because he's not with the right girl." Always the optimist, Lizzy pointed out a possible silver lining to Gil's behavior. "Maybe he's not ready for anything serious?"

Maggie sighed again.

"What about you?" Selah asked Lizzy. "Any action?"

Lizzy scowled. "No. This dry spell is worse than the Sahara. The last guy I kissed was Roger. Have you ever noticed how much he looks like a Monchichi doll?"

We all groaned. I think everyone had kissed Roger at some point. He got around more than Dylan on *90210*.

"Sounds to me like we need to go out and find some entertainment off campus." Selah raised her cup.

"We should go dancing in Seattle or something. It's only an hour away. We could get dressed up." Lizzy's dark eyes twinkled with excitement. "No boys allowed."

We lifted our cups and toasted to a *girls only* adventure. I didn't want to point out it was kind of sad how none of us had a boyfriend or any romantic prospects.

Maybe only I found being hopelessly single depressing.

TWENTY-ONE

"Groove is in the Heart"
Deee-Lite

QUINN SUSSED OUT our plan to go dancing and insisted on joining us as our driver and chaperone. Ignoring the "no boys allowed" rule, he suggested a gay club in the Capitol neighborhood of Seattle with the best DJ in the area.

Some chaperone he turned out to be.

Within five minutes in the club, he danced in the middle of the floor with some gorgeous black guy with a shining bald head and biceps the size of softballs. Occasionally, Quinn would catch our attention and wave. At some point he acquired a whistle.

Selah smiled at him and waved back. "I'm confiscating the damn whistle and shoving it down his throat if he starts blowing it in the car. I'm saying it now, giving the three of you time to come up with an alibi for me."

As Quinn promised, a gay club was the best place for four girls, who were over dumb straight guys, to dance themselves silly without having to deal with getting picked up or harassed.

All the "you go girls" and compliments flattered our egos. Not to mention most of the guys in the club weren't boys. They were men. Hot, fit, really good looking men. Some didn't wear shirts. Others wore the tiniest jean shorts.

"Oh look, leather pants. I've always wanted a pair of those." Lizzy pointed out a couple of guys a few feet away. She screamed when they turned around and exposed their bare asses.

"What is the point of ass-less pants?" I asked, not really wanting the answer.

"You don't want me to explain it to you, do you?" Selah raised an eyebrow at me.

"No, no that's okay. I get it." I didn't want to get it. Not at all.

"I feel like I'm in a candy shop, but I can't eat sugar." Maggie leaned over to me and pointed at two beautiful men making out a few feet away.

Lizzy's mouth hung open as she stared. "I . . ."

I lifted her chin with my index finger. "Careful, you're drooling."

"Condoms?" A thin man with tan skin highlighted by silver eye shadow presented a tray filled with condoms to us. He wore the little hat and outfit of a vintage cigarette girl. "Rubbers, prophylactics, French umbrellas . . ."

"We don't really have the right equipment." Lizzy picked up a neon package.

"Girl, unless you're lesbians, you need these." He focused on me and Maggie. "Are you?"

I sputtered out a no.

"Hmm. Too bad. You'd make a great lipstick lesbian. Pity." He handed us each two condoms in a reverse form of trick or treating. "Wrap it or don't tap it." Off he went like a condom fairy on roller-skates.

"What did he mean by lipstick lesbians?" I'd never heard the term.

"Meaning, we're pretty and girly. It's a compliment," Selah explained.

"Have you ever kissed a girl?" Lizzy asked the group.

"I have." Selah raised her hand. "Seriously, none of you ever experimented by kissing your friends?"

Maggie and I shook our heads.

"I practiced on my own hand." Lizzy volunteered. "And the mirror."

With a big sigh, Selah mumbled something about prudes, grabbed Maggie by the back of the head, and kissed her. On the mouth. For what seemed like ages. Long enough for some random guy to take a Polaroid and hand it to me.

Maggie looked more than dazed when they broke apart.

"I'm not going to stand here like a wallflower." After stuffing the condoms in her bra, Selah pushed her way into the throbbing mass of bodies on the dance floor. The crowd swallowed her, leaving only her hands swaying above her head still visible.

"How was it?" Lizzy asked.

Maggie slowly blinked herself out of the haze. "Much better than Roger. She's an amazing kisser. Soft." She pressed her hand to her mouth.

I shook the Polaroid as it finished developing. "It's a great picture of you both." Flipping it over, I showed them. Even though both Maggie and Selah were out of focus, I could identify them, and they were lip-locked.

"Keep it for prosperity," Lizzy suggested. I tucked it into my little bag with my ID and money.

A cute Filipino guy bumped into Lizzy, spilling his drink on her arm. Apologizing profusely, he called her Audrey Hepburn, and bought her a fresh cocktail.

"This is the best place for my ego." Lizzy sipped the new drink. "Let's dance."

She was one-hundred-percent right. We danced like wild women, not caring who saw, because they didn't care. The night flew by, ending at last call with a rainbow of balloons dropping from the ceiling while Kool & The Gang's "Celebration" played.

Laughing, sweaty and starving, we stumbled down the street to an all-night diner.

"It's like *Pretty in Pink* out here," Selah purred. "Look at Duckie over there."

Standing ahead of us in line, two guys in creepers and mohawks smoked clove cigarettes.

"Clove cigarettes always remind me of the Goth kids smoking behind the biology building in high school." Quinn inhaled the spicy secondhand smoke.

"I was one of those Goth kids." Selah gave him a high five.

Lizzy snapped her fingers. "Speaking of John Hughes' movies, you know, Ben's a total Jake Ryan type. Rich, bored . . ."

"More like Steff. Kind of a fuck up." I'd managed not to think about him for the past few hours. Lizzy's mention broke my Ben-free bubble.

"Gil looks more like Jake. Except now his hair is growing out, he's more like Bender." Maggie sighed.

"And he got rid of those terrible frames he had freshman year. I kept worrying Sally Jessy Raphael would press charges for theft." Selah laughed at her own joke.

"They weren't terrible. They weren't even red." Of course, Maggie defended him.

"Maybe they weren't red, but they were terrible." Quinn made a sourpuss face.

Everyone nodded in agreement.

Since Ben had been brought up, I wondered what he was doing tonight. Maybe he had a date. The thought made my chest hurt. I didn't want him, not as a fuck up, but I didn't want some other girl to have him either.

I wanted him to be my Jake Ryan who showed up in his Porsche and rescued me. Forget the white horse, I'd take a red Porsche any day.

Wait, did I sound materialistic? I didn't really want to be rescued by some rich guy. Or any guy.

"Do you think I'm shallow and materialistic?" I asked, beginning to freak out I was both of those things.

"You are a little Barbie in the looks department, but you have the brains hiding behind the blond and pretty." Quinn pulled on my ponytail.

Lizzy thoughtfully studied me. "Do you think you're shallow and focused solely on material things?"

Maggie nudged her. "Two sections of psychology and human behavior are a dangerous thing."

"What if you are?" Selah shrugged. "Own it."

"I think Selah is saying you are, but I disagree. You tutor people. If you didn't care about others, you wouldn't bother," Maggie said.

"Then there's the whole volunteering with the underprivileged kids stuff." Lizzy shared how I spent last summer. I forgot I had told her.

I didn't explain how in elementary school I had been one of those kids after my dad got laid off at the factory. We pretty much lived off of Bisquik recipes, casseroles, and peanut butter sandwiches until he found another job a year later.

Mom had started working as a secretary at our church to help with the bills. At the time I thought she wanted to be a church secretary, but later realized it had been the church's way of giving us some help without it appearing as charity.

Anyone looking at our family wouldn't have seen anything different. Mom bought our school clothes at thrift stores or on super-sale with her friend's employee discount. Same house, same cars. From the outside, we were exactly the same as before. We hid our poverty behind closed doors.

I never wanted to go back there again and promised my nine-year-old self I wouldn't. Hard work, goals, and yes, even an ambitious, successful husband were part of my life plan.

An entitled, spoiled rich kid didn't fit into my goals. No matter how handsome he was.

TWENTY-TWO

"THE GUY I'M not supposed to mention called again." Jenni slid a piece of paper across my desk. "He insisted I write down a note and make sure you saw it."

I fought the instinct to crumple it up and throw it in the trash without reading it. My fingers twitched on the paper.

"He also told me if you threw away the note, I should tell you the message next time I saw you. What's it going to be?" Exasperation edged her words.

"Fine." I read the note. All six words of it. "That's it?"

"He insisted it was important and you'd know why."

I reread the sentence.

Then crumpled up the paper and threw it away.

THE BOY WHOSE name I didn't want to hear sat outside my door after classes on Thursday. I spun on my heel to head back down the stairs.

"Jo!"

I kept walking. I didn't need him or his sweet words.

"I know you saw me. Don't run away."

"I'm not running." I sped up into a jog. Although I'd thrown away his note, Ben's words had haunted me for four days.

Now he called my name and literally chased me. I raced down the stairs, aiming to hide out in the laundry room in the basement.

His sneakers slapped the stair runners as he followed me. Bracing his hands on the railing, he jumped down the last flight. He landed a few feet away from me with a loud thud.

"Ouch!" Another thud followed as he crumpled to the ground. "Shit. I think I broke my foot."

I stopped. I wasn't heartless.

"Are you okay?" I slowly moved toward him, cautiously, like I was approaching an injured animal.

He held his foot, rocking back and forth. "I'm not okay. Not even close to okay."

"Do you need to go to the ER?" I had no idea where to find the nearest hospital, but he hurt himself chasing me. I felt responsible "I'll take you. Can you stand?"

He extended and bent his left leg before bracing his weight on the other foot. With a hop, he stood up. Tenderly balancing his left foot, he winced. "I'll be okay."

I shot him a doubtful look. "Try walking."

He took a step with his good foot and then did a weird kick-ball-change move when he stepped with his left.

"Nice dancing. Now try again." I crossed my arms.

This time he managed to take two steps. I could see the effort not to wince in his eyes and the way he appeared to be biting the inside of his cheek. Or his tongue.

"Where's your car parked?" He could say he would be fine all he wanted, but he needed an X-ray.

"In the lot behind this building." He stood on one leg, resting the toe of his other shoe on the linoleum floor.

"Stay here, I'll be right back." I ran up the first flight of stairs.

"Jo?"

I paused and faced him.

"You'll need these." He tossed me his keys.

"Oh, right." Duh. I mentally slapped myself. "I'll be right back."

LUCKILY I KNEW how to drive a stick. His Audi had faux wood de-tails and lots of beige leather. I felt like I was driving someone's parent's sedan.

We arrived at the local ER, sat in two uncomfortable chairs, and the wait began. Given Ben wasn't bleeding from the head or imminent-ly dying, he wasn't a priority.

"Is it swollen?"

He shrugged. "It's not too bad."

"You should elevate it." I patted my legs. "Here, rest your foot across my lap."

"If you're sure." He paused, uncertain. No more cocky arrogance.

"Come on."

He lifted his leg and I placed his foot on my thigh.

Other than when he wrapped his arm over my shoulder on the way from the dorm to the car, this was the second time we'd ever deliberate-ly touched. Halloween didn't count. I wondered if he felt the connec-tion as acutely as I did.

"Now you're pinned down, can we talk?" He pressed his leg against mine.

I raised a shoulder, but didn't speak.

"I'll take your silence as acquiescence." He shifted to see my face.

I braced myself for his words. I could remain distanced. His words didn't have to have any power over me unless I let them.

"I'm sorry." He held my gaze, giving me a shy smile.

"You've said that already."

"I'll keep saying it until you accept my apology."

"I'm not even sure what you're apologizing for anymore."

"I can make a list if you'd like. I wrote a lot of them down." He slid forward to reach his back pocket. Removing his wallet, he opened it and pulled out a well-creased piece of notepaper. When he unfolded it, it tore along one of the edges.

"Looks like you've been carrying it around for a long time."

"Since the afternoon of the disciplinary hearing. A few months ago." He lifted his shoulder in a shrug.

Mouth hanging open, I stared at him in disbelief.

"You think I'm kidding, but I'm not. Look at the first thing on the list." He pressed the worn paper into my hand. The pencil had been rubbed and smeared with dirt and the oils from his hands.

"Never attend another judicial council."

"That's a good life goal." I tried to hand the paper back to him, but my name caught my eye. I traced the words with my finger: *Win Jo back*. "Back? A little presumptuous, don't you think?"

His shy smile spread into a familiar confident grin. "I believe in setting my goals high."

"You have goals other than getting high?" The sarcasm flowed out of me before I could edit myself.

He flinched a little. "Touché. I earned that."

I bit my tongue to resist apologizing. "I was never yours."

Exhaling, he rubbed his hand over his jaw. "You keep reminding me."

"We never went out—" I stopped him from interrupting by lifting my hand. "Let's not argue over the semantics again."

"Okay, we never went out on a date. I accept I messed up. But have you ever met someone and known within the first five minutes of meeting them you would become friends?"

I nodded.

"You didn't question it, you knew. Something in you matched up. Your edges fit together and you clicked." He ran his fingers over the knuckle of my hand resting on his shin. "I knew. With you."

"We'd be friends?"

"And more."

"Looks like you were wrong. On both accounts." His touch tickled and I moved my hand away.

He grabbed it and wove his fingers between mine, resting both our hands on his armrest. "I'd only be wrong if this was the end of us."

"Again, there is no us." I watched as he unfolded my hand and traced the lines of my palm.

"I want there to be an us." With his chin tucked, he peeked up at me. He looked like a young boy trying to get out of trouble.

"Ben . . ."

"We're stuck here for now, hear me out. Unless you want to leave. I won't keep you against your will. You can take my car back to campus and I'll catch a cab later." His words ran together like he was out of time and options.

"I'll stay."

"You told me you wouldn't go out with me because I didn't ask. I should've asked you. I'm a jerk, because until you called me out on it, I didn't think I had to. I thought we had something between us, and we'd hang out, you know, and fall into things."

"Things? Like your bed?" I bristled and felt myself begin to shut down. Not saying I hadn't fantasized about his bed and him naked. Hypocrisy, thy name is Josephine.

"Honestly? Yes. You're beautiful. Any guy would be stupid or blind not to be attracted to you. Even a blind man would think you're beautiful if you let him feel your face."

I gave him a sidelong look. "Got it. You wanted to sleep with me because I'm pretty."

"There's more. You're also super smart, probably smarter than me." He gave me a little cocky wink.

"You've yet to prove your intelligence."

"That's the thing. Ever since last November, I'm turning things around. Did you see my final grade in global economics?"

"You got a ninety-four. Congrats." I admitted I knew his grade, which he could figure out meant I'd asked McDonald about him. "I take partial credit for you passing."

"You totally should. You motivated me to get my shit together. I got rid of the bong and the pipes. I haven't smoked since winter break."

An older woman in a terrycloth housecoat sitting across from us scowled at Ben's confession.

"For the first time in my life, I'm working on goals." He pointed at his list lying on my lap. "No more coasting. No more being a jerk because I feel entitled. Rebelling against the life I've been gifted only hurts myself."

"That's deep."

"My very wise grandmother called me out at Christmas."

"She yelled at you on Christmas?"

"Two spiked eggnogs into the evening and the white gloves came off. I didn't think anyone in the family paid attention to my antics."

I imagined a small woman wearing white gloves and pearls in a boxing ring. "Did she give you a lump of coal in your stocking?"

"No, I received a new cashmere sweater."

Of course he did. Getting back on topic, I brought up something still bothering me. "You were kind of a jerk for going out for coffee with Jenni and getting her hopes up."

"I never told her it was a date. I suggested we get coffee because we had you in common."

"Coffee is girl code for a casual date."

"It is?" He slowly blinked in realization. "Oh shit. Really? Explains a lot of things. Wow. Okay. I am a jerk." He took the paper out of my hand. "Do you have a pen?"

I found one in my purse. "What are you writing down?"

"I need to apologize to Jenni."

"Are you doing some sort of twelve step program?"

"Sort of." He paused in his scribbling. "I didn't go to rehab, if that's what you're implying. I'm not an addict. I just like smoking pot."

"And you can quit any time." My sarcasm returned.

"I have. Ask Gil. Or Maggie. They'll tell you."

I frowned, but Maggie's story corroborated his words.

"My friends aren't going to cover for me. If that's what you're worried about."

"No, I trust you. Maggie told me as much the other week."

He bit down on the end of the pen, but his lips curled in a grin. "You talked to Maggie about me?"

I sighed. "Your name has come up in conversation. Mutual friends and everything."

"Right, right." After folding the paper, he replaced it in his wallet. "Where was I?"

"You have goals."

"I do. One of those goals is to go out with you. I assume you got my last message from Jenni."

Six words floated through my mind. "I did."

"What's it going to take for you to say yes? I've apologized. I've stalked you. Waited outside your door. Returned your lost glove. Given you space and time. I even asked. Nicely, I might add." He tucked the pen back into my bag, then picked up my hand again.

I couldn't keep avoiding him. No matter how much I wanted to protect my heart, I believed him.

"Okay."

"What are you agreeing to?" Amusement and hope sparkled in his eyes.

"I'll stop avoiding you." My heart beat faster. I wanted to scream yes, but I also wanted to play with him a little. Honestly, I enjoyed feeling powerful.

As awareness coursed through me, I smiled. This wasn't about me denying myself. Or worse, giving the guy all the power over me.

This was about saying yes to something I'd denied myself for months. From the moment he walked into the study room—late, cocky, and assuming the guy at the head of the table was me—I'd wanted him. Even when I thought he was an aimless screw up and the worst idea ever. My heart had wanted him, no matter what reasoning my mind presented. No evidence could change the reaction my body had to his presence.

"Will you go out with me? Let me be specific. Out with me on a date. The two of us. I'll pick you up and drive us to a restaurant where I've made a reservation. I'll pay the check with no arguing about going Dutch and splitting the bill because you're a modern woman. A real, old-fashioned date." His earnestness grew contagious.

"Will there be a goodnight kiss on this date you have planned?"

"Up to you. A peck on the cheek would be nice."

I narrowed my eyes at him. "Nice? You'd be happy with nice?"

He nodded happily. "We can go as fast or as slow as you want."

I mirrored his happy expression.

"Let's get out of here." His hand brushed my hair over my shoulder.

"We can't. You still need an X-ray for your foot."

He stood up without wincing. "Look, it seems to be fine."

"Sit down! You're probably in shock or something." I pulled him down toward me.

He caught himself, bracing his hands on my chair's armrests. "I'm fine," he whispered a few inches from my face.

"Benton Grant . . ."

"Yes, Josephine Asotin?" I liked the way he said my name, but I wasn't going to let him know that.

I scowled at him, raising my hand in the air. "Are you telling me we've been sitting here in a germ infested ER full of sick people for the past two hours for no reason?" Angry little arrows burst my happy bubble.

His signature cocky grin returned. "I wouldn't say for no reason, but my foot is okay. I swear."

I glowered at him.

"I needed to get you to listen to me. I did a risk assessment when I chased you down the stairs."

"You faked hurting yourself and lied to me?" My voice rose to a shout.

A soft gasp told me the older woman had continued eavesdropping on us.

"You're too much. This is your idea of winning me over?" I lowered my voice to a whisper and shoved him away from me.

He caught my hand. "I fibbed. A little white lie. Nothing major."

I stormed out of the ER with him shadowing me. "Maybe I had plans tonight. Or homework or a test to study for!"

"Jo." He stopped walking once we got to the parking lot.

"What?"

"The car is over there." He pointed to the opposite side of the hospital.

"I knew that." I stomped off in the new direction.

"Remember five minutes ago when you liked me? You smiled at me and everything." His voice sounded happy, despite my mood change.

Arriving at the car, I paused. He got under my skin like no other guy. One minute he lit up my world. The next, he riled me up like he knew where every single one of my buttons were located and what set me off.

"I'm so mad at you right now."

"Only right now? You've been angry at me for months. In fact, have you ever not been mad at me? Pretty sure at this point, mad is the status quo. I'm not sure what you would do with yourself if you weren't in a constant state of being annoyed at me."

Despite all of my protests and doubts, he also made me laugh.

His brows lifted higher on his forehead and he pouted out his lip in some fake innocent expression I'm sure he thought would get him out of any trouble. "I'm sorry I faked a non-life threatening injury to get some alone time with you. However, I'm not sorry we talked. The motivation was honest, even if the injury was a lie. Forgive me?"

"You say sorry a lot."

"I'm working on it."

"Being less apologetic?"

"No, doing fewer things resulting in an apology. Starting with you." He stepped closer. "Instead of more apologies, I'll tell you what I don't regret."

I backed up until my thighs and bottom pressed against the car.

"I'm not sorry we spent the evening together." He took another step.

"I'm not sorry I made you laugh." Another step.

"I'm not sorry I held your hand." He stopped walking when only a few inches separated our bodies. Reaching between us, he wrapped both of my hands in his.

"I'm not sorry for the way I feel about you." He leaned closer.

I rested against the car and closed my eyes, my breathing shallow as I waited for whatever came next.

"And I'm never going to regret doing this." His lips brushed against mine in the softest, most tortured kiss I'd ever experienced.

He groaned, and for a brief moment, he pressed himself against me. Then the kiss ended.

I slowly opened my eyelids, feeling as stunned as he looked.

"Wow," he whispered.

I simply touched my lips in response. The feel of his kiss lingered and its memory tingled along the tender skin.

"Go out with me tonight." It wasn't a question.

"It's the middle of the night."

He glanced at his watch. "It's almost midnight. I'll ask you again in fifteen minutes."

TWENTY-THREE

"Two Princes"
Spin Doctors

HE KEPT HIS word. When the clock on his dashboard showed twelve o'clock, he asked me to dinner.

I said yes. With no regrets.

Ben arrived right on time at my door to escort me to dinner. He apologized to Jenni about misunderstanding the underlying code for coffee and told her he'd set her up with his friend Roger if she wanted a fun time.

He opened my doors all evening, including the car door. He'd morphed into the perfect gentleman. In fact, almost too perfect. Like Eddie Haskell on *Leave it to Beaver*—super smooth with all the right things to say.

He slipped the maître d' a folded bill and we were seated at a table with a view of Lake Union in Seattle. Thick white cloths covered the tables and a harpist played in the corner. A real live woman plucking away on a gold harp while people chewed their food. Talk about over the top.

My menu didn't have prices on it, but he assured me I could order anything, and it would be fine.

I had the crab. He had the steak. We shared and created our own version of surf and turf.

Everything was perfect.

No clowns.

No punches thrown.

It all seemed very grown up and sophisticated. Like something I'd experienced at senior prom, but without the shiny pink lamé prom dress with extra puffy sleeves and satin pumps dyed to match. No wilted wrist corsage either.

I still felt like a princess. Not because of the harpist, although she played beautifully. No, because the entire evening, Ben focused on me like I was the center of his world.

It was a pretty incredible world, too.

As of now, it included crab and harpists.

And my favorite part, slow, tender kisses I felt everywhere.

BEING COURTED, AS Ben called it, was as similar to modern dating as the horse and buggy were to race cars.

In other words, we took things slow.

Very slow.

The kiss at the car and another equally slow, restrained goodnight kiss following our first date were all the action I got from him. In one sense, it felt like months of flirting and sexual tension had been building up between us. In reality, we'd only gone on one date and spent the evening in the ER, which didn't count.

It had been only a week since our date, but my patience had frayed to nothing. We talked all the time, even spending time on the phone when we weren't together.

Talk. Talk. Talk. No action.

I knew he wasn't above manipulating situations to his greatest advantage. I wouldn't let him out-maneuver me. We didn't fight, but we both loved to negotiate everything. It became our own kind of foreplay.

I spotted him outside the CAB chatting with Selah. Perfect timing.

After interrupting their conversation, I made my first move. "Selah, what do you think of the traditional dating structure? Girl sits by the phone waiting for boy to call to ask her out?"

Her green eyes blazed while her mouth twisted into a scowl. "I think it's bullshit. What is this, the nineteen-fifties? It's almost the twenty-first century. Women have jobs and birth control. We don't have to be pregnant and stuck in the house all day taking care of screaming babies, watching soaps about lives we'll never lead, and wondering where our dreams went while folding some man's stained tightie-whities . . . unless we want to. Then, more power to you, sister."

Ben shot me a confused look. "Why are you riling up Selah?" he whispered as she continued her rant.

She accidentally slapped his arm when she brought up the suffragettes and the ERA. "I mean, it's all unbelievable. In my women's studies seminar—"

I stopped her before she really blew a gasket. "Okay, thanks for proving my point."

She harrumphed and mumbled something about patriarchy.

Smiling, I made my next move. "Ben, I'd like to ask you out for tomorrow night."

"But . . . I'm the guy. I should be—" He stopped himself from going any further. A smile lit up his face and he nodded with realization. I'd outmaneuvered him. Plus, I had a witness to back me up.

"You're the guy? What do you mean by that? Because you have tender, delicate genitals hanging outside your body you're better equipped to make decisions?" Selah's face began to deepen with color. "Don't make me go all riot grrrl on you."

Ben slowly backed away from her. Grabbing my hand, he pulled me with him, using me as a human shield. "I don't even know what a riot girl is, but I'm afraid."

"You should be, Benton Grant, the second. You and your white patriarchy are falling like Rome." She jabbed her finger at him. "You're going down."

"I think her women's studies class on the history of feminism is doing strange things to her brain," I whispered without shifting my focus. I didn't want to lose sight of Selah until I knew we were out of range in case she decided to karate chop Ben's oppressive manhood.

Selah stomped away, still talking about feminism and riot girls.

"What was that all about?" he asked once she entered the building.

"Collateral damage." My eyes tracked Selah's departure while I fought a smile of triumph.

He spun me to face him. "I would've said yes to your proposal. You didn't have to use Selah as a pawn to ask me out."

"Would you have? You've been acting traditional about everything."

"I was going to ask you out for Friday night when we saw each other today. You beat me to it."

"You were?"

Shock flashed across his face. "Of course. Why wouldn't I? Didn't you like dinner last week?"

"Of course. It was amazing. I'd never eaten to the sounds of live harp music before."

"The harp was a little much, I admit."

I pinched the air between my thumb and index finger. "A little."

"Did you think I didn't have fun?" Worry furrowed his brow.

"No, it's not that."

"What is it?"

I inhaled and then exhaled all my thoughts into one long sentence. "It's been a week and I'm impatient. The whole flirting thing started months ago, and you've only kissed me twice, not complaining about the kisses because they were very nice, amazing, but there have only been two, yet we've known each other for ages, and that's making me impatient for more."

His lips silenced my rambling. Then his tongue found mine and I forgot what I was trying to say. When his hands wrapped around my braid, and gently tugged, angling my head exactly where he wanted it, I couldn't have told him my own name because I suddenly had no idea what it was.

Benton Grant had kissed me stupid.

I rubbed myself against him like a cat, complete with a soft purr deep in my throat. My hands roamed over his shoulders, down his arms, and under his jacket. I needed to touch more of him.

His thumb brushed my cheek, grounding me and calming my frenzy. He slowed down the kiss, balancing me upright on my feet before releasing me.

"You should ask me out more often." He kissed the corner of my mouth.

I let my focus stay on his mouth a moment before meeting his eyes. "What are you doing right now? My roommate is working until seven. I have the space to myself."

"Oh really?" His cocky grin returned.

I nodded.

"I'd be happy to accept your invitation." He held out his elbow for us to link arms.

"So formal." I shifted my bag to my other shoulder and accepted his gesture.

"For some reason, I like being formal and old-fashioned with you." He gave me a peck on the cheek.

"You know I asked you back to my room to fool around, right?"

"Doesn't mean I respect you any less." He stopped and pulled me to face him. "In fact, I like your honesty and directness." A quick kiss to my lips turned into more when I wrapped my arms around his neck.

Still pressed against him, I whispered, "I'm thinking Jenni needs to find another place to sleep tonight."

His eyes widened comically and his eyebrows shot north toward his hair. "Okay. Then why are we still wasting time standing out here?"

He took off at a jog in the direction of the dorms, towing me behind by the hand until I found my footing and ran ahead of him.

Before I could make it through the doors, he caught up with me and pinned me to the glass. Laughing, our chests rising and falling, we tried to breathe through our noses as we kissed again. Unfortunately, the need for oxygen won, and I reluctantly pushed him away. Dizziness hit me as the image of him before me blurred.

"Hold on." I bent at the waist to catch my breath. Placing my hands on my knees, I inhaled and counted to ten. After the world stopped spinning, my eyes focused again.

Ben's jeans were barely constraining his very obvious arousal mere inches from my face.

"Get a room," someone yelled. A few yards away on the path, some pimply faced hippie bounced a hacky sack on his foot. In his Grateful Dead tie-dyed shirt, he looked like the ultimate college cliché.

"Thanks for the sage advice." Ben waved at him with a sarcastic grin. "Shall we?"

If kissing him made me stupid and almost pass out, I wasn't pre-pared for more. All my confidence disappeared as we climbed the stairs to my room. At my door, I fumbled and dropped my keys, my fingers shaking.

He picked up my key ring and stuck the right one in the lock, but didn't turn it.

"Jo?"

I met his concerned eyes.

"We don't have to do anything. Remember in the ER when I said we could go as fast or slow as you wanted? I meant it. That's why I haven't done more than kiss you goodnight. You're the one in control here."

I wasn't sure if I believed him. "You're not going to do the classic guy move and shove my hand on your crotch or push my head down to let me know you want a blow job?" I wished I were kidding about those moves. Those were two of my perfect-on-paper high school boyfriend's favorites.

"What? No! I wouldn't force you." His eyebrows lifted again with shock. "Please tell me no guy has ever done that to you."

Pressing my lips together, I nodded.

"I knew you hadn't been with the right kind of guy. We're not all cavemen who don't have the language skills to ask for what we want. Or even more important, ask what you want."

No guy—not the high school boyfriend, not the random guys I'd dated freshman year—had ever asked me what I wanted. If they weren't completely consumed with their boners, they might have responded to a subtle shift, a hand placed in the right spot, a change in pressure or an-gle guided by me. Sadly, directions didn't work for most of them.

Ben touched my face and traced from my temple to my jaw. "What do you want, Jo?"

"You. I only want you." I turned the key in the lock and the door opened.

TWENTY-FOUR

"American Girl"
Tom Petty

I FLIPPED ON my desk lamp instead of the awful overhead fluorescent. If I had candles, I would have lit them.

My palms felt clammy and my heart flew around in my chest. Rubbing my hands on my jeans, I talked myself into calming down.

I wasn't a virgin, but I didn't have a lot of experience. Only my high school boyfriend really. The other semi-sexual encounters had always ended before the full shebang. Literally.

Ben wrapped his arms around me from behind and rested his chin on my shoulder. I swore he sniffed my hair.

"You always smell like fresh flowers."

"I bathe regularly and use perfume?" It came out like a question.

He chuckled and kissed the little bump on the top of my shoulder. "I wasn't questioning your hygiene. It's not perfume. It's you."

He buried his face in my neck. This time I knew he sniffed me. I tilted my head to give him more access. Not knowing what to do with my hands, I held onto his forearms. His front pressed against my back from thighs to shoulders. Everything made contact.

I shifted and deliberately arched back into him. I'd caught a glimpse outside the building, but I wanted to feel all of him.

Sensing my goal, he spun me around and backed me up until my calves hit my mattress. I tumbled onto the bed and he followed, rolling onto his side next to me on the twin.

He ran his fingers through my hair, spreading it out on the pillow. "You're beautiful."

I stared into his eyes, seeing the honesty behind his words. Lifting my hand, I stroked his face. "You're the most handsome man I've ever seen."

"Ever?" His smile lit up his face.

My hand paused at his jaw. "Okay. Not ever. In person."

"Ouch. You wound my delicate male ego." He held his other hand over his heart. As if my words had stabbed him, he flopped dramatically onto his back. Lying partially across me, his weight pinned my arm beneath him.

"Sorry, but have you seen River Phoenix? Or John F. Kennedy, Jr.?"

"Those two are my competition? An actor and a Kennedy heir? Both are liberal democrats." He faked his disgust well.

"On looks only. Although if John-John called, I might switch parties." I poked his side and he shifted, kneeling to keep his weight off of me.

"You love to rile me up, don't you?" He nipped my exposed collarbone, finally pressing his hips to mine. Unfortunately, as much as I liked to provoke him, he enjoyed teasing me more. Lifting back on his knees, he straddled my thighs.

I pretended to pout.

He ran his thumb over my bottom lip. "Beautiful. I can't believe you agreed to go out with me, let alone the fact you're here with me now."

My face heated under his intense stare. I'd never felt as cherished as I did with him. His warm brown eyes held emotion we hadn't spoken out loud or dared to hint at.

Afraid of what might come out of my mouth if I spoke, I pulled him down to me, kissing him.

In response, he was everywhere at once. His hands unbuttoned my shirt, exposing my pink lace bra. He traced the lace with a knuckle before reverently kissing the small swell of my breast.

I tugged at his rugby shirt, yanking it up his back. He took over removing it, leaving his torso bare.

He shoved my shirt down and off my arms. In only our jeans, we looked like a Calvin Klein ad.

My palm skimmed his denim, brushing against the hardness beneath his fly. He moved my hand out of the way and undid his buttons, revealing plaid boxers.

"My turn." With a single finger he flicked the top button and then pulled the zipper on my jeans.

I shimmied out of them.

"So beautiful." His mouth kissed whatever exposed skin he encountered next.

My shoulder.

My navel.

My thigh.

The inside of my knee.

The curve of my calf muscle.

The delicate bones of my ankle.

Then he retraced his path back up my body, finding new places to explore.

A mole on my inner thigh.

My hip bone.

A middle rib.

The hollow at the base of my neck.

A soft spot underneath my chin.

The shadow behind my ear.

I squirmed and sighed, needing more, but not wanting him to stop.

Soon the thin material separating us landed on the floor. He reached into his wallet for a condom.

"Are you sure?" he whispered against my lips.

I'd never been more sure in my life.

I inhaled at the moment we joined together. When he began to move, I wrapped my arms around his lower back, pulling him closer to me, angling my hips.

Slowly, I lifted my eyelids to discover him staring at my face. The reverence I'd felt before in his gaze greeted me again. His shy grin played on his lips for a moment before he bit the bottom corner.

I smiled up at him, happiness cresting over me with each movement of our bodies together.

An unfamiliar pressure built in my lower abdomen. I'd never had an orgasm during intercourse before. Ben shifted and small stars appeared behind my lashes.

"Again." I wasn't sure if he could hear my whisper.

He repeated the new angle and I tightened my legs around his thighs.

"There?" Restraint tightened his voice.

Afraid of doing anything to lose the promise of pleasure beyond my grasp, I barely nodded, hoping it would be enough to encourage him.

His thumb added enough pressure above where we were joined to push me over the edge into a whole new world of pleasure.

I gasped, still chasing the fading bliss he brought to my body. He faltered, his rhythm erratic before his face broke into ecstasy.

Joy bubbled out of my mouth as a giggle. I'd never experienced bliss before.

TWENTY-FIVE

"All I Want is You"
U2

BEN'S CURTAINS FILTERED the bright May sunlight. Like a cat, I lay in a pool of its warmth, my sociology textbook sitting open in front of me. Behind me, Ben ran his hand up my bare leg, distracting me.

I stared over my shoulder at him. From his expression, he knew exactly what effect he had on me. His fingers reached higher, skimming the hem of my boxer shorts. Well, his boxers I stole. I kicked my legs when he tickled me and rolled over to my back.

He crawled up my body to kiss me.

"No way. I need to finish studying for the test next week." I gave him a closed mouth kiss.

He responded by wiggling his hand under my shirt. "You know you'll wait until the day before to cram, and then you'll ace it. Like you always do."

I stopped his hand moving. Beneath my palm, he squeezed my breast. I closed my lids as the sensation flooded my body with warmth, concentrated in pulses between my legs.

"Ben." I intended to chastise him, but my voice came out pleading and husky.

"Shh." He quieted me with another kiss. "Study later."

I would never have been able to focus with him so close, knowing he felt as turned on as I did. My willpower evaporated.

AFTER OUR AFTERNOON spent not studying, we napped and lay around. Ben wore his boxers and I put on one of his prep school T-shirts. It hit me mid-thigh, providing more decency than being naked all day like he'd suggested. I had my sociology book open again and took notes.

"I have a brilliant idea." Ben leaned against the wall with my legs across his lap.

"Hmm . . . what?" I was starving and hoped he would suggest we order pizza.

"Let's move in together."

I jumped up, my head spinning with his words. "Are you insane?"

"Never been more sane in my life. I know. Without any doubts, I know I love you."

"See? You say crazy things and expect me to believe them." My heart raced and my palms felt clammy.

"You do believe me, because it's the truth. Who cares if it's only been a few months. This is different than anything I've ever felt. I know it's the same for you."

"Means we dated the wrong people. Like the stupid teenagers we were."

"Exactly. My point is we know this isn't anything close to what we experienced before."

Memories of how his skin felt against mine flashed through my mind, causing those places to fire up with anticipation. "I'll agree with you."

"I love you. Never been more sure in my life." He stepped close to me. "Now's when you say it back, Jo."

"I love you." Finally saying the words out loud was as easy as breathing.

He touched my cheek. "I thought you might."

"What are you proposing?" I hadn't meant to use *that* word. No way would he have been proposing right now. That would be insane.

"If we do this, for real, it's forever. Not some random college fling for a few weeks or a quarter. I'm talking lifetime. Marriage, kids, house, dog, family car, summers at the beach, ski trips, European vacations . . . the whole enchilada. Both feet, arms, and legs, all in."

"I think you described the hokey-pokey." I fought a smile struggling to burst across my face.

"Fine. If you want the hokey-pokey, that's what I'll give you." He backed up and did a mini-version of the children's dance. Putting himself all in, he kissed me, then jumped away.

I threw myself at him and he supported my legs under my thighs. Wrapping my ankles behind him, I held onto his shoulders while he kissed me. In a slow spin, he twirled me around, never breaking the contact between our lips, his hands resting on my naked butt.

"This summer I'm taking you to Europe. Then we're finding our own place."

"Europe?"

"Do you have a passport?"

I responded with a shake of my head. I didn't. I'd never had a reason to get one before.

"Well, that's the first thing we'll do." He kissed me. "I can't wait for whatever comes next with you."

TWENTY-SIX

A WEEK LATER a group of students staged a protest in front of the library over the scant number of books by female authors in the fiction section. I recognized Selah's favorite combat boots amongst the group of women wearing gorilla masks.

"I FOUND AN apartment in Olympia where we can all live for the summer." Quinn slapped a newspaper on the table. A big red circle had been drawn on the middle of the rental page. "Three bedrooms, plus a formal dining room, and a screened porch the landlady said we could use as additional bedrooms at no extra charge."

"But there are seven of us." Selah turned the paper to read the description.

"I figured whoever doubled up could have the biggest bedroom. Maggie and Gil spend enough nights sleeping in his bed in our room, they could even share." He gave Maggie a devilish look, which she responded to with a blush and her middle finger.

Gil ignored him. "Quinn and I could share. I know how you girls like your privacy."

"I call dibs on the sun porch. Unless it's moldy. I want all natural light." Lizzy claimed her room.

"What about Ben and Jo?" Selah asked the group, but looked at me.

"We're going backpacking in Europe for the first part of the summer, and then we'll move into an apartment in July."

Maggie's deep blue eyes widened, exposing more of the white. "Your place?"

I nodded.

"Wait a second." Lizzy jumped into the conversation. "You two are going to shack up? Live in sin? Won't Ben's WASPy grandmother kick him out of the will?"

"We're not telling her." Ben rested his arm on the back of my chair. "It's highly improbable she would ever come to Olympia. I'm not sure she could even find it on a map. The only Washington she's concerned about is D.C. And as long as Republicans hold the White House, she's content."

"Is she the one who has the framed photo of the Ronald and Nancy on her piano amongst the family photos?"

"That's her. When I made Presidential Scholar and received the signed letter from Reagan, she asked for a copy for the downstairs hall." Ben beamed. He loved his letter. The original sat framed on his desk back in the dorm.

"Now I know where you get your love for the Gipper." Quinn laughed. "It's genetic. You can't help yourself."

"Q, don't get him riled up. You know the two of you will end up squabbling over politics. Hasn't it gotten old yet?" I prepared myself to play referee again.

"Fine," they both said at the same time.

"Dukakis," Ben mumbled under his breath.

"I heard you!" Quinn shot him a dirty look. "This is why we could never live together in peace."

"I say we go look at the apartment this evening." Maggie ignored the guys' glowering contest.

"Right after we burn those disgusting germ riddled things on your feet." I pointed at the slimy green fur-balls a cat coughed up and she decided to wear as shoes. I nudged one with the toe of my tennis shoe. The plastic eyeball gave up the fight and fell to the floor. "The sooner the better. Let Kermit rest in peace."

I looked around the table at this funny group of friends, smiling as I thought how improbable it was we found each other.

Ben squeezed my hand before kissing the back.

Even crazier, I found my forever.

GIL

Gilliam Morrow, 20

American History
Junior

What moment do you regret most in college?

Not speaking up when I had the chance changed everything. I assumed I had all the time in the world. We were young and our futures were endless.

No decision was so important it could change the course of my life.

I learned the hardest lesson by doing nothing and waiting for the perfect moment. Only later did I realize the perfect time had passed.

My cautious nature, playing it safe, cost me everything. I waited too long.

TWENTY-SEVEN

"Maggie May"
Rod Stewart

SMOKE POURED OUT of the apartment's kitchen and triggered the alarm in the living room.

"What smells so terrible?" I waved my arms above my head, dispersing the cloud around the squawking smoke detector. After knocking it open, I pulled out the battery to silence it.

"I'm baking," Maggie hollered from a spot in front of the oven, the source of the smell and smoke. In her oven-mitt covered hand, she held a tray of charred disks.

"Why are you putting hockey pucks in the oven?"

"They're biscuits. For strawberry shortcakes later." She frowned at the tray. "Or they were. I think the oven temperature is wrong."

I sniffed the so-called biscuits. "Did you make them from scratch?"

"I used the scary pop kind."

I raised an eyebrow in question.

"The ones in the tube. I hate sticking the spoon into the crease and waiting for the explosion. It makes me jump every single time."

I took the tray from her and tipped it into the garbage can. "Maybe you should stick to chocolate chip cookie dough."

"You know we never get to baking the actual cookies when we make dough." Her sad eyes followed the sad trail of each puck as it fell into the trash.

"That's my point exactly. Maybe avoid the oven all together."

"Nice. Really nice." She hit me with the dish towel, making a sad thwap sound upon contact.

"You need to twist it to make it snap." I grabbed and twisted the other towel, aiming for her ass.

The towel snapped, creating a satisfying sound when it contacted with her shorts.

"Ouch! Gilliam Morrow. You're mean." She rubbed her butt. I wanted to do it for her, but the boundaries of our friendship prevented me.

"Here, let's hug it out." I scooped her up in my arms and squeezed. She wiggled and squirmed, making me mindful of my body's reaction to having her close.

I couldn't decipher her muffled mumbles from where I had her head pressed against my chest. "Speak clearly. I can't understand what you want if you don't enunciate."

She pinched my side. I held her tighter. Her teeth nipped my pec, too close to my nipple for comfort.

"Ow. You bit me." I released her.

"You were smothering me."

"With my friendship. Only with my friendship." I rubbed my chest and looked down. "You left a mark on my favorite Jane's Addiction shirt. Does drool stain?"

"Are your pillowcases stained? Because you drool like a fountain." She scampered around the breakfast bar, out of towel and smothering range.

When I lunged at her, she squealed and ran into the living room.

"Maggie May, you know you're the drooler. Next time we watch a movie, you have to bring your own pillow," I called after her.

Smoke still lingered in the air. I opened the windows, letting in fresh air and sunshine. The day promised to be warm and sunny. A perfect afternoon to do nothing on the roof where we'd set up a bunch of beach chairs and a hibachi. It was also where the girls decided they had enough privacy to sunbathe.

Sometimes they even went topless.

I'd gathered this information from their conversations, but had yet to witness it for myself. Most of my time I spent at rehearsal or the print shop.

However, today I had the afternoon off.

"Maggie, are you free this afternoon?" I strolled down the hall to her room.

Her door stood partly open and I lightly knocked as I pushed it open. Not loud enough apparently.

With her back to me, she stood bent at the waist, exposing her purple underwear with green polka dots as she pulled on her cut-off shorts.

My new favorite pattern.

After getting an eye-full, I quickly yanked the door closed, and knocked louder.

"Hold on! I'm changing." Her voice carried through the wood.

"Okay." My voice cracked. I rested my head on the door, softly banging my forehead for good measure.

"What?" Her long hair stuck out at funny angles when she opened her door. Her shirt's tag poked out the front of her chest.

"Your shirt's on backward and inside out."

She tucked her chin and looked at her chest. "Turn around."

I obliged. Behind me I heard the soft rustle of fabric as she fixed her shirt. A foot or two away, she wore only her bra. I shut my eyes and named various ski mountains back home, willing myself not to get hard. Ajax, Buttermilk, Snowmass, Steamboat, Vail . . .

"Okay. Decent. Did you come to smother me some more?"

I faced her and did a double-check of her chest. Her nipples perked through the thin fabric of her tank top. I scratched my ear trying to remember why I'd come to her room.

"If you are thinking about smothering me, can you at least move out of the way? I need to go to work."

Right. Maggie and Lizzy both worked at a local café as baristas. The upside? They often brought home day old baked goods and sandwiches. The downside? They always smelled like coffee after their shifts.

"Are you working this afternoon?"

"I'm off at two. Why?"

"It's supposed to be sunny and warm all day. I thought we could hang out on the roof."

Her face lit up like the sun itself. "That's the best idea ever. I'm over all the rain we had last weekend."

"You know you live in the Pacific Northwest, right?"

"Har har. Remember, I grew up spending summers on the beach here. I know it can be sunny." She tucked her hair into a loopy ponytail as she gathered her keys and purse. "I'm going to be late, but rally the troops, and I'll see you on the roof later."

"It's a date." The words slipped out without thought. "No, not a date-date. More like a plan."

"You're weird." She waved and walked out the front door.

My plans to become a rock god and be slick had evidently failed. I collapsed on the couch. When it came to Maggie, I either said something weird—making things awkward—or I did stupid shit in front of her as had been my pattern from our first meeting.

Quinn pushed open the sliding doors to his room. His hair stood up in all directions, messier than Maggie's had been. In a pair of old man style pajama pants and no shirt, there was no doubt we'd woken him up. "What's all this ruckus about sun and roofs?"

"It's going to be hot today. Thought we could drag our pale bodies to the tar beach and hang out if anyone is around."

Quinn ran his hands over his face. "I can see right through your suggestion, man. But I'm going to give you credit for your earnest hetero attempt at game." He patted my head on his way past the couch.

"Gee, thanks for the approval. Just friends hanging out."

"Keep lying to yourself, Morrow. Someday you might convince yourself the truth right in front of you is all a lie."

He amazed me. Obviously barely awake and he was already more astute and articulate than most of the guys I knew.

He shuffled into the kitchen. "What died in here?"

"Maggie played with the oven again."

"Oh, no. What did she destroy this time? I had no idea brownies could smell horrible. Burnt chocolate smells like ass."

I snorted.

"Not that I would know," he said.

"Sure. Okay." I held up my hands. "Not judging."

"Why are there hockey pucks in the garbage?"

"Those are biscuits?" It came out as a question because I still wasn't convinced they were made of dough.

Something hard hit the floor and skidded across the wood. "If it looks like a puck, sounds like a puck, moves like a puck . . . it's not a biscuit. We should save this and play street hockey."

"You got plans this morning?" I rolled off the couch and stood up. "We could play in the driveway."

Quinn and I spent most of our time working. Him at some art space gallery as an intern. Any free time I had I spent practicing with the band. Mark found a rehearsal space for us in an old warehouse. At least Ramirez didn't have to lug his drum kit around unless we had a gig.

WE'D MADE A goal in front of the row of carports with two chairs. I pulled out a couple of old tennis rackets and we taped them to broom handles to bat the puck-biscuits toward the goal. The rollerblades hadn't been the brightest idea, but definitely upped the complication factor of our new game.

We declared Quinn the winner based on an arbitrary and complex point system. Road rash bloomed on his forearm and a small tear in the shoulder of his T-shirt. I sported a nice scrape on one knee where I'd slid trying to steal control of the biscuit.

"We need a better name than Biscuit Ball if this is ever going to take off." Quinn and I sat on the front steps of the apartment building, nursing beers and our wounds.

"How do you apply to get a sport into the Olympics?" He picked a tiny piece of gravel out of his arm. "I'm imagining sleek unitards or singlets, and matching shin guards. Maybe a cross between what the speed-skaters and wrestlers wear."

"I think you need sleeves." I gestured to his bloody arm.

"Maybe wrist guards, too. Something inspired by *Tron*. Or maybe Storm Troopers."

Ignoring his costume designs, I waved at Maggie, who was walking up the sidewalk.

Smelling of coffee, Maggie gave us a tired wave and joined us on the steps. I offered her my beer and she took a long sip.

"Are those my biscuits broken up all over the driveway?"

"We had some issues with inconsistency in the structural integrity." Quinn ignored her scowl. "For next time, I think you need to burn them a little longer until they're harder. Go for full charcoal, please."

"I'm never baking for you two again."

I held up my palm for a high-five with Quinn. "Our diabolical plan worked."

"How are we supposed to take over the world when you keep announcing our plans? You are the worst Bond villain ever." He shook his head in disgust. "Maggie on the other hand would make an excellent Bond girl. We only need to find her the right bikini."

Maggie gave him a side-long stare. "Speaking of bikinis . . ."

"Yes?" My voice sounded as overeager as I felt. At least this time it didn't crack.

"Are we roof beaching? Or did your plans change to bleeding all over the front steps instead?" She pointed at my knee. It looked worse than it felt.

Q jumped up. "I'll meet up with you in a bit. I need to see a man about a plan." We watched as he pulled his bike key out of his pocket and unlocked his bike from the rack. With a wave, he sped off across the lawn and down the block.

"He's a strange man," Maggie murmured.

"If you haven't noticed, we're all a little weird around here." I bumped her shoulder with mine.

Selah arrived home from her latest temp job and joined us on the steps. "I feel like we need a theme song if we're going to sit here much longer. It's like the opening scene for a rom-com movie or sitcom about a puckish group of friends."

"You know what would be awesome?"

"Like, let's go to the roof and totally soak up some gnarly rays." I imitated a surfer.

"Only if you stop speaking with that accent." Selah scrunched up her face in disgust. "What happened in the driveway?"

The girls giggled as I explained the rules and cleaned up the first and last Biscuit Ball course.

"You know, Ben would be ultra competitive about winning this game." Selah tossed the last of the broken biscuits in the dumpster.

"It's not even a real game."

"He has to win at everything. If you want to mess with him, challenge him to a title match."

TWENTY-EIGHT

"Spinning Around over You"
Lenny Kravitz

I'D BEEN PRETENDING to read the same two pages of *Hitchhiker's Guide to the Universe* for the past ten minutes. Sweat rolled off my forehead and blurred my vision. Hotter than a sauna up on the roof, tar paper absorbed and reflected the heat beneath my chair. I would never be able to smell either coconut or baby oil again without remembering this summer.

The only slice of shade fell on the far side of the stairwell, but no way would I move. Not now. Not when Maggie had loosened the strings to her bikini top. Sure, she lay on her stomach and I couldn't see anything, but my body still reacted.

There was hope she'd forget she untied her top, and roll over, or sit up. Where there was hope, existed possibility. I'd been living in Hopeville for the last two years.

Also known as the Land of Friends.

I didn't even know how it happened. Or when.

That wasn't true. The *when* happened when I walked by her dorm room freshman year. I heard her laughter down the hall, spilling out of her open door. When I looked inside, I couldn't see her at first. My focus caught on a giant Bryan Ferry poster on one wall, my then favorite musician. A loud thump had drawn my focus to the floor where a tousled mane of red hair flowed over the side of the twin bed. Legs kicked in the air as the laughter turned to cackling and I found myself smiling at the ridiculous creature in front of me. When I'd worked up the courage to go back to meet her, she was gone, but her cute, and very forward, roommate had been there instead. I let my hormones take over.

Maggie's same crazy laughter broke through the haze of memories. I dropped the book and bent to pick it up, setting my beer on the arm of the chair.

Maggie shifted on her towel. My eyes instinctively focused on the strip of exposed skin below her clavicle.

"Enjoying your book?" Selah asked, tilting her head back to stare at me. Her towel lay next to Maggie's, but she rested on her back. The straps of her bathing suit had been rolled down to avoid tan lines. Her boobs strained to burst free from the black fabric. I'd seen them enough times to know they were amazing, but not the ones I'd been obsessed with.

"Yeah. It's hysterical." I turned the page, pretending to pay attention.

Selah laughed. "I'm sure it's even better right side up."

I glanced down and realized she was right. Embarrassed, I quickly flipped the book and brought it closer to my face. "Shut up."

She snickered and rolled over.

"I'm too hot." Maggie tied the strings of her top and sat up. Her suit had shifted to expose a pale pink half-circle on her left breast.

I swallowed heavily before offering her my tumbler of water.

A few drops spilled on her chest as she chugged the liquid. Two droplets sped down the curve of her breasts. I traced their path and envied them.

Selah fake coughed and underneath the sound I heard "staring."

I needed to escape. "I'm going to get more water. Maybe a beer. I could go for a beer. Anyone else want anything?"

The girls asked for wine coolers. Anything they wanted, as long as I could get off the roof before fully tenting my shorts.

I raced down the stairs to the slightly cooler apartment. Standing in front of the fridge, I rolled my neck and let the cold air chill my skin.

"Everyone up on the roof? I was thinking we could play dirty Scrabble." Quinn passed me while I stood there with my head in the fridge. He didn't wait for an answer. The door closed behind him with a loud thump.

Once I had my body under control again, I grabbed a beer and the remaining three wine coolers in the four-pack.

The sun blinded me when I kicked open the door to the roof. I quickly clamped my eyes shut and nudged my sunglasses down before reopening them.

I screeched like a girl and clamped them shut again to block out the scene in front of me.

Quinn was naked.

Again.

His ass looked like two dinner rolls browning in the oven. The image seared itself onto my brain. I could never forget the visual as long as I lived.

Attempting to cross the space between him and the girls, I navigated with my eyes closed. Something hard slammed into my toe. Or more accurately, my toe slammed into something metal. Like a chair or table leg. I screamed a stream of obscenities and set the drinks down on the ground. Straightening up, I finally peeked out one eye.

"Why are you screaming like a little girl?" A few feet away, Quinn rolled over onto his back.

Nope. Never forgetting that image either. I groaned. "Damn it, Quinn!"

Quinn walked over to me, completely nonchalant, not caring that he stood naked on a roof in broad daylight. "Are you hurt?"

"This isn't a locker room, Q." I rubbed my forehead with the back of my hand while standing on one foot. "Put a towel on or something."

"Something bothering you?" He turned his back to me to grab one of the wine coolers.

"Your naked ass, as a matter of fact," Selah said. "No man should have such a perky ass. It's unfair. No cellulite. Doesn't jiggle."

"Why thank you, Elmore." Quinn chuckled. "I fully believe in *Omnia Extares* if you've got it."

I covered my face with my arm. "I don't think the college's founders meant 'let it all hang out' literally when they chose our motto. Put on some shorts."

"Can't you respect a man's need for a lack of tan lines?"

"I'm sorry, but I really can't. Who cares if your ass is tan or not? It's called 'where the sun don't shine' for good reason." I groaned again. Beer. I needed my beer.

"I think you must be jealous. Do you have ass envy, Gil?" Quinn wrapped a beach towel around his waist. "Show us yours and the girls will vote on who has the nicer butt."

I ignored his wiggling eyebrows and resumed my seat in the beach chair.

Maggie lifted her head and gave me a wink. "My vote would be for you."

I leaned over her and whispered, "You've never seen my ass."

A slow, wicked smile spread over her face. "That's what you think." With another wink, she rested her head on her folded arms.

Wait, when could she have seen me naked, or at least my naked ass? I ran through two years of memories in my head and came up blank. Maybe she meant in jeans. Or shorts. She probably meant clothed.

The conversation changed to which actor had the best butt. I didn't participate. Instead, I picked up my book and went back to pretending to read while staring at Maggie's perfect, round ass.

It would be a long summer.

TWENTY-NINE

"You Can Call Me Al"
Paul Simon

I REACHED OVER the counter to turn up the volume on the radio.

"Let's dance, Betty." I grabbed Maggie's hand.

She grinned at me as she hopped out of her chair. "You got it, Al."

"Here they go again," Jo groaned. "How often do they need to play this song?"

She and Ben had been home from Europe for only a couple of weeks. How annoyed could she be?

Every time Paul Simon's "You Can Call Me Al" came on the radio, Maggie and I danced. It had become our thing after seeing the video on MTV. I played the Chevy Chase to her Paul Simon.

I swung her around the kitchen in a fast-paced and awkward swing dance. The awkward part came from me trying to avoid pressing myself against her, lest she figured out I sported a semi.

I blamed the close quarters and all the sunbathing she and Selah did on the roof. A twenty-year-old guy could only handle so much skin.

I took very long showers most days. I had the cleanest dick in Olympia.

And probably the bluest balls.

I'd made a vow to finally pursue Maggie. Make a move or die from embarrassment trying.

Weeks of cohabitation had already passed. We'd lived together almost a full month before I'd made my vow. Time was running out. She and Lizzy left in the middle of August for France. For the year.

It was now or never.

The lyrics about being pals didn't encourage me. Maggie was my best friend and had been pretty much ever since our road trip to see the Bryan Ferry concert freshman year. I'd proposed like an idiot. I didn't mean it. What kind of idiot proposes over Spinal Tap quotes? The words had spilled out of me without any sort of conscious effort. I'd been embarrassed as she stood there gawking at me, but deep down I didn't care. She was beautiful, and the coolest girl I'd ever met.

And I'd blown things before I ever met her by fooling around with her roommate Jennifer. No wonder Quinn put the kibosh on us dating right then and there.

I'd earned the label tongue masher. A month into college and I had the reputation of being a Romeo—with one girl one moment and proclaiming my love for another right after. Sadly, the role fit.

I was no more ready for a relationship at eighteen than I was to kill a man in the name of God and country. Hell, I hadn't ever done my own laundry.

Add to everything else, I'd been a complete dork. Glasses, skinny . . . not a cool guy at all. I liked history, music, video games, and books. In high school band, I picked up the bass because it was easier than guitar. I learned a few chords, enough to audition when a couple of guys on campus were looking to form a band.

Mark and Mike told me upfront they wanted to be in a band to get girls. They didn't really care about fame or music as much as they saw it as a gateway to easy sex with groupies. I'd laughed at the thought.

Turned out, being in a band, any band—even as bad as us—pretty much guaranteed girls saw me differently. We'd gotten better over the past year, but in comparison to some other local bands getting signed to major deals, we still sucked.

When not rehearsing, or playing video games, I worked in a

printing shop. The trade off to sweating my ass off all day in the heat from the printers meant the band got free flyers for our shows. Quinn designed everything and offered to distribute them around town.

The new flyers and stickers must have been working. Last months' shows had a bunch of new faces and fresh groupies for Mark and Mike.

One girl seemed very eager on becoming my groupie in particular. I'd been polite and flattered, but not interested.

Unfortunately, Mark slept with her best friend and kept inviting them back to our shows. I'd smile and thank her for coming, keeping my distance. Somehow she always managed to find a way to be in my personal space and touch me.

Heidi wasn't ugly. Different time and headspace, I might've been interested. It kind of freaked me out how easily I could have gotten laid if that's what I wanted.

But my one and only girl this summer was Maggie, whether she realized it or not. Majority of nights I preferred to go back and hang out with her. We'd watch movies on my crappy TV and VCR, then fall asleep on her bed or mine. Always fully clothed.

Sometimes I'd wake up before her and find us in a compromising position. Once she threw her leg over mine and there was no way she didn't feel the hardness in my jeans.

Basically, for the past two years, I'd been living in a state of perpetual torture.

I was willing to risk our friendship for a chance at more.

After I made the vow to act, I also told myself I'd be okay if it all fell apart.

Pretty sure I'd never be okay if I ruined the most important relationship in my life.

However, I had to try for more.

THIRTY

"Hey Jealousy"
Gin Blossoms

THE GIRLS WERE due to come home Sunday from their week on Whidbey at Maggie's family's cottage. It had been a girl's only trip because there were only two guest rooms and her family didn't believe in boys and girls sleeping in the same room unless they were related by blood or marriage.

Quinn and I hung out Sunday evening, eating cold pizza and playing games on my old Atari. I kicked his ass.

Quinn tossed his controller and pulled another slice out of the box. "We should plan a party. With Ben and Jo finally home, it will be the first time all of us are together since finals."

"Sounds like a good idea." A party might be the set up I'd been waiting for. Okay, I'd been stalling all summer, but a party did sound fun.

Around seven, our buzzer rang.

"It's probably the girls being too lazy to find their keys." Quinn hit the button to unlock the door downstairs and undid the lock before returning to his seat.

With two quick knocks, Mark walked in, with Heidi and Tammy in tow.

"Hey, were we supposed to rehearse tonight?" I wrinkled my brow in confusion.

He grabbed a slice of pizza and flopped into one of our chairs. At first, Tammy sat on the arm before sliding down to sit across his lap.

"Hi, Gil." Heidi sashayed over to my side of the couch. She squeezed herself between me and Quinn, making Quinn squish himself up against the opposite arm.

Q shot me a look of annoyance.

"Nah, no rehearsal. We were bored at my place and thought we'd come hang out over here. You always have something going on." Mark took another bite of pizza.

I offered the remaining slices to the girls, but both declined saying they were on diets. Whatever. Girls always said that. More pizza for me.

Heidi twisted her body to tuck her legs under her, essentially curling up against me.

When she "accidentally" kicked Quinn, he shot me another dirty look and stood up. "I'm going to go for cigarettes. Anybody need anything?"

I stared at him. He knew I wasn't interested in the woman coiled around me. Now he left me alone with her.

The girls made conversation and giggled a lot. I half paid attention, but most everything they brought up went over my head. Mark happily chomped on our pizza. A telltale redness rimmed his eyelids—he was totally stoned.

The same redness tinged Heidi's and her friend's eyes. Nice. They'd gotten stoned at his place and came over here looking for munchies.

I should've kicked them out and told them to go to the McDonald's down the road.

When the door swung open, I expected Quinn to return with cigarettes and maybe beer if he didn't get carded.

Instead, Maggie, Selah, and Lizzy, and all their bags, poured into the room. Laughter followed them. They looked sunburnt and sandy. Maggie was a sight. Her nose had more freckles and sunburned pink. She looked beautiful.

They all stopped short when they spotted our little foursome in the living room.

Heidi pressed close against me. She might as well have been in my lap. My back pressed against the corner of the couch, with nowhere else for me to go to give her space.

"Oh, hi." Always polite, Maggie stepped forward. "Hi, Mark. Who are your friends?"

He introduced the girls.

"Gil's more my friend." Heidi's nails dug into my skin as she wrapped her hand around my upper arm. With her words, she left no doubt about her perceived claim on me.

Maggie's smile faded from polite to fake.

Knowing this looked bad, I jumped over the arm of the couch and stood up. "Anyone want a beer or soda? You guys need help with your bags?"

My roommates shook their heads.

"We won't interrupt. It's been a long drive." After a silent conversation with their eyes, Lizzy pulled Maggie down the hall, leaving a pile of sandy bags by the door.

Selah remained standing there, shooting daggers at the new additions. "You look familiar. Didn't I have an art theory class with you?" She directed the question at Heidi.

Heidi giggled. "Oh, we don't go to Evergreen. We're studying cosmology."

"I think you mean cosmetology. Or are you studying the origins of the universe?" Selah's voice had gone icy.

More giggling followed. "No, silly. We're going to be hair stylists. Duh."

Selah's eyebrow arched like a cartoon villainess about to go in for the kill.

I stepped between her and the girls. "I didn't invite them over," I whispered.

"Then get rid of the STD Twins," she whispered back. "Not cool to have a party on a Sunday night when most of us have to work in the morning."

She gave me the out I had been looking for. "Listen, Mark, I've got an early shift at the printers. Better call it a night."

He glanced at the clock on the wall. It barely read nine o'clock. Nodding in understanding, he agreed.

Heidi leaned back into the couch cushions. "I don't have to go do I, Gilly?"

Gilly wasn't my name. Or a nickname.

"It's Gil. Or Gilliam."

"Willy's short for William. So Gilly is short for Gilliam?" She twirled a permed lock of hair around her finger.

"She's got you there." Mark and Tammy stood up. "Come on, girls, let's find some real food and let the old people go to bed."

"I thought you'd be more fun." Heidi exaggerated her bottom lip into a pout so deep a bird could've perched on it. Her hand grazed the front of my jeans as she walked by me on her way to the door.

I jerked back my hips to avoid full contact. More than obvious, she'd made her intentions clear. I locked the door behind them to be on the safe side.

THIRTY-ONE

"These Are Days"
10,000 Maniacs

THE DAY OF the big going away party we all hung out on the roof one last time. A couple other friends joined us early before things got out of control as our parties tended to do.

"We need a group picture to capture the moment," Lizzy announced as the sun began to sink, casting us all in a golden light.

"Nothing gold can last." Maggie butchered the quote, but we all understood her reference.

"Pony Boy, go get one of your cameras." Selah pointed at Quinn.

He disappeared down the stairs. Returning, he carried one of his many Polaroid cameras. He had a collection of them from old Land models with the peel-back film to this snappy black model with built-in flash. He called over Mike to take a group pic.

"Which way should we face? I don't want to be squinty." Selah stood with her hands on her hips.

"Do the sun in the background." Quinn stepped around her and faced away from the sun.

We shuffled together. Maggie and I in the middle with Lizzy to her left. Selah and Quinn in their matching flannels and cut-offs flanked Lizzy's other side. Ben stood beside Jo, who squeezed in next to me, her golden hair glowing in the late afternoon light.

"Should I stand between Q and Selah to break up their dynamic super hero twin flannel powers?" Lizzy asked.

My arm around Maggie, I patted Lizzy's head in a weird dog version of a high five.

Maggie giggled beside me.

"Form of a grungy college student," I whispered to Maggie.

She tilted her head back and really laughed as the flash went off. "We should redo it. I was laughing and my lids were closed," she said as the camera spit out the exposed print.

"Too late." Quinn studied the back of the camera. "No more film."

We waited for the print to finish developing. Quinn shook the white-framed photo.

"Shaking it doesn't do anything." Lizzy stood on her tiptoes to see the image.

"It makes the wait go by faster." He held up the Polaroid. "It's a keeper."

"Let us see!" Selah demanded.

Ben didn't even look at the camera. He stared at Jo, who looked like her head was on fire from the way the light played on her hair. Maggie's eyes were shut and she'd angled her head back. My hand covered most of Lizzy's head and kind of looked like I squished her down. She'd been right about the flannel. Next to her, Quinn and Selah did look like twins whose mother dressed them alike, right down to their matching combat boots.

My own shoulder-length hair could be pulled back into a decent ponytail, but I wore it down unless it was too hot, or in the way when I played bass.

"It's a terrible pic. My head is glowing like an alien." Jo sighed.

"Says you. I think Selah and I look amazing. My legs look fantastic in these shorts." Quinn held up his palm for a high five with his twin.

Selah slapped his palm. "We'll never be this young or fabulous again. These are the days, my friends."

"I plan to grow more fabulous as I age." Quinn puffed out his chest.

Maggie pulled his short ponytail. "Aslan, I'm not sure any of us could handle you being more spectacular than you already are."

Ever since Quinn grew his hair out, he resembled a lion. One night of too much cheap Mountain Rhine wine, he'd let Lizzy braid his hair and tie it with red scrunchies like the mean girls wore in *Heathers*.

I thought he looked more like the Cowardly Lion in the Emerald City than the beloved king of Narnia, but I knew enough not to delve into a pointless debate about lions.

Anytime anyone brought up a lion, he'd break into the king of the forest song from *Wizard of Oz,* proving what an incredible drama queen the lion really had been. The last time it happened, he and Lizzy had skipped across the quad singing at the top of their lungs about wizards.

PEOPLE SPREAD OUT all over the apartment and roof as the party hit its peak. I'd lost track of Maggie and needed to find her. Tonight was my last shot. She and Lizzy left early tomorrow morning.

Once I made sure she wasn't on the roof, I continued my search for her in the overcrowded apartment. I followed raised voices, including Maggie's, into the hall to the bedrooms.

"What are you even doing here? Who invited you?" With crossed arms and a scowl, Maggie blocked Heidi's path.

"What are you doing here? Who invited you?" Heidi parroted Maggie's words.

"Oh, you're a charming one in your crop-top and acid-washed jeans. First, I live here. In fact, the room you were attempting to enter is mine. The first explains the second question."

Heidi's expression went blank as she processed, or attempted to process, Maggie's explanation. "Prove it."

I took a step closer to the hall, but Lizzy stopped me. "Let Maggie handle this. She's been wanting to take down your groupies for months. Think of this as a parting gift when she'll be on the other side of the world for a year."

"She what?"

Lizzy shushed me.

"Listen, Heidi, is it? You crashed this party and you should probably go back to whatever corner you came from."

Ignoring Maggie's dig, Heidi pushed back her shoulders. "Mark invited us."

"Mark doesn't live here. He didn't have the authority to invite you to *my* going away party."

"You're a real uptight bitch." Heidi got up in Maggie's face.

Instinctively, I stepped forward. Lizzy yanked me back by my T-shirt.

"And you're a skank. Gil's never going to sleep with you. Ever." Maggie jabbed her finger in front of Heidi's face.

Heidi lunged at Maggie. I lunged at Heidi. Lizzy got dragged along behind me because she still held onto my shirt.

Maggie slapped my groupie.

"Whoa," Lizzy whispered over my shoulder. "I didn't think she had it in her."

Unfortunately, Heidi swung her arm to retaliate. And missed, stumbling into the wall. As she fell, she tried to pull Maggie down with her.

"Enough!" I raised my voice over the music. Stepping around Heidi, I checked on Maggie.

"Gilly," Heidi whined from the floor. "Did you see that bitch hit me?"

"Who are you calling a bitch, skank?" Maggie made a fist.

Trying not to laugh at her tough girl act, I closed my eyelids and shook my head. I pulled Maggie to my side and addressed the mess on the floor. "You need to stop calling her a bitch and maybe she won't slap you again."

"Why? Is she your girlfriend?"

Maggie's arm curled around my waist and she tucked two fingers into the front pocket of my jeans. "It isn't any of your business, but I am."

I held my face as still as possible to avoid showing my shock. I kissed the top of her head to hide my ridiculous grin. This was the best moment of my life and I wasn't going to spoil it by questioning anything.

Lizzy caught my eye and mouthed, "Ohmygod."

I shrugged in response. The crazy situation could always be used as an excuse for my actions.

"Mark said you didn't have a serious girlfriend."

"Mark doesn't know anything."

Heidi sneered and scrambled upright.

"We live together. How stupid can you get?" Maggie wrapped her other arm around my front, holding onto me like a koala. Perfect analogy. I heard they're vicious in the wild. I wouldn't want to go up against Maggie right now either.

"There's like twelve of you living here. Unless it's some sort of sex commune, I'm calling bullshit." Evidently, Heidi didn't know when to cut her losses and back down.

"Maybe this will shut you up." Maggie grabbed the back of my neck and pulled me down to her level. Our eyes met for a second, and the world paused. She blinked. Once. Twice.

Before I knew what happened, her lips pressed to mine.

I sucked in a breath and kissed her back. I didn't care if she was putting on a show to prove a point. I'd wanted to do this to her and with her for two years.

"You're both assholes." Heidi's heels stomped off down the hall.

Lizzy's voice broke through my Maggie haze. "You two can stop now. She's gone."

We moved apart, but I squeezed Maggie's shoulder, trying to keep her close.

"You're welcome." She touched her finger to her lips, her voice distant. Emotion softened her expression.

"Impressive display." Lizzy gave us a thumbs up. "Should keep the groupies at bay once she tells all her slutty friends you're taken. Brilliant move with the kiss, Mags."

I half listened to Lizzy's praise. Part of me replayed the kiss over and over. The other part of me wanted to press Maggie against the wall to do it again. Or open her door and lock it behind us.

"After all the excitement, I need a drink. Maybe even a shot." Maggie's voice rose in a fake attempt to be chipper.

"Celebratory shots for everyone!" Lizzy led her away. I followed like a puppy.

"Tequila!" Quinn shouted from the kitchen. He poured a row of shots.

"Ding dong, the skank is dead!" Lizzy lifted her glass.

"To friends sticking together." Maggie downed her shot.

I raised my glass and silently toasted to her. To the girl who captured my heart and owned my body. To bravery.

THIRTY-TWO

"With Tomorrow" ~~Creepion Twins~~ This Mortal Coil

I KEPT TRYING to get Maggie to talk to me after the fake-not-fake kiss in the hallway. Twice she giggled and brushed me off by either walking away or changing the subject.

Damn it. Time was running out.

I'd wasted two years waiting for the perfect time. She kissed me. I wasn't going to let her leave for an entire year after our kiss.

The party began to wind down around one in the morning. A few of Lizzy's friends hung out in the kitchen discussing *The Godfather* movies. Ben and Jo had already gone to bed. I had no idea where Selah went, or who she was with.

Quinn and Maggie sat on the couch. He said something I couldn't hear and she rested her head on the arm, laughing.

"What's funny?" I sat on the coffee table in front of them.

Maggie sat up and tucked her toes under Q's legs. "He was telling me his idea for an installation project involving little rhinestone mice and Eva Gabor."

I cocked my head, waiting for the humor to hit me.

"It's funny because of *The Rescuers*. The Disney cartoon. Get it?"

I faked a laugh. I didn't get it. I didn't get most of Quinn's weird cultural references. The guy was a walking pink pie piece from Trivial Pursuit.

What I did understand was I had only hours left with Maggie. "Mind if I borrow Magpie?"

Quinn studied me.

I stared at him, willing for him to understand the importance of this to me.

He tilted his head back, focusing on Lizzy's group. "I totally disagree. The cannoli are a metaphor for innocence in *The Godfather*."

Following his non sequitur, he jumped over the back of the couch and joined the party in the kitchen.

Finally, Maggie and I were alone.

"I have a going away present for you."

"You didn't have to buy me anything." She focused on the hem of her shorts, pulling at a long string where her jeans had been cut off.

"I know. But I wanted to get you something." I stood up and held out my hand. "Come on."

She paused before uncurling from the couch and standing. I reached for her hand, entwining our fingers. At first her grip remained soft before she mirrored my pressure.

I led us down the hall to my room. Selah and Maggie shared, but with Quinn in the former dining room, I had my own space.

Once inside, I flicked on the desk lamp and locked the door with a quiet click. If she heard it, she didn't react.

Maggie being in here wasn't strange. Our normal meant being together. Last week we'd rented an old black and white French film, and both fell asleep on my bed in the first ten minutes.

Quinn joked the two of us could sleep in a twin without touching. Truthfully, we could sleep in the small space, but touching was the whole point. At least for me. Sleep made me brave.

"You lured me in here with the promise of a present." She gave me a shy smile, and held out her hands.

"Who are you and what did you do with my best friend? First, you're having a big, old-fashioned cat-fight over my honor. Next you've gotten all demanding. Do I need to check the back of your neck for signs of alien abduction?"

She held up her hair and turned around to show me her flawless neck.

I opened my desk drawer and pulled out the small wrapped rectangle. From its shape and weight, she should immediately guess what it contained.

I tossed it to her, and surprisingly she caught it.

"Ooh, is it a new car?" She shook the box.

"Why would I buy you a new car when you're leaving the country?"

"Excellent point. Is it a dog?" She tapped the paper wrapped plastic. "You should've added some air holes for the sweet little guy."

"It's not a puppy. Again, do I need to remind you this is a going away gift? Not really fair for the puppy to be quarantined because France is afraid of American dog germs." I made a face over the word France.

"You're really emphasizing the whole 'leaving the country' part of this gift." She frowned and her dark blue eyes shone brighter with tears she quickly blinked away.

"Merely stating the facts." I tried to sound like her leaving wasn't a big deal.

"When I signed up last fall, seeing the world, or at least Europe, on my parents' dime, and enriching my life sounded like the perfect thing." Her voice grew softer the longer she spoke.

"Hey," I stepped closer to her, "It's a wonderful opportunity. Don't ever regret following your dreams, Maggie May."

She sat heavily at the foot of my mattress, still holding the wrapped gift. I knelt on the floor in front of her.

"Open it." I placed my hand over one of hers. "It won't bite."

"It's not the boa constrictor I asked for?" She faked her sad face.

I pouted. "It's not. Because you would never, ever, ask for a snake as a present."

"You know me too well." Finally, she ripped the paper in one quick tear. She held the mixtape up to look at the handmade cover.

"Quinn helped with the collage." Seven floating heads, one for each of our friends, decorated the paper. Five sat on a red blob vaguely resembling America and two floated on a green square on the other side of a blue ocean.

This time her tears spilled over her eyelids and down her cheeks. "You made me a mixtape?"

I nodded before wiping more tears threatening to fall off the edge of her jawline. "You'll need some decent music over there. For all I know they listen to Jerry Lewis comedies and old Marcel Marceau albums." I winked at her.

Understanding my mime joke immediately, she laughed. "I think you mean Maurice Chevalier."

"I doubt it. A really old guy thanking heaven for little girls is trés creepy."

She flipped the tape over and read my tiny script of the song list. "You put 'You Can Call Me Al' on here."

I moved from the floor to the mattress next to her. "It's our song. I have one favor to ask."

She rested her head on my shoulder. "Anything."

"Never dance to our song with anyone else."

Leaning back on her elbows, she stared into my eyes. "Never anyone else."

"Deal."

Silence followed our underlying promise to each other. Even in the moment, I didn't believe we would manage to keep our word, but I wanted to. I wanted to believe space and time wouldn't change our friendship.

"Maggie?"

She gazed up at me and wet her top lip with the tip of her tongue.

"I'm really going to miss you." I blinked away the sting of tears.

"Me too." Her voice lowered to a whisper.

Unconsciously, my own breathing slowed and matched hers while we stared at each other.

Slowly, we moved closer, a magnet pulling us together.

Her hand rested on my thigh. My fingers wove into her hair at the nape of her neck.

Everything moved incredibly slowly.

Our touches. Our breathing. Time.

"Gil."

I kissed her, softly pressing my mouth against hers. Unlike the kiss in the hall, her lips parted, soft and wet. Inviting.

I wet my bottom lip before sweeping my tongue across her lips. A soft moan escaped her throat.

Exhaling, I changed the angle, brushing my nose along hers. Her tongue peeked out and gently touched my lip. Accepting her invitation, my own tongue responded, gliding into her mouth and following her lead.

As the kiss intensified, time zoomed ahead. Everything sped up. She leaned forward, pressing me back against the bed. Her hair formed a curtain around us as she kissed me, her hands exploring my chest and shoulders.

Wanting more, everything all at once, I rolled over her, settling my knee between her legs.

She opened them to accommodate me. With her fingers in my hair, she tugged me closer to her mouth. Her other hand pulled my torso against hers. I let my arm collapse and pressed my weight down on her.

A million thoughts fired in my brain. Behind the impulses to touch, taste, and feel everything I could on her body, a small voice kept reminding me she was leaving. To stifle my doubts, I listened to my body demanding more and more and more.

My finger hooked around the top button of her shirt. I paused before slipping the button through the hole. Her hands found their way under my T-shirt, and she gently scraped her nails along my spine.

The entire time, our mouths never broke contact. Once her shirt lay open, I moved my hand to cup her breast through thin fabric and lace. Her nipple responded, rising to meet my touch. I slipped my finger under her bra and tugged it down. Only then did I stop kissing her mouth.

Bracing myself on my forearm, I teased her skin with my tongue before sucking on the rounded peak. Gasping, she arched her back.

With my other hand, I reached behind her and unclasped her bra. I needed her shirt off to remove her bra. I lifted her up with my hand on the middle of her back.

She responded by raising the hem of my shirt. I reached behind my shoulder and pulled it off with one hand before returning my focus to her. Naked from the waist up, her eyes held a little nervousness and her hand moved to cover what I'd only had glimpses of before.

"You're beautiful." I whispered, gently bending her arm and placing her hand on the bed next to her shoulder. "You have no reason to be shy around me."

She interlaced our fingers, holding my hand and stretching her arm above her head, pushing her chest toward me again.

Time paused as I explored her body. In the background, the stereo switched over to the Cocteau Twins' *Treasure*. I paused, thinking I should change it to something sexier.

"I've always loved this album." Maggie pulled me to her mouth, our skin touching from shoulder to hips. Hers felt warm and unbelievably soft.

"Maggie." A sudden urge to tell her everything crashed over me.

"Shh." She pressed a finger to my mouth. I kissed the tip.

"I—"

She wrapped her legs around mine. "It's okay"

What's okay? I loved her? Did she mean she felt the same?

Her tongue in my mouth and her hand skimming the fly of my jeans stopped my mind from thinking. She snuck a finger beneath the denim, brushing against the skin by my hip. Reacting on instinct, I thrust against her, seeking more. A low moan reverberated in her chest. I did it again and the sound grew louder. Shifting to lie beside her, I drew a wide spiral down her stomach with my finger, slowly watching her skin react, leaving goosebumps in my wake.

The top of her purple underwear peeked out above the faded denim of her shorts. I followed the line with my finger from one hip to the other. Under my teasing touch, she twisted and squirmed.

Unwilling to torture myself any longer, I undid her shorts' button fly. She bridged her hips, and I shimmied them off of her.

A small white bow centered her underwear. The tan line from her bathing suit left a pale shadow around the cotton. Freckles dotted her arms and legs, but not her stomach.

I committed every detail to memory first with my eyes, followed by my fingers, and mouth.

Hovering above her, I breathed warm air over the tops of her thighs.

"Gil," she whispered like a plea.

I answered her by kissing the bow. My fingers splayed over her hips and pushed her thighs apart. My nose skimmed down the center, inhaling her. I'd wondered and dreamed about her for forever. Every sense memory needed to be recorded.

With a sharp inhale, she tried to close her thighs. I braced my hands, preventing her from hiding herself from me. "Every part of you is beautiful, Maggie. Let me show you."

Her hands clenched the sheet beside her hips when I dipped my fingers under the edge of her underwear and pulled it down. I had to shift again to slip them off her legs completely. I dropped them to the side of the bed. Part of me hoped she'd leave them behind.

Kneeling again on the floor, I dragged her body closer to me. Her lids flew open.

"It's okay. Let me show you."

I waited for her to relax before doing anything more. Her hand swept down my arm and found my fingers, holding on to our point of contact.

Given the approval I'd wanted, I squeezed her hand before returning my focus to her pleasure.

"Tell me what feels good." I kissed her inner thigh and made eye contact. "I want to make you feel amazing."

She nodded and squeezed my hand again.

I followed her body's responses as I explored her with my tongue and fingers. She liked long sweeps and light pressure at first, before building up the intensity with the tip of my tongue and gentle sucking. I slipped a finger inside and matched my rhythm until she told me with the tightening of her legs I found the spot and the right pace.

I could have stayed there forever. I wanted to be nowhere else in the world.

With a soft inhale and a clenching of her fingers around mine, her body fluttered around my fingers. I rode out each wave of pleasure with her, slowing my pace and releasing the pressure.

She went limp on the bed, stretching out her legs, curling and uncurling her toes. I smiled in satisfaction and kissed her hipbone.

To relieve some pressure, I undid the top few buttons of my fly. My erection popped free and I sighed.

I felt her hands on my hips, reaching around my arms to shove at the denim.

"These need to come off." Her voice sounded determined.

I stood, never breaking eye contact, and undid the final buttons, letting the jeans fall to the floor. Hooking my thumbs into the waist, I lost my boxers next.

Standing naked in front of Maggie could have been awkward, but not tonight. Seeing her satisfied smile and the pink flush of pleasure on her chest from my actions, turned me on like nothing ever had before.

Against the red of her hair, her pale skin glowed. A blush spread on her cheeks, down her neck, ending slightly above the deep rose of her nipples.

Nothing would ever be more beautiful to me than Maggie in this moment.

She crooked her finger at me. "Come back."

I obliged, and crawled over her as she scooted farther up the bed. When her hair spread across my pillows, she enveloped me in her arms.

Our bodies aligned and for a brief moment, I thought about going without a condom. It would be easy, natural, to slide inside of her without breaking this connection. I stilled and exhaled as I brought myself back from the edge.

Shifting, I reached into the drawer of the table next to my bed and found a condom.

Maggie quirked an eyebrow at me. I shrugged. Too many after school specials about teen pregnancies and news hysteria about AIDS had sunk in over the years. I didn't think either of us had ever been exposed. We knew we were clean when we'd all gone to get tested after Selah and Maggie's sexuality class. Never did I want to put Maggie's future at risk for my own, short-lived pleasure. She was too important.

And she was leaving.

"Are you having second thoughts?" She touched my arm.

I'd paused too long, lost in my own head. "No. Never. Why?"

A thousand emotions swam in the depths of her blue irises. "I feel like we're crossing a line and things will never be the same between us."

I ran the back of my hand over her cheek. "The line is already behind us. Somewhere over there with our pants." I pointed to our heap of clothes on the floor. "Nothing will ever change what's between us. Not sex. Or not having sex. Or miles. Or time. Promise."

She sat up and kissed me, throwing her arms over my shoulders. Leaning away, she stared at me. "Promise."

I kissed her again and tilted her into the pillows.

This time I didn't stop. I kissed her as I thrust forward. She sighed into my mouth and entwined herself around me.

We shifted positions, rolling to our sides and then I pulled her over me. I wanted to watch her body and face, and it allowed me to touch more of her. My hands set a rhythm on her hips as she glided above me. Her hair tumbled down her back. I took handfuls of it and gently pulled, exposing her neck to my mouth. Sitting up more, I kissed the length of her throat before finding her breasts again.

I needed time to still. *Better yet, it should stop all together.*

My body warned me this moment would be over long before I could have my fill of her. I shifted us again, prolonging the inevitable climb and tipping point. My movements slowed, delaying my pleasure as I sought to give her more.

The CD stopped and the room fell into quiet, the only sounds from our bodies moving against the sheets. In the silence, our breathing and soft moans echoed louder than any screams of pleasure. My own heartbeat slammed into my ears. I placed my hand over her chest and felt the rapid flutter of her heart beneath my palm.

We existed in the bubble as long as we could.

Time didn't stop for us.

It raced forward, sweeping us along with it.

My primal instincts took over, driving me toward orgasm. I enfolded her in my arms, wanting to consume her, seeking to crawl inside of her. I wanted to exist in this state of oneness. My nerves fired and I no longer knew where she ended and where I began.

All I knew was I felt. I existed as physical pleasure in pure form, speeding toward explosion.

Everything ceased except my blood thrumming in my ears and the euphoria expanding through my body.

I stilled, trying to stay in the moment. Beneath me, Maggie sighed and anchored me to her.

Time slammed into me.

Realization hit as I came down from the high. An unbearable heaviness crashed over me. I gave into its weight, lying on top of Maggie. Panting, I tried to catch my breath. Attempted to center myself before the moment slipped away.

I rolled to my back, bringing her with me and curling her to my side. She rested her thigh on my leg and placed her hand on my chest. Beneath her touch, my heart pounded against my ribcage, begging her to take it with her when she left.

I fought the tears forming, and I swallowed against the truth of our reality.

She would still be leaving in a few hours. I had no right to anchor her to me the first opportunity she had to spread her wings and fly. I wouldn't hold her back.

I could do the right thing. I could let her fly away, soaring with the joy of a dream come true.

I could hope she'd understand the message of the lyrics on the tape I'd given her.

I could hope.

I could pray she would come home to me.

Our time together could begin.

The future I'd imagined a hundred times would be more than a fantasy.

For her, I could wait.

Because I loved her.

HER BREATHING DEEPENED into a soft snore beside me. Unable to sleep, I stared at her, committing everything to memory. Filing away the tiniest details of her and this night, I wouldn't forget.

I debated waking her and telling her my feelings.

If I were selfish, that's what I'd do.

Instead, I whispered the words, practicing for our good-bye in the morning. I'd say them to her tomorrow before she left. I'd look into her eyes so she would know I meant every word.

"I love you, Maggie May. From the very beginning. Please come back to me."

Feeling a huge weight lift off of my heart from saying the words out loud for the first time, I smiled as I spooned behind her

Tomorrow morning wouldn't be good-bye. It would be a beginning for us.

Hope filled my chest as I drifted off to sleep.

LIZZY

Lizzy Jackson, 21

Art History
Senior

What experience will you remember most about college?

Oh boy.
I want to remember everything.
Only one?
Hmm …

Junior year in France.
All of it.
It's when I realized the world held an infinite number of love stories.
A few with happy endings and ever afters.
Some had limited potential and heartbreaking endings.
Some could take more than a lifetime to be told.
For others, the story ended before it began.

THIRTY-THREE

"Right Here Right Now"
Jesus Jones

MAGGIE REFUSED TO tell me what was wrong. Not in the car, not on our flight from Seattle to JFK, not during our three-hour layover, or on the overnight flight to Paris. Her eyes were puffy and red when we finally arrived. Then again, mine were, too.

She played the same mixtape over and over on her Walkman until the batteries ran down.

I counted fifty-seven sighs from the time we left Olympia to when we finished immigration and gathered our bags. On the train into Paris from the airport, she stared out the window, but I had the feeling she didn't really see the beautiful French architecture passing her by.

Replaying the last twenty-four hours in my head, I searched for clues. We'd had a teary, long good-bye with our friends at our going away party. Selah even shuffled out to the living room this morning in a kimono to say a final good-bye with a promise she'd see us over winter break.

Maggie didn't want to wake up the rest of our housemates with the excuse we were running late and might miss our flight. That had been a little odd. Maybe she'd snuck into Gil's room earlier to say good-bye. I couldn't imagine her leaving without doing so. They'd been inseparable at the party. In fact, two different people asked me if they were a couple.

Plus, their fake kiss looked pretty real to me. The last I saw of them, they'd been going into his room.

However, she sat in her room this morning when I went in to wake her. Her suitcase and backpack were neatly stacked by the front door and she'd already taken a shower.

Sigh fifty-eight and counting escaped from Maggie. It would be a very long year in France if she moped about being here the entire time.

Although, sighing did seem like a very French thing to do. I studied the couple across the aisle from our seats. He wore a sour expression like he smelled something terrible or someone had insulted his wife. The woman opposite him, who I assumed to be the maligned wife, frowned as she read her book. Neither smiled the entirety of our short train trip. Nor did they speak to each other. Maybe they were strangers after all.

Arriving in the station, he handed her a small bag from the luggage rack above their heads. She passed him his hat and I noticed a thin gold band.

Exhaustion washed over me as we lugged our suitcases up the stairs to the street. The director of our program had arranged to meet us outside and escort us to orientation.

Maggie tromped along behind me, in even more of a daze than I felt. I didn't know if it was the moping or jet lag. Probably both.

A guy on a scooter whizzed past us, nearly hitting my large suitcase. I jumped back from the curb, pulling Maggie with me.

Next to us, a woman in a chic pencil skirt and red lipstick scowled and whispered, "Stupid Americans," under her breath in thickly accented English. I knew the only reason she spoke English was to make sure we understood her insult. Delightful welcome to the city of love.

An older woman with dark hair streaked with white waddled up to us. She reminded me of a little penguin with her small pointed nose. Her round belly stood in stark contrast to the ultra slim Parisienne woman who insulted us.

Maybe the snooty woman only felt hungry. I could get very cranky when I was hungry, too.

The benevolent penguin greeted us in a mix of French and English. "*Bonjour*! You must be Maggie and Lizzy!"

Maggie snapped out of her walking coma and said, "*Bonjour, Madame Picou.*"

Madame's bobbed hair bounced with her excitement. "Welcome to France! *Bienvenue a Paris!*"

I wondered if she would repeat everything in both languages.

Maggie gathered herself together and introduced us. Jet lag had erased my language skills. I smiled mutely and made awkward hand gestures.

Madame Picou smiled at us, then gave us double kisses, one on each of our cheeks. She smelled of old roses and hairspray, with a lingering layer of strong body odor.

I immediately nicknamed her Madame Pee-ew in my head and giggled. I'd have to tell Maggie later.

We were among the final students to arrive for our program's orientation. The rest had departed by private bus earlier in the day. Madame Picou stuffed as much of our luggage as she could into her small Renault's trunk. Our backpacks sat on the seat next to me.

All of our possessions fit into this tiny French car. We each shipped over a couple of boxes of winter clothes a few weeks ago. We were basically gypsies for the next nine months.

Madame Picou drove like a Formula One driver. She cut across lanes and barely slowed down unless she encountered a red light. Out the window, Paris blurred past us as we headed to orientation at a château outside of the city.

"We need to pick up one more student." She swerved around a bicycle close enough I could've reached out and stolen the baguette in the basket on the back.

I thought about where we would put more luggage and wondered if I'd missed a roof rack.

The car came to sharp halt in front of a café on the corner of two quaint streets. Everything appeared charming to my American sensibility.

A tall blond man warily approached the car with a rucksack type bag on his back.

Madame Picou prattled something in French at him and unlocked the door behind her. Unless he planned to sit on our backpacks, I had to shift them closer to me. One I put on the floor between us and the other I held on my lap, barely able to peer around it.

"Hello." He shoved his pack into the car and squeezed in behind it. His own bag filled the middle of the seat, creating a wall between us.

"Introduce yourselves while I drive." Picou put the car into gear and we lurched away from the curb.

Maggie rotated in her seat and stuck out her hand. "I'm Margaret. The tiny woman smothered under the bags is Elizabeth."

I peeked around the tower of backpacks. "Hello."

It was all I could do. My hands were trapped, and even if they weren't, I wasn't sure I could stretch around his bag to shake hands.

"Christopher. Christopher Liddell. Delighted to meet you both." His accent wasn't American. Who said delighted? Besides Quinn?

"You sound like James. James Bond." Maggie emphasized the pauses in between his first and last name. "No double-o-seven?"

"Sadly, no. A simple university student."

"*En français,*" Madame Picou commanded.

Jet lag overtook me and I rested my head on the window. The sun poured in through the glass and something smelled of fresh laundry and spices. I sniffed myself. Nope, it definitely wasn't me. My clothes held the faint aroma of stale airline air and public transportation.

I would only close my lids for a minute while I listened to the conversation *en français* around me. I didn't want to be rude, but my brain was too tired to translate and conjugate.

A GENTLE TOUCH shook my shoulder. "Elizabeth? We've arrived."

I jolted awake at the sound of a male voice close to me. Completely confused, it took me a minute to realize I sat inside a car.

While I attempted to shake off my impromptu nap, concerned gray-blue eyes came into focus. They belonged to the handsome face of a stranger with a British accent who leaned into the back seat of this tiny sedan. He rested his elbow near my head.

"How did I end up in England?" I attempted to blink away my confusion. "How long was I asleep?"

He chuckled. "You're in France. Outside Paris."

"Why are you calling me Elizabeth?"

His left eyebrow dipped while his right arched, making him appear almost comical. "You were introduced as Elizabeth. By Margaret?"

"Who's Margaret?"

"Did you hit your head?" Maggie peeked around him. She disappeared, and then my door opened. Her head reappeared in front of me. "You fell asleep on the drive to the château. You were out completely, even snoring."

I hung my head. Great first impression. Confused, snoring American girl charms no one. Despite my recent snooze, I wanted to close my lids again. I could have slept like the dead for days.

Maggie tapped my nose. "Don't fall back asleep. We're in France!"

At least I thought it was her. My lashes fluttered as I lifted my lids.

With a tug, she pulled me out of the backseat. I managed to get my feet under myself before I splayed out face first in the gravel of the drive.

"I'm up. I'm awake." Planting my feet, I spread out my arms.

Applause came from behind me. I spun at the sound.

Prince Charming and two other guys clapped. After a bow followed by a curtsy, I stuck out my tongue. "In the fairytales, the prince awakens the sleeping princess with a kiss."

Christopher arched his eyebrow again. I wondered if he practiced in the mirror. Honestly, he seemed the type. Now that we were out of the car and no longer squished by luggage, I could examine him more.

He wore a slightly rumpled pale yellow button-down Oxford shirt, tan pants, and very crisp white sneakers, without socks.

I swore if I had my copy of *The Preppy Handbook*, his picture would have been in there. His dark blond hair hung almost to his very high cheekbones unless he pushed it back. The ends brushed his collar in the back.

Angular cheekbones. Check.

Ruddy, prone to blush, pale English skin. Check.

Patrician arrogance. Check.

Mr. Darcy school of charm. Check.

"If the lady insists upon a kiss, then a kiss is what she'll receive."
He strode closer and kissed my cheek. I froze, holding my breath. Then,
slowly, deliberately, his breath brushed across my lips as he moved to
kiss the other cheek.

Dumbstruck, I silently blinked at him as he stepped back.

"Kit's not a prince. He's not even a baron, poor bastard." A short,
dark haired guy slapped Christopher's shoulder.

Standing next to me, a wide-eyed Maggie observed the subsequent
scuffle and play-fighting between apparent friends. Or blood enemies. I
couldn't tell.

"Who's Kit?" she whispered. "Is he the one who kissed you?"

"I have no idea, Margaret." I clasped her elbow. "What's with the
formal names?"

"Maggie and Lizzy sound too American. Our given names are
more sophisticated."

"We sound like Thatcher and the Queen."

"Or the youngest Dashwood and elder Bennet sister in Miss Jane
Austen's novels." Christopher interrupted our conversation.

"Dashwood and Bennet could be lady crime fighters. I like it."
Maggie beamed a smile in his direction. I realized I wasn't the only one
of us to notice his arrogant charm.

It had to be the accent. Maybe it was ingrained in us from a young
age to find British accents appealing. Our generation had stayed up all
night, if we were lucky, to watch Princess Di marry a future king in a
real life fairy tale wedding. Even I had the Princess Di haircut in elementary school. Something in our blood must have remembered the old co-
lonial days of British rule. Maybe somewhere deep down, some of us
still wanted to be told what to do by a British man.

I thought about my first real crush on a fictional character. It hadn't
been Mr. Darcy or a prince, but Sebastian Flyte and his teddy bear
Aloysius in *Brideshead Revisited*. I could still recall watching the mini-se-
ries on PBS with my older sister and parents. We'd been allowed to stay
up later than our normal bedtimes to watch classic literature and be
educated.

At eleven years old, I'd missed all the homosexual overtones in

Sebastian's sad story. All I saw was dreamy Anthony Andrews ~~Edwards~~. He was a charming blond, too, and the first in a long line of bad boys who stole my heart.

"Come on, let's help the American girls with their bags." Christopher pointed to our luggage piled near the bumper.

"Anything else in the boot?" a short freckled redheaded guy asked, tapping the trunk.

"You mean the trunk?" I asked.

He looked at our suitcases. "You have a trunk, too?"

"No, the car's trunk."

He regarded me in confused silence.

"The thing your hand is resting on right now?"

"That's the boot."

"This is going to be a long year if we can't communicate while all speaking English, let alone French." Maggie shrugged her backpack over her shoulder.

"Why are you in this school? Don't British colleges have their own study abroad programs?" I didn't mean to sound nosy, but I was curious.

"Study abroad is a thoroughly American idea. Joe and I are here for international business studies and language immersion. Different program, but we share the château for a week of orientation and immersion." Christopher pointed at the boot-trunk guy.

"And him?" I gestured to the dark haired one.

"He's Joe's twin, James. And a complete prat."

James attempted to trip Christopher by sticking out his foot. Christopher nimbly jumped over the obstacle without breaking his pace.

"Why did he call you Kit?" I followed behind the trio of guys carrying our bags into an enormous mansion.

"Kit's my old name from nursery days. I prefer Christopher."

"I prefer Lizzy, if I'm being honest."

He set my bag down at the bottom of an enormous stone staircase. "Then Lizzy is what I shall call you. Girls' rooms are upstairs and to the left. Your names should be on the door. Leave your bags here if you don't want to heft them up the stairs. Someone will bring them up for you later."

The three of them said good-bye and left us.

"This place is a palace." Maggie's voice was hushed like we were in a church. The château dated back to the eighteenth century. Its pale plaster exterior with enormous shutter-flanked windows and long gravel drive were understated compared to the ornate interior.

"I feel like I'm in a fairytale." She spun around in a small circle, her head tipped back to take in the high ceilings and carved moulding. "This is definitely not Olympia, Washington."

Watching her face light up for the first time since we woke up yesterday morning restored my faith this would be our greatest adventure yet. "Let's go find our room. Maybe there will be rows of little twin beds like in Madeline."

We giggled and raced each other up the stairs like little girls. When we got to the top, something golden below caught my eye. Christopher and his arched eyebrow still stood in the foyer, his face impassive with the exception of the aforementioned eyebrow. I couldn't tell if it arched in amusement or judgment. I gave him a little wave like I'd seen the Queen of England make to her loyal subjects and another curtsy.

He smiled, shaking his head, but returned the wave with a slight bow. I didn't know what about him made me want to curtsy, but if he gave me his gorgeous grin again, I'd keep doing it.

THIRTY-FOUR

"Keep Young and Beautiful"
Annie Lennox

OUR ROOM HAD four twin beds lined up in a row along one wall. A mural of a blue sky covered the middle of the ceiling. Fat cherubs holding ribbons decorated the corners of the room. Every single roll of their chub had been carefully detailed, a reminder not to over-indulge in all the amazing buttery, fattening food in France. As much as I wanted to eat everything in sight, I also didn't want to gain back all the weight I'd fought hard to lose in high school and kept off so far in college.

Maggie and Jo were lucky. They seemed to be able to eat anything and never really work out yet never gained weight. Selah embraced her curves. Hell, she flaunted her breasts like prizes she won at a carnival. Meanwhile, I carefully monitored calories, the scale and how my clothes fit on a daily basis.

The other beds in the room had been claimed. Our two roommates were from different colleges. Tall Amy went to Middlebury and glasses wearing Lara attended Antioch. In an attempt to memorize all the new names, I began assigning physical characteristics to names. Ginger James. Brown Joe. Eyebrow Christopher. I couldn't forget his name.

The four of us wandered down to the dining room for lunch. My catnap in the car had given me a second wind. Maggie moaned about it being the middle of the night and the wrong time for sandwiches.

The longest dining room table I'd ever seen centered the equally enormous room. Three chandeliers twinkling with crystals hung above it. A buffet lined one wall, filled with tiny sandwiches and cold sides.

"I feel underdressed." Maggie wore a sundress and sandals. If she felt underdressed my jeans and Chinese Mary Janes were probably some social faux pas.

We followed Amy and Lara through the line and sat across from them at the long polished wood table. I glanced around for the three other familiar faces and spotted them clumped together at the far end. Christopher gave me a small wave, and because I was already sitting and couldn't curtsy, I bowed my head.

"Are you saying grace?" Amy asked me.

Maggie snorted into her hand.

"Amen," I whispered while pinching Maggie's thigh under the table. She pinched my hand in retaliation.

I moaned loudly when I bit into what appeared to be a cheese sandwich, but tasted of creaminess and butter surrounded by delicious bread. It probably had a thousand calories, but I didn't care.

Apparently my moan had been louder than I thought. I lifted my gaze and met the cocked eyebrow of judgment. I didn't care. Butter!

Madame Picou and an older man in a neckerchief entered the room, calling everyone's attention to them.

"Is he wearing an ascot?" Maggie whispered to me.

"It's a neckerchief."

"I am awed and disturbed you know the proper name for men's neck fashions."

"You forget my uncle works in fashion in Miami. He's educated me on all things having to do with style."

Madame Picou cleared her throat. "This is Monsieur Laurent. He's the coordinator of the château and our sister programs in Paris. Please welcome him."

He spoke in a rapid stream of French and I caught about every third word. Even though it sounded like he said *haricot vert*, I felt pretty confident his speech didn't include the topic of green beans.

Everyone chuckled and I joined them, lost in confusion but laughing. My laughter continued after the others stopped. All thirty faces turned to focus on me. I ducked my head, but not before my eye caught the arched eyebrow of judgment.

I focused on folding and refolding my napkin on my lap until the speech ended.

Maggie, sensing my discomfort, summarized the introduction in a way that sounded like she had questions she wanted me to clarify.

I reached under the table and squeezed her hand in thanks.

The Paris program enrolled students from all over the US, whose own colleges didn't have study abroad campuses. We'd only be roomies for the week of orientation. When we returned to the city for the semester, we'd be assigned to live with a French family. I hoped Maggie and I wouldn't end up on opposite sides of Paris. Even with the Metro and bicycles, the city sprawled for miles.

THE FIRST SEVERAL weeks of classes were a blur. I had beginner's level language classes while Maggie took intermediate. Our host families lived about six blocks from each other not far from the Pantheon in the 5th *Arrondissement*.

Christopher and the twins lived in the same beautiful beaux art apartment building close to *Les Invalides* in the 7th. Unlike our host families, their situation involved tiny studio apartments and a shared hall bathroom on the top floor. An older grand-mere figure fed them breakfast and dinners in her grand apartment two floors below. Their living arrangement sounded romantic, like struggling American authors and painters who moved to Paris in the early twentieth-century.

My own host family lived in a more modern building without all the character and ghosts of artists past. Julie, Sebastien, and little Olivier were all trés nice.

Quickly, I figured out part of my housing situation would be to tutor Olivier in English while they taught me French. I soon discovered my French was worse than I thought. A precocious five year old regularly beat me on vocabulary tests.

Mags' family consisted of a single mom, Bernadette, and her daughter. When the daughter went to stay with her father, the mother went out. And typically took us with her. She knew the coolest clubs and jazz bars. Bernadette turned out to be one of the best parts of Paris.

She also knew of a broken payphone along the Seine near Shakespeare and Company, the famous bookstore and gathering place for English language ex-pats and homesick exchange students. The phone wasn't really broken. It allowed international calls for domestic rates. Knowledge of the phone was top secret, carefully shared, and protected.

The nine hour time difference made calling the West Coast almost impossible. We decided middle of the night our time would be best to reach our friends in Washington.

One night, Maggie and I rode our bikes to the secret phone at one in the morning. Tucked near the fence of a small park on a narrow street, the phone appeared the same as any of the hundreds of others scattered around the city.

We huddled with our heads next to the receiver in order for both of us to talk and hear at the same time. The phone rang and rang before Quinn finally answered. Maggie cried when she heard his voice. I got a little teary, too. He passed us around to Ben and Jo. Selah picked up last and told us Gil was at work. Seeing the disappointment in Maggie's face at the news, I wrapped my arm around her waist and gave a squeeze.

A short line formed behind us, despite the late hour. I recognized Christopher's tall form at the end with the twins. He waved at us. I smiled at him.

We promised to call back soon, giddy we could call home on our limited budgets. After hugging, we pulled our bikes from the fence and walked toward our friends.

Christopher greeted Maggie with the standard double-cheek kiss. When it was my turn, I went right instead of left. His lips brushed against mine for a brief second before he corrected himself and kissed my cheek. He held my shoulders still as he repeated the kiss on my other cheek, never acknowledging our kiss faux pas.

My giggle and the heat on my cheeks betrayed my surprise. Was this a first kiss? "I'll get the double-kiss right eventually."

His own laugh sounded cocky, confident. "Let me know if you need a practice partner."

I stepped back and slipped on a cobblestone, righting myself as I laughed nervously.

"Out past your curfew, young ladies?" Christopher tugged on my coat sleeve, drawing my attention back to the conversation.

"I'm staying with Maggie tonight." Everyone knew about my host family's strict policies. I felt twelve instead of twenty.

Christopher nodded, looking serious. He brushed his fingers against the cuff of my jacket.

"You don't seem the type to need discounted international calling." I prodded. "What brings you out in the middle of the night?"

"We were at a pub down the street that serves proper pints and wanted to try out the magical phone for ourselves."

"Maybe he thought you'd be here." James elbowed Christopher and got a headlock in return.

Maggie cleared her throat as the guys scuffled around. Clearly they'd been drinking. "We should go back to the apartment."

I leaned my bike against my hip. "I'm kind of enjoying the show."

Somehow Joe had involved himself as well. Two against one, but Kit held his own, ending with both twins in headlocks.

"Sorry about these wankers. They're pissed," Christopher apologized, looking embarrassed and flushed.

I twisted a lock of hair around my finger, staring at his handsome face and messy hair.

"Lizzy?" Maggie spoke.

"Hmm?"

"We should get going."

"You must stay. Kit's been hoping to run into you all night." Joe jumped a few feet away from Christopher's reach.

I studied their faces, trying to see if Joe's words were true.

"We could go for a ride along the Seine," Christopher suggested, his voice full of hope.

"Now? In the middle of the night?"

"It's Paris. The city of lights. You can't see those lights during the afternoon." His logic was sound.

"It's really late." Maggie yawned, or more likely fake yawned, to make her point.

"Then Lizzy and I'll go together. I'll drop her off at your apartment in one piece." Kit's expression turned serious and his hand reached for my sleeve again.

I stared at Maggie, weighing my options. Roaming the empty streets of Paris for free long distance was one thing. Riding around in the wee hours with a guy, something else entirely. And completely outside my norm. Both were mad ideas, but the latter felt decidedly more reckless.

Maggie tilted her head and pressed her lips together for a second, telling me it was my decision.

He tugged on my sleeve again.

"Maybe a short ride?"

"Sure. We can meet back here. Margaret can hang out with the boys, who will promise to be perfectly behaved." He directed his words at the twins, who were occupied with kicking each other.

With a pleading look, I begged Mags to agree.

"I suppose I could call my parents." She sounded reluctant, but didn't say no. "Okay. Do you have a bike?"

He brushed his hair back. "A flaw in my otherwise brilliant plan."

Maggie pushed her bike toward him. "It's too small for you, but it'll have to do."

Sitting on her bicycle with its wicker basket, Christopher looked silly. He lifted the seat to accommodate his long legs. It helped. A little.

"Off we go. Once around the island?" He glanced back at me as he pedaled in the direction of the nearest bridge.

I kicked away from the curb and pedaled after him over the Seine.

He pointed out obvious landmarks any tourist would recognize, gesturing widely with both hands off the handlebars. I laughed, pedaling to keep up with him as he swerved through the empty streets. Reaching the buttresses behind Notre Dame, he slowly coasted. Holding onto my bike with one hand, his shoulder brushed against mine.

He might have been drunk, or at the very least, tipsy, but I liked this carefree version. All too soon, the bridge to return us to our friends came into view. Silently, I begged him to go straight for another lap, but resigned myself when he took the turn. I'd left Maggie for too long already.

We passed the green shuttered book stalls along the river before making the final turn to end our adventure.

Maggie stood at the phone, lost in conversation. The line from earlier had disappeared, leaving only her and the twins. I felt grateful they were with her.

After sliding off the bike, Christopher leaned it against the fence. I slipped down from the seat, resting my feet on the ground, but still straddling my bike. Maggie finished her call and joined us, reclaiming her bicycle from him.

He pulled on my jacket. "A delightful expedition. We should do it again. Meet here in the middle of the night and have an adventure."

"Maybe next weekend?" I mirrored his gesture and touched his sleeve.

"Until then, Elizabeth." He bowed, making me giggle.

I gave him an awkward curtsey while holding my bicycle.

His laughter followed us as we rode away.

Unfortunately, like all good things, the practically free payphone ended too soon. On Monday, word spread the phone had been fixed.

SATURDAY TWO WEEKS later found me studying at Bernadette's dining table with Maggie while we smoked cigarettes and drank tiny cups of silty coffee.

Conjugating verbs and assigning gender to pronouns made me sleepy. I yawned and stretched, then rested my head on my French book.

The telephone in the hall rang, sounding like an old movie. Maggie jumped up to answer it. I only heard her side of the conversation, but could decipher she made plans for the evening. I understood:

"Allô?"

"Oui."

"C'est soir?"

"Merci."

"*À tout à l'heure!*"

She resumed her seat at the table, twisting her red hair into a loose bun at the nape of her neck. "We're going to a party."

"We?"

"*Oui,* we."

I snickered like a little kid. "You said wee-wee."

With a smirk, Maggie acknowledged my joke. "That was Sabine from the school. It's a social mixer between the English programs and French students. *Seulement en français.*"

"Wonderful," I moaned. Despite living in Paris and studying, my French lacked a certain *je ne sais quoi* of comprehension and fluency. I relied too heavily on Maggie to be my translator.

She tsked and purred, "*En français.*"

"*Superbe!*" I scowled at her smug expression.

"Maybe there will be cute French boys there. The kind who smoke unfiltered *Gauloises* cigarettes and madly discuss Sartre." Her expression took on a dreamy, unfocused quality.

Both of us smoked more in France than we ever had in Olympia. Everyone smoked here. I wouldn't have been surprised to see well-coiffed little dogs smoking. Not only did everyone smoke, they did it everywhere. I decided if my hair and clothes were going to reek of cigarettes, it might as well come from my own doing.

Inspired by Bernadette, I'd taken to wearing dark red lipstick and vintage dresses we found at flea markets, or *marché aux puces*. Like many things in France, it sounded glamorous, but literally meant market of fleas, which only made me itchy.

Maggie said I looked like a vamp. I took it as a compliment. Much better than a typical American college girl. My favorite pink mohair coat from the fifties, another street market find, complemented my new persona.

"I wonder if the Brits will be there tonight." I attempted to sound nonchalant. I hadn't seen Christopher since I bumped into him at Shakespeare & Company over a week ago. I didn't know what to do with myself when he wasn't around to tease me.

"Sabine said everyone had been invited. I imagine they were, too. You shouldn't spend all your time with them. You'll never learn French."

"*Je suis un parapluie,*" I apologized.

"You're not an umbrella." Maggie chuckled. "See my point?"

I shrugged. "Maybe I am."

THIRTY-FIVE

"Hey Jude"
The Beatles

THE MIXER WAS held in a large dining room on our little campus. It looked exactly the same as it always did, with the exception of missing tables and a disco ball sadly spinning in the center of the ceiling.

"Let's dance."

"To the Beatles?" I remained perched on the banquette along the wall of the party, tilting my head to study Christopher's expression. He appeared serious, sans the judgmental eyebrow.

"Why not? They're British, I'm British. If you say no, you'll be insulting England and the Queen."

I arched my eyebrow. "The Queen? Really?"

"Yes. Dance with me." He extended his hand, his palm up and bent two fingers in a gesture of command. My gaze lingered on his long fingers, his wide palms. I attempted to resist the images flitting behind my eyes of how they would feel on various parts of my body. He flexed his fingers again and I pressed my thighs together.

I wondered if his polite demeanor would remain in place when he was naked. Or would he finally crack and let go, exposing a wilder side that simmered under the surface when he argued? Would he speak French in bed? Cursing a soft *merde* if I put my mouth on him . . .

"Lizzy?"

I let my focus drift up his arm to his face. He stared at me, sharp blue eyes waiting for an answer.

"Yes?"

"Dance?"

"Hmmm . . ." It wasn't a yes, or a no. I forgot what he'd asked. *Que sera, sera.*

Instead of waiting for me to give him a response, the hand I'd been fantasizing about grabbed mine and pulled me upright. After wrapping his fingers around mine, he set them on his shoulder, then settled my other hand on his waist.

"Do you know how to properly dance? Waltz?"

"We can't waltz to this song. It's not in three-three."

He gave me a sly, sweet smile. "Fine, the fox trot it is."

While everyone else danced like normal people, Christopher moved me around the floor as if we were at a V-Day celebration at the USO.

Okay, the song wasn't that old, but the way we danced was. When the music changed, he started to jitterbug.

I couldn't keep up for laughing at him. And myself. The French must have thought we were imitating Jerry Lewis, because they stopped dancing altogether to watch and applaud, big grins on their faces.

"Stop." Breathing had become difficult. A wheeze rattled in my chest whenever I stopped laughing long enough to take a breath.

He set me down gently. "You sound like a pensioner with a chest cold."

I opened my mouth to say something sarcastic to him, but the French students swarmed him, slapping him on the back. Who knew a Brit jitterbug dancing like a fool would be the thing to mend the centuries old rift between the two countries?

Rather than fight for his attention, I slipped away to the little refreshment table in the corner. Rows of small glasses of red wine and sparkling water lined the surface. No red solo cups or cans of cheap beer here.

Maggie stood in the corner near the table, arguing loudly in French with a cute guy. I admired how well she'd picked up the language.

He gestured wildly with his hands. Fire burned in his eyes and manly sexual energy rolled off him like waves on hot sand in the desert. Not super tall, he made up for it with his handsome face and full lips. With his dark hair and dark eyes, he definitely seemed like Maggie's type.

I was curious over his evident passion. I grabbed two extra glasses of wine and walked over to them with my peace offering.

"Oh, good! I need a drink." Maggie took both glasses from me, but didn't offer either to her new friend. Or enemy. It wasn't clear where he stood at the moment.

With his eyes, he shot imaginary arrows at the extra glass of wine in her hand, mumbling in French about rude Americans.

"Did you want a glass of wine?" she asked him in English.

He scowled at her, but took the glass. After swallowing most of it in one long sip, he noticed me. *"Merci."*

"De nada." I covered my mouth. "That was Spanish. *De rien."*

"Pas de problème." He finished his wine.

Feeling very much a stupid American, I changed the subject. "What were you two arguing about?"

"Cheese." Maggie briefly focused on the ceiling.

"Cheese?" My voice rose two octaves. "But you were shouting and arguing."

She finished rolling her eyes. "Over *le fromage*, yes."

Staring at both of them like I was watching the French Open, I waited for further explanation. Cheese itself wasn't enough for what could have been mistaken for a passionate lover's quarrel.

"She thinks those little squares wrapped in plastic you eat qualify as cheese."

"They do. The word cheese is in the name. American Cheese. You can't call something cheese if it isn't cheese." She gulped her wine in exasperation.

He glowered at her. It was all sorts of sexy. "You can if you are American."

"How do you even know about cheese slices? Have you been to the States?" I attempted to diffuse the tension.

"No. I have seen this *cheese* on your television shows." He sneered.

I didn't need to ask what he thought of those shows because his frown was the very caricature of disgust.

"Oh, stop it. You told me you loved *Family Ties* not more than twenty minutes ago." Maggie huffed, and this time her eyes made a complete circle when she rolled them.

"Fine. Some of the shows are not terrible." His "terrible" sounded more like "tear-e-blah." The emphasis clearly on the blah.

Christopher joined our little circle, draping his arm over my shoulders. "What are we discussing?"

"Terrible American cheese and television shows."

He lifted his hands and took a couple of steps away from the group.

"Where are you going?" I asked.

"Anywhere but this conversation." He spun around in a circle, seeking a reasonable escape. "Oh, look, it's a . . ." His unfinished sentence hung in the air as he raced to the opposite side of the room. He literally ran away.

Maggie whispered something in French to Le Fromage, and he stopped frowning. When not making faces like someone nearby him farted, he was handsome. Surprisingly good looking, especially when he smiled.

He politely asked if we'd like more wine before leaving to refill our glasses.

"He's rather passionate," I whispered to Magpie.

"He's insane."

"Is he this passionate about subjects not involving dairy products?"

"I don't know. We met tonight. He's here with a friend."

Le Fromage returned with three glasses of wine. A short guy with a very long nose followed along behind him. What he lacked in overall height, he made up for in impressive nose cartilage.

"This is my friend, Oscar." He pronounced it less like Oscar the Grouch and more like NASCAR with an "O."

Uh oh. This was the friend. My focus flicked to Maggie. A set-up brewed and I needed an escape plan.

"*Bon soir.*" I managed to not butcher the words.

A stream of French flew out of Oscar's mouth like a flock of pigeons flapping around my head. I had no idea what he said. His thick accent thwarted any attempt on my part to decipher his words. I nodded, hesitantly, hoping I wasn't agreeing to anything nefarious or sexual.

Seeing my blank expression, Maggie translated, "He said your dancing was unlike anything he'd ever witnessed before in person or in the cinema. I mean, movies."

I smiled. *"Merci."* I had no idea if he paid me a compliment or insulted me. After the cheese conversation, insult seemed more likely.

"I am sorry for your friend's rudeness for not introducing us." Le Fromage extended his hand. "I am Julien Armand."

Maggie's eyes bugged out. "You didn't really give me a chance. You went from bashing my country's food to insulting our culture." This time she spoke in English.

Oscar looked on in confusion. His English was probably as good as my French.

Julien huffed and swore a string of expletives in his native tongue. I caught a few of the more colorful expressions. I couldn't conjugate in subjunctive tense to save my life, but the swear words were seared on my brain.

Oscar handed me another glass of wine. I held my existing glass up to show him but he gestured for me to drink mine first, and quickly. While our mutual friends continued to argue about *fromage* and hamburgers, Oscar and I silently drank red wine.

Without preamble, their arguing turned into kissing. The passion Julien had for defending the sanctity of dairy products paled next to his zest for kissing my best friend.

"Zut alors!" Oscar gulped down his wine.

I thought only Pepe Le Pew said those expressions. Oscar stared and bounced on his toes, not unlike the little cartoon skunk.

Zut alors indeed!

Avoiding the PDA in front of me, I scanned the room, telling myself I wasn't searching for Christopher.

Very few men in attendance at this little fête stood anywhere near as tall or as blond as my new friend. He shouldn't have been difficult to spot.

Unless he'd gone. Maybe he thought I'd left. I wished I had. Instead,

I found myself stuck in a corner with Oscar, Julien the Grouch, a flustered Maggie, and my wine.

"Scanning the room for suitors?" A warm breath hit the back of my neck along with the crisp British accent.

"No, as a matter of fact I was searching for you." I spun to face him. The wine heated my cheeks. Or perhaps it was his close proximity.

His laughter rumbled in his chest, rich and throaty. "If only I believed you."

"Dance with me."

"To this?" He jerked his head toward the dance floor.

Nancy Sinatra's "These Boots Were Made for Walking" played on the speakers.

"Sure." I pulled him by his shirt cuff to the floor. I knew all the words and sang them loudly while I danced a weird shimmy-twist.

He pretended to be shocked, but his smile lit up his entire face as he laughed at me.

Finally, my charms wore him down and he joined my dancing. Jerking his fists over his head, he stomped around in a circle.

The uptight, proper British private school educated boy disappeared as he let himself be ridiculous. I suspected this was a very rare moment for Kit Liddell, not a baron by birth order.

We giggled ourselves silly, attempting to outdo each other with archaic dance movements. I held my nose and pretended to sink to the floor. He followed with an impressive Charleston. When he lifted me over his shoulder for a spin, tears ran down my face.

"I can't breathe!" I slapped at his back. "Put me down."

Instead, he carried me off the floor and set me on my feet by a chair in the corner.

"Where did you learn to dance?" I rubbed the back of my hand across my damp brow, hoping he didn't notice.

Along his hairline, sweat darkened his hair. He pushed it back and ran his fingers through it a couple of times to get it to stay in place. "My grandmother loves to dance. She taught me so she'd have someone to dance with."

"Not your grandfather?" I sat and patted the empty chair next to me.

Slouching down on the chair, sadness passed behind his eyes. "No.

Not for a very long time. He died when my father was a young man. I never met him."

"I'm sorry."

He acknowledged my apology with a small nod of his head. "No need for you to be sorry." I swore I even saw his upper lip stiffen. "What about you? What's your family like?"

"My father is in sales. My mother is a school nurse."

"Very respectable."

"Very middle class you mean."

"We can't control who our parents are." He sounded resigned.

"No, but we can create our own lives, follow our dreams."

"That's very American of you. Pluckish optimism." His tone didn't infer his words as a compliment.

"We're in Paris. The city of light. The city of love. Even you can't be immune to its charms."

"The English have a love-hate relationship with the French. It's in our blood."

"Is it really hate?"

"More like envy."

"For the food?"

"No, the passion." He threaded his fingers through his hair, leaving it more tousled.

"Maybe you should take a French woman as a lover."

He choked on nothing. "That's not the kind of passion I meant."

"Oh." I blushed.

"Everything in my life is planned out for me. Even more so for my brother, who will inherit the estate and title. Months like these are small holidays from reality and responsibility."

"Kind of like your very own Rumspringa?"

"I have no idea what you mean."

"The Amish? Like the movie *Witness*?"

"With Harrison Ford?"

"Aha, you have seen some American movies." I bumped his shoulder. "Yes, the one and the same. The Amish have this thing where at a certain age, teenagers are allowed to leave their society and explore the modern world."

"Oh, like our gap year."

"Yes. What did you do on your gap year?"

"Nothing. My father thought it would be a waste of time. I went straight to uni." He drummed his fingers on his knees and stared at the floor.

I couldn't help but think of how young and resigned he seemed.

No grand adventures loomed on the horizon for him.

THIRTY-SIX

"Whatever Will Be, Will Be"
Doris Day

I REACHED INTO my bag and touched a thin paper cylinder. With the tips of my fingers, I traced its familiar shape and texture.

Ohmygod.

Ohmygod.

Maggie dozed on the row of seats across from me in our six-person train compartment, which we had all to ourselves. I gently kicked her to wake her up.

"What? Are we back in Paris?" Her words came out muffled and groggy.

"No, we only crossed the border about ten minutes ago."

She balled her coat under her head and closed her eyes again. "Shh, more sleep. Wake me up when we get to the station."

"Maggie," I nudged her with my boot again, "We have an emergency."

She lifted her head and shoulders, but didn't sit up. "What's going on? Is there a strike or fire or something?"

I tilted my bag in her direction and showed her the joint in my hand.

"Where did it come from?" Now she sat up, fully awake.

"Selah probably. She asked me to hold it for her when we went to the Van Gogh museum after the café." Getting stoned and looking at art had been one of Selah's goals when visiting us over winter break. We'd spent a couple of days going through the Louvre, and other museums in Paris, before deciding to hop the train to Amsterdam.

"Do you know what this means?" Panic spread across her face. "We're international drug smugglers."

"Shh!" I leapt across the narrow space and covered her mouth. "Don't say that out loud."

Moving my hand, she whispered, "They don't bug the trains, Lizzy. No one else is in here but us."

An older man walked by down the main corridor of the train on the other side of our glass door.

Her eyes widened. "So close."

"We need to get rid of it." I nodded.

She frowned. "It's really good stuff."

"What are the possession laws in France? Are you willing to go to French jail for a little buzz?" The more I talked about it, the more anxious I became.

"I have no idea! All I know about French jails is from *Les Misérables* and *A Tale of Two Cities*. We don't want to end up in those kinds of jails. Trust me."

"I bet they have better food than American jail. Maybe croissants and at least baguettes with cheese and butter. Or the ham ones, with lots of butter. I could live off of those. Or simply butter and bread wouldn't be too bad. As long as there is butter." My stomach growled in agreement.

"I wonder if they have wine in prison." She rubbed her finger across her lips in thought.

"It's France. Fraternity is right there in their version of the Declaration of Independence. Have you ever heard of a frat party that didn't have booze?"

She wrinkled her forehead and stared at me. "Your logic and Latin are terrible, but I'm going to agree. Even if there is wine and creme brûlée, I really don't want to end up in jail. We need to get rid of the joint. And the sooner the better."

"We could throw it out the window." I studied the smudged glass. Standing, I tried to tilt it open, but it wouldn't budge. Maggie helped, but the thing was jammed shut.

Sitting back down, she sighed. "We could flush it."

"That's brilliant."

"Walk down the aisle with your purse. That's totally legit."

"Come with me," I begged.

"The two of us going into the toilet only makes it more suspicious. You can do it."

"Rock, paper, scissors?" I held out my fist.

"Okay." She balled her hand. "One, two, three."

I threw paper. She did scissors.

"Two out of three?" I asked.

"Fine. One, two, three."

I went with scissors. She did rock.

"You can do this. I have complete faith. And if for some reason you do get caught, I'll bring you filtered American cigarettes and People magazines. I know how you can't live without both."

I gave her a small salute. "If I don't make it . . ."

She shook my shoulders. "Do it for Johnny."

With a laugh, I opened the sliding door and stepped out.

I turned to say something to Maggie and the train swayed, sending me off balance. As I straightened, I ran right into a conductor, and dropped my purse.

"*Pardonnez moi,*" he said, handing me back my bag.

"*Bien sur,*" I replied, incorrectly. Facing Maggie, my eyes widened and I mouthed "help."

She waved me down the aisle. I sped away from the conductor.

"*Mademoiselle,*" he called from behind me and then said something else in French.

I froze, but didn't turn around.

"Is this yours?" he repeated in English.

The joint must have fallen out when my bag dropped. Two plans of action formed in my head. The first involved jumping off of a moving train. I mentally practiced my drop and roll. This train chugged along at full speed. It definitely wasn't the best option.

My second thought was to play dumb American girl. The idea involved less chance of broken bones, but an increased opportunity for humiliation and possible arrest.

I'd gone twenty years without breaking a bone. So far in my life, I'd tried to avoid both pain and living on the lam. I had no idea where we were in France and knew no one to hide me from the law.

Making up my mind on option two, I turned around, plastering a huge smile on my face.

"*Oui, Monsieur?*"

He held up a white paper covered cylinder. I glanced at it briefly, but focused on his face.

"Did you drop this?" he repeated

I held up my hand to my throat in some damsel in distress gesture like I was on the verge of fainting. "Why would you think it belongs to me?"

He pinched the end in disgust with a look of confusion on his mustached face. "I saw it roll out of your bag."

"Oh, no, it couldn't have. I have no idea what that is. I've never seen anything like it before." My voice continued to rise in panic.

He studied his hand for a second. "It is a . . . tampon. I believe the word is the same in English?"

"What?" Shocked, I actually looked at the object in his hand. Sure enough, I recognized it as one of my Tampax.

Nothing embarrassing about this moment at all.

"*Pardonnez moi,*" I mumbled and claimed the tampon from his hand. "*Bon Anniversaire!*"

Once in the safety of the tiny bathroom, I realized I'd wished him a happy birthday instead of a happy new year.

I dropped the joint into the bowl, flushed, and breathed through my mouth while I sat on the seat long enough to make my bathroom visit seem legit.

Someone knocked on the door after a few minutes.

"Occupied," I shouted.

"It's me," Maggie whispered from the other side of the door. "I thought you might have fallen in. The conductor came back to check on you. He said he thought you might have died from embarrassment."

I flushed again and rinsed my hands in the tiny sink before unlocking the door.

"What happened? Is it gone?" She peered over my shoulder.

"Nothing other than I told a very nice mustachioed French man I'd never seen a tampon before." I led the way back to our compartment.

Once inside, I retold the entire conversation.

Maggie about peed herself from laughing. "I'm never ever going to forget this trip."

"So, I learned a new vocabulary word." I joined her in giggling. The panic over doing hard time passed into fits of laughter. "At least no one is going to prison."

"As punishment, they probably make prisoners eat McDonald's."

"Or American cheese, which is apparently the worst thing ever to exist in the history of the universe according to some people." I reminded her of the ridiculous argument she'd had with Julien Armand at the party a couple months ago.

She wheezed with laughter. "Pompous French pricks!"

Her words echoed around the little room, loud enough an ancient widow in the corridor heard her and scowled at us.

Her disdain only sent us into another round of laughing until tears streamed down our faces.

We collapsed on the benches, panting with the occasional giggle. The train click-clacked along the rails while we gathered our breath.

"What's the deal with Le Fromage anyway?" I whispered.

Maggie's face stilled. Then she bit her lip before answering. "Nothing really."

"Nothing at all or nothing serious?" Julien had showed up outside classes a few times after the party, and taken her to coffee or the movies. She always said it was to practice her French, but they went alone and didn't invite me. Felt more like dating.

She sighed. "I don't know."

"You don't know if you like him?"

"I do like him."

"What's the problem? You don't know if he likes you?"

"That's not it either. He's made it clear he likes me."

"Then what's the issue?"

Briefly she met my eyes, then stared out the window at the passing bare fields and gray winter sky. Another familiar sigh escaped her.

I remembered those sighs from our trip over here.

"Does this have anything to do with Gil?" I'd avoided asking her for months, figuring she would bring it up. Then I decided if she hadn't, I didn't want to get involved.

She exhaled, her exasperated breath lifting her bangs. "Maybe."

"You know you can always tell me anything. We're in a tiny room of honesty here."

"Promise?" Tears collected in her lashes.

"Oh, Mags. What happened?" I crossed the narrow space to hug her.

"I swore I wasn't going to tell anyone and make it a big deal. Or be one of those girls who say they're cool and then turn out to be the opposite of cool."

"You mean hot?" I went for a little humor to lighten the mood.

"No, uncool. Clingy. Reading into things and seeing emotions and commitments where there are none because of sex."

Whoa. "Sex?"

I'd seen their anti-groupie kiss at our going away party. I'd even given her imaginary high fives for finally making a move. One of them had to.

She nodded and the tears spilled down her cheeks in two sad, salty rivers.

"Oh, Mags." Hugging her to my side, I let my sweater absorb her tears. "You're not one of those kind of girls. You and Gil are best friends."

"I know. And I ruined everything by hitting on him."

"He kissed you back."

"He didn't really have a choice. He had to either kiss me back or be the target of Slutty McGroupie for the foreseeable future. I wanted to protect him."

"Gil doesn't need protecting. He's a big boy and can handle

himself. You wanted to mark him as yours before you left. I completely understand."

She nodded and her wet nose rubbed on my arm. Snot probably covered the wool of my former favorite sweater.

"Not to pry," I was totally breaking my no prying rule, "but you said sex?"

"We had sex after the party. I threw myself at him in some desperate last ditch moment." Sitting up, she rubbed her nose with the palm of her hand. "It's humiliating."

I tilted my head to the side in a silent question.

"What?" She wiped at her cheeks, her fingers coming away stained with black mascara.

"Why was it humiliating? Did he want to do weird stuff like *9 1/2 Weeks*?"

She shook her head and covered her face. "No, nothing weird. It's the desperate, throwing myself at him part."

"I didn't take the same biology class you and Selah did freshman year, but I'm pretty confident he had to be somewhat interested to . . . you know."

Her eyes widened with shock. "Oh. No. He. No. He was into it. Really into it." Pink spread across her cheeks.

"Got it. Let's agree you didn't force him into doing anything he didn't want to do, and move on from there, okay?"

Her head bobbed in agreement.

"Okay. Nothing to be humiliated about. You two had been dancing around each other all summer. Hell, probably since freshman year. I never understood why you didn't get together."

"Was it obvious? I know everyone liked to tease me about it."

"Not only you. Quinn and Ben brought it up to Gil, too."

"Now that's humiliating. Everyone talking about us behind our backs."

"Only because we could all see how you two acted around each other. I don't think this was ever a one-way thing on your side. It's pretty obvious the feelings are mutual."

Tears flowed freely.

"Why are you crying again?" I rubbed her back.

"Because we missed our moment. I didn't tell him how I feel. Or even say good-bye to him."

I pressed my lips together. "Oh."

"I know. I'm a terrible person. I just left."

"No note? No good-bye?"

Her breath quivered as she tried to inhale. She covered her face with her hands.

Poor Gil.

"Oh, Maggie."

"I know." Her voice shook. "I'm horrible."

"You're not horrible."

"I was embarrassed when I woke up naked in his bed. I snuck out while he slept so it wouldn't be awkward when we left. I didn't want to see his regret."

"Why do you think there would've been regret?" I couldn't follow her thought pattern, but I felt her pain. My own tears threatened to fall.

"We promised each other to always be best friends. Not hook up buddies."

"When did you make this promise?"

"Freshman year."

The train slowed as it approached a station. People filled the corridor on their way on or off the car. A man in a hat and overcoat opened our compartment door, took one look at two crying girls, and apologized before backing out.

I found an old napkin in my purse and handed it to her. With a loud honk, she blew her nose.

"Lots of things changed since freshman year. We all grew up a little more."

"I didn't want to lose him as a friend." She grabbed another napkin and wiped her eyes. "And now I have."

"Have you told Selah? Or Quinn?"

"No!" She curled up on the seat. "I don't want anyone to know. You have to pinky-swear you won't tell anyone else. Promise."

"I swear. I'll take it to the grave." I held up my pinky.

She hooked her finger around mine and pulled.

"Want to hear my thoughts? You don't have to. I can listen if you want to tell someone and not have to hold the secret anymore."

"What would you do if you slept with your best friend and then disappeared to the other side of the planet?"

"Tough question since you're my best friend and we're on the other side of the planet together." I nudged her with my elbow. "In all honesty, there's not much you can do right now to make it better. Did you write him? Call? Have you heard from him?"

"No. I tried calling him from the free pay phone, but I'd get a busy signal or he was never there. I've wanted to call again, but I never had enough change for an overseas call." She made the saddest frowny face.

I sighed. What a mess. It had already been months of no communication between the two of them. Selah had been pretty vague about Gil when we caught up on gossip. Maggie had asked about him, but in hindsight she acted pretty disinterested.

I exhaled and whistled while I formed a plan. "I think you need to set Gil aside."

"What do you mean?"

"You two have had years to get together. Neither of you ever crossed a line until faced with separation. That tells me you were both pretty happy in the friendship and not wanting to lose it. Agree?"

"Sure." Her voice sounded wary.

"Now you're in Paris. Being flirted with by a gorgeous, albeit pompous, Frenchman."

"I'm following, but what's your point?"

"*Que sera, sera.*"

"Still confused." She furrowed her brows and sniffled.

"I think it's Latin for whatever will be, will be. Or it's a Doris Day song."

"Okay, I'm supposed to follow Doris Day's love advice? Wasn't she always married to Rock Hudson in all her movies? I'm not sure she's really a good judge on men and relationships. Maybe I should date Quinn instead."

"He wasn't gay in the movies. He was charming in an abrasive, yet dapper way." I poked her. "That's not my point. I say don't pine, stop moping and enjoy your year in Paris. Date the Frenchman. Hell, fall in love. It's kind of mandatory when you are living in the city of love, right?"

"You make it all sound easy." She dabbed her cheeks again, but the tears had stopped.

"Why can't it be? Be a fish, go with the flow."

"But what about Gil?"

"Whatever will be, will be. If you two are meant to be together, a year won't make a difference. Hell, you've already waited twice as long. If he's yours, he'll wait for you."

"And if he falls in love with someone else?"

"What if you fall in love with someone else? Le Fromage for example."

"I'd still want him to be my friend." She didn't look thrilled at the prospect.

"Then that's your answer." I wrapped my arm around her shoulder. "We're young. We're beautiful. We're in Paris."

She nodded and hugged me back. "You should take your own advice."

I froze and then laughed. "Maybe I should."

"Although an affair with a Brit in France seems a little traitorous."

"If Oscar wasn't a little Napoleon, maybe we could double-date."

"He's not terrible."

I slowly blinked at her.

"Okay, he is. He's very bossy."

"He's not at all sweet like the dessert."

THIRTY-SEVEN

"Heroes"
David Bowie

A GROUP FIELD trip took us out of the city into the countryside to visit the small city of Rouen. Maggie ditched the trip, claiming she had a headache. The headache had a name: Julien. Being the best kind of friend, I'd promised to cover for her if anyone asked.

Christopher loped down the aisle of the coach and grinned when he saw me by a window. He lifted my bag out of his way, groaning under the weight, then folded himself into the aisle seat next to me.

"What do you have in here?" He spread open the top and peered inside.

I attempted to steal it back from him, but he held me at bay with his forearm. "Didn't your mother tell you it wasn't proper to paw through a lady's hand bag?"

"Are you calling yourself a lady now?" He grinned at me again, his hand still in my bag. The smile faded as he pulled out Donnie.

"What's the story with the Ken doll, darling?" Kit's face displayed his disdain.

"It's not Ken." I snatched the doll from his hand and stuffed it back in my bag.

"Don't be embarrassed about carrying your poppet with you."

I wanted to wipe his smug dolly smile right off his handsome face.

"It's not a poppet. If you must know, he's Donnie Wahlberg."

He stared at me with a blank expression.

My brows rose in disbelief. "Donnie Wahlberg?"

"Yes, I heard you. I have no idea who that bloke is. Someone from one of your American television series?"

"You've never heard of New Kids on the Block?"

Another shake of his head.

"Seriously?"

"Why would I joke about something as serious as a little shirtless poppet you carry around in your bag?" His lips twitched with amusement. "What other childhood souvenirs do you have in there? Jacks? Teacups?"

"Why would I have teacups in my purse?"

"For your doll to have a tea party."

It made complete logical, illogical sense.

Like ninety-percent of our conversations I couldn't tell if he flirted with me or teased me. Or both.

For the first week at the château, I swore he disliked me, maybe even hated me. After the party, I knew I at least amused him in a "silly American" way. I didn't think much in his life amused him.

From our conversation at the party and subsequent ones, he seemed resigned to his life. Study business, work in business. Marry the right kind of girl, preferably with the right kind of family, bonus for nobility. Have perfectly respectable British children, preferably boys, who would wear short pants and knee high socks for most of their childhood. Everything had been planned for him as soon as he was christened Christopher Winston Liddell.

AFTER LISTENING TO Madame Picou explain the importance of Rouen, its history and role in various political upheavals over the centuries, we were left to wander through the cathedral on our own.

I trailed behind the twins, half-listening, half-trying to ignore Christopher ahead of us. I didn't think Joe or James knew I stood behind them while I pretended to study the tomb of Richard the Lionheart and read the sign. The tomb contained only his heart. The rest of him had ended up elsewhere. I could sympathize. Like many of us, he'd left his heart in France. I sighed over how silly my crush made me feel.

"Katie phoned twice yesterday. Kit's grandmother is in hospital again."

"Katie's a saint to be concerned about his family . . . given what happened last summer."

"You can't be in someone's life for years, have a long history, and not care."

"The bastard doesn't deserve her."

"And you do? Sod off. You never stood a chance with her." Joe knocked James off balance and the two of them scuffling caught the attention of an old woman in one of the pews, who stopped praying to shush them.

Breaking apart, James did a silly penguin waddle and salute in my direction. "Hello, Liz. Didn't see you there."

"I wasn't eavesdropping. I swear."

"It's okay, love. We know Kit fancies you." Joe received an elbow to his shoulder from James.

"Is everything okay?" I wanted to ask who Katie was.

"Nothing to worry yourself over." James closed ranks. "Bit of family drama back home for Kit."

Joe threw his arm around my shoulder. "The Liddells are a close, but estranged family."

James walked on my other side. "Emphasis on strange."

"He's seems very normal to me."

"If normal means boring, then yes, Kitty is."

"Kitty?"

"Old nickname from our school days. You should have seen him then. All ears, teeth, and knobby knees." James stuck out his front teeth and bounced his knees together as he walked.

I stifled a giggle, remembering we were in a church.

"Pity he never grew out of it. Have you ever seen him in shorts?" Joe made a very serious face.

As a matter of fact, I hadn't. "It was fall when we met and then winter."

"Yes, Elizabeth, that's how the seasons work. First comes autumn, next winter." He dodged my elbow and locked his arm around my shoulder.

"It's a terrible curse to look like Kit. His mother suffers with worry over finding him a suitable bride. She frets the grandchildren will be as hideous."

"Joe." Christopher spoke from a few feet away, his voice unmistakable.

Joe turned us as one unit, awkward conjoined twins. "Ah, there's Quasimodo now."

Calling a man as beautiful as Christopher Quasimodo was too ridiculous for my self-restraint. Church or not, I burst out laughing, the sound echoing off the stone floor and pillars. Joe quickly stepped away and pretended to study some carvings.

Above me, some saint looked down from his stained-glass in disapproval. I squinted to see the figure more clearly. Oh, great. Not some random saint. No, she was Joan of Arc.

I said a silent apology to her for being a silly girl, then made the sign of the cross like I saw the little old ladies do in every church we'd visited.

"No curtsy for Joan?" Christopher whispered next to me.

"No, but I felt I owed her an apology for the giggling. I bet she never giggled around boys. Or in church."

"She was human, not a robot. She probably laughed at some point. Maybe even liked a charming farm boy or two. You know, before going to battle and martyring herself."

I stared up at the young face composed of glass. "I hope so."

"She was burned not far from here."

"That's uplifting."

"For her it was. Figuratively, speaking."

I frowned at him. "That's a terrible joke."

"I know something to make you smile." He bent his index finger to bring me closer.

"What?" I leaned in.

He mirrored me, bringing his face close to mine. "This church has a butter tower."

I grinned. "Tell me more. Is it made out of butter? Or where they hoard the butter?"

"Neither."

I pursed my lips at him.

"It was funded with butter. The church allowed its patrons to continue to eat butter during Lent if they promised to donate money for the tower."

"Not nearly as good as actually being made of butter, but I approve."

Amusement crinkled the corners of his eyes. "I thought you might."

"I really love the stuff."

"I know you do. Shall we ditch the tour and go see Joan's church?"

Christopher breaking the rules delighted me. How could I say no?

He held out his arm and I took it, hooking mine around his forearm.

I didn't expect the modern building of St. Jeanne's church. Nor to cry visiting it.

After our tour, we stood outside in the golden evening light. Christopher, being the proper gentleman, had a tissue for my tears.

"Joan is my new patron saint."

"I support this idea. After all, she is the patron saint of badass girls and strong women everywhere." He put his hand on my shoulder and I leaned into him.

"She changed history and died at nineteen. I'm twenty and have nothing to show for it."

"You're a late bloomer, love. I have faith you'll change the world or at least the hearts of a few men."

"Do you call every woman love?" I stood up straighter.

He thought for a moment before responding. "No. Only the ones I fancy."

"Do you call Katie love?" I had no right to be jealous of any woman in his life. He wasn't mine and I knew he never could be.

He stepped away abruptly and I almost tumbled over. "Who told you about Katie?"

I twisted my ponytail over my shoulder. "Joe and James."

"Bloody hell. Those two couldn't keep their mouths shut for all the ale in England."

"Is she your girlfriend?"

"It's complicated."

"That's not a no."

He chewed on his bottom lip. I watched as it went white and then deepened red. Color ruddied his cheeks

"Lizzy." His voice sounded pained. "I never imagined meeting a girl like you."

I held my breath. The way he spoke my name reminded me of being back inside the church. It held reverence and awe.

"You've probably figured out by now my life is not my own. Unlike you, who has always been taught you can be anything you want, do anything, go anywhere, my path is more narrow. There are expectations for me to live up to, or fail trying." Resolved sadness cloaked his face. The sweet smile and wicked spark in his eye disappeared.

Pulling at my ponytail, and feeling even more awkward, I tucked my hands into the pockets of my pink coat.

"Katie, or Catherine, is someone I've known since nursery. Her grandparents and my grandparents grew up together."

"Are you betrothed to her?"

He chuckled. "No, this isn't an arranged marriage situation. But my mother and grandmother would be delighted about the match."

The meaning of his words sank in. "And you? Will you be delighted?"

"Katie's a great girl. The best."

He didn't say he loved her.

"What do you want?"

He sat on a bench and held out his hands to take mine, pulling me between his knees. "What I want is of little importance."

"Says who?"

He dipped his chin, then peered up at me. "Everyone."

Removing my hand from his grip, I pushed the lock of hair off of his forehead. He hummed at my touch, encouraging me. I scratched my nails across his scalp. I felt him grip the back of my thighs right above the knee. Through the thin material of my pale green floral dress, the heat from his palms blazed on my skin.

With my other hand, I lifted his chin. "I believe in you. Everyone deserves to have their own dreams come true."

His fingers flexed against the back of my knees, sending waves of something electric up my body. "Don't."

My head jerked and my hands dropped like I'd been physically shocked.

"I'm sorry. What?" I needed to hear him say it again.

"Don't waste your time on me, Elizabeth. I'm not worth it." Pain so real it had to have physically hurt clouded his eyes. Unshed tears reddened the whites, making the blue irises stand out even more.

"That's the biggest lie I've ever heard spoken. And my father is a salesman."

He let his gaze drift to the ground. "I wish . . ."

I stilled and waited.

Suddenly, he stood up, towering over me. Determination blazed in his set jaw.

Without another word, his hand framed my cheek and his lips found mine. I stood on my tiptoes to even out our height difference. He pulled me closer with his arm braced against my lower back while keeping one hand on my jaw.

My arms rested on his shoulders, my fingers reclaimed their spot in his hair.

Air felt like water and the only thing to save myself from drowning was his kiss. I inhaled him instead of oxygen, feeding something deep within me with his essence. My body sung along to the beat of his heart and the rhythm set by his mouth on mine.

"I can't."

When he stopped, everything I'd been feeling ceased as if it never occurred. I held my breath, my blood rushing in my ears and my lips on fire from his kiss.

"I wasn't supposed to meet someone like you. No, that's not right.

Not someone like you. Only you."

I gasped, oxygen burning my lungs. His words didn't make sense. Feeling dizzy, I sunk onto the bench.

Christopher paced in front of me. "I'd ruled out your existence ages ago. I resigned myself to a life of duty, being a good Liddell. Companionship and the kind of love you grow into with time and age. Then you showed up, crashing into my carefully constructed façade with all your American brashness and silly notions about dreams."

I frowned at his harsh words. "You have the oddest way of insulting me. I don't know whether to thank you or slap you."

"I deserve the slap. I shouldn't have kissed you."

"Is Katie your girlfriend?"

He shook his head while crouching in front of me. "It's complicated. Yes, we've dated, and at times she's been my girlfriend."

"Do you love her?"

In his silence, my heart broke a little.

"It's complicated. The simple answer is yes. The longer answer qualifies that love. Like a friend. Sometimes a sister. Once upon a time as a lover."

I wanted to shove him away for his honesty. I pushed at his shoulders, needing more space. He didn't budge. Instead, he grabbed my hands and held them to his chest.

"Let me go." My voice remained steady even as my heart angrily shook the cage of my ribs.

"You were never mine to hold onto." His hands dropped to his thighs. "You deserve to be happy. I envy the man who gets to be the one you love. He'll be the luckiest bloke on the planet."

I didn't want some other man.

My heart wanted him.

"If . . ." He stood again, but this time he stepped away. With a shake of his head, he mumbled something to himself.

"Pardon me?"

"I was about to go down an impossible path of hypotheticals. If is a dangerous word. I'm sorry, Lizzy. More than you can ever imagine."

I nodded because I was sorry, too. If the Duke of Windsor could give up his throne for a divorced American, why couldn't he stand up to his family obligations? Maybe he wasn't the prince charming I'd first imagined.

"I shouldn't have kissed you, but I'll never regret it. Or meeting you. Even if your memory is a reminder of everything I can't have." He stuffed his hands in his front pockets. His hair flopped down over his face. I wanted to brush it back again. With his ruddy cheeks and sad expression, he looked completely lost.

I hoped his loyalty and sense of duty would be rewarded. He deserved happiness.

"Fortune favors the brave," I whispered.

"Be brave for both of us, Lizzy." He leaned down and kissed the top of my head. It was both endearing and crushing.

THIRTY-EIGHT

"If I Ever Lose My Faith in You"
Sting

CHRISTOPHER SAT ALONE on the ride back to Paris. Pretending to sleep, I leaned my head on the window and watched the twinkling lights of the most romantic city on earth pass by. Rain sprinkled the windows and the shadows of the drops sliding down the glass hid the tears on my cheeks.

I declined the offer to join the Brits for a drink after we arrived. Christopher gave me a small wave a la the Queen. I curtsied.

His grandmother took a turn for the worse later in the night. He flew out the next morning to be by her side.

The following week, a small article about her funeral appeared in the *Sunday Times*. I went to Notre Dame and lit a candle in front of Joan for the woman Christopher loved so dearly.

He never returned to the program. James told me Kit had worked out a deal with his professors to finish from England.

Weeks later at the good-bye party Joe gave me the letter. He apologized and said Kit had left it for me, but it had gotten lost in his room.

Those few weeks wouldn't have changed anything.

Part of me wanted to throw it away and never know. What weight would his words have? Nothing had changed. I decided to wait to open it. Maybe with an ocean and time between us, it would no longer break my heart to remember he existed.

TWO WEEKS BEFORE the end of the program, Maggie announced Julien would be coming back to Washington with her. It wasn't a total shock. They'd been inseparable for months. I guess she took my advice and opened herself to the possibilities.

How ironic.

The night she told me she loved him, I decided to read Christopher's letter.

Two things I knew about myself.

One, I was an emotional masochist.

Two, I was a hopeless romantic.

If Maggie could fall head over heels in love, there had to be hope for me. Someday. If not charming Christopher Liddell, then someone else was out there waiting for me.

I tore open the envelope and pulled out a piece of thick linen stationary. It felt expensive in my hand. My finger traced his neat penmanship before I let my mind translate the shapes into letters and words.

> *Lizzy,*
> *I'm happier knowing you exist in the world.*
> *Be brave and love deeply.*
> *For both of us.*
> *Yours always,*
> *Christopher*

There wasn't a return address. Nothing about staying in touch. No hint at a hypothetical future.

I kissed his name and said good-bye to the first man who stole my heart.

Like Richard the Lionheart, my heart would forever be separated from my body. A piece of it remained in France; another part now lived in England. At least I had enough remaining pieces to put back together and carry on.

QUINN

Quinn Dayton, 22

Studio Art

Senior

What do you want to be when you grow up?

An artist with a capital A.

Pop culture has always been my muse and my lifeblood.

It was my safe spot when I didn't fit in anywhere.

Even the summer in high school when I ran away and lived on the beach for a couple weeks "camping," I could still fit in by mentioning some pop culture trend.

"I love Madonna's 'Holiday,' but what was she thinking with 'Like a Prayer?'"

"You know Miss Piggy and Kermit could never consummate their marriage."

"Vader is Dutch for father."

"Is there anything MacGyver couldn't get himself out of with some tape and a box of paper clips?"

See? Conversation starters were the key to surviving any situation.

That's what art is for me. A way to engage and not be invisible.

I knew I could be an artist when I first heard about Keith Haring. He changed everything for me. Like me, he loved pop culture. Like me, he was gay.

He broke down the lines between low and high art. He wasn't too proud to slap his work on a mug or T-shirt to help pay the rent. Plus, he had the coolest friends ever. He hung out with Warhol.

Haring was my idol.

Was.

He died earlier this year from AIDS.

THIRTY-NINE

"Bizarre Love Triangle"
New order

LIZZY CAME HOME from France a month ago looking like a chic Audrey Hepburn with bangs and shoulder-length hair. The suitcase of pretty vintage dresses added to the similarity.

When I asked her about any romantic affairs, she said it had been more *Casablanca* than *Sabrina*. I reminded her Bogart had been a love interest in both films, to which she replied something about the beginning and end of a beautiful friendship. We often communicated in the language of film quotes. Easiest way to get our point across was to use the perfect line, even if it belonged to someone else.

Labor Day rolled around and classes lurked on the calendar when Maggie was finally due to return from France. No one had seen or spoken to her in months. She sent a couple postcards from the South of France and Barcelona.

Lizzy filled us in on the details of the grand romance. It sounded passionate and whirlwind, the exact thing a girl—or boy—dreams of having while living abroad. I couldn't get a clear read from Lizzy if she liked the guy or not. If anything, she seemed a little envious and a smidge overprotective.

Even though Mags had stayed in Europe longer than originally planned, she had committed to live with all of us for senior year. We'd saved her one of the bedrooms in the old Victorian house Jo and Ben found. Six bedrooms and three bathrooms, it was a big improvement over the crazy apartment we rented last summer. No one had to sleep in the dining room or on a porch. Plus, compared to the dorms, it was a palace.

The kitchen had an eating area where we hung out most nights. Surrounded by ancient pale green linoleum flooring, minty cabinets and avocado-colored appliances, the room provided an institutionally calm gathering place.

Above the enamel topped kitchen table hung Jo's chore wheel, a leftover from last summer. Looking like a bossy, demonic roulette wheel, each slice of the pie contained some form of domestic torture: vacuuming, dishes, kitchen, dusting, bathroom one, bathroom two. Jo and Ben had the master and were in charge of their own bathroom. Even so, odds were heavily stacked on someone having to clean a toilet once a week.

Jo had a real thing about messes. Leave a dish or ten in the sink and suffer her wrath. That's why I locked the cupboards with padlocks, and set out paper plates and plastic utensils during my week of dish duty.

I stared at the wheel, plotting to burn it after graduation. Let Jo be someone else's house mother. I imagined the flames curling up around the edges of the wheel and bursting through the center like the opening credits of Bonanza.

I loved that show as a kid. Michael Landon was incredibly dreamy. Then he grew up to be Pa Ingalls. The sexiest homesteader there ever was in high-waisted pants and suspenders, holding those reins like he meant business.

Humming the theme from *Little House on the Prairie*, I made a shopping list for the party.

"Fantasizing about Mr. Ingalls again?" Selah stole one of my double-stuff Oreos.

"How'd you guess?"

"You were humming the song. It's your tell." She opened a cookie, licked out the center, and set the two empty halves on the table. Like anyone else would eat them without their delicious cream filling.

I moved the package out of her reach. "I can't help it. He was my first crush as a kid."

"Really? I can't remember mine." She jumped up on the counter and thumped the lower cabinets with her feet. "I think it was probably Christopher Plummer as the Captain in *Sound of Music*. My entire family watched it every year when it came on TV. We were allowed to stay up late and my mother would make Jiffy-Pop."

"No crush on Rolf, the cute but soulless Nazi?"

"Too blond and too virginal. Couldn't think for himself, but bossy at the same time. All talk, no action. I need a man willing to stand up for what he believes in. Plus, blonds have never done it for me. Too Ken. I'm definitely not Barbie."

"You're more like an evil Tinkerbell." She'd cut her hair shorter and gone darker a la Winona Ryder.

She ignored my pixie reference. "Who carries a riding crop around for no reason? Did you see him on a horse in the movie?"

"Never. Not a single horse." Of any of us, my money had always been on Selah to be kinky. This conversation proved it.

"Why do you think I loved him? The authority rolled off of him in waves." Sighing, she jumped off the counter and stole another cookie.

Tucking the package closer to me on the bench, I scowled at her. "How do you think Gil is going to take Maggie showing up with Julien?"

Selah cringed. "He's been super stoic ever since she left last summer. He's either excellent about masking his emotions, or it's not a big deal."

We made eye contact for a beat.

"Exactly. I think the former, too."

"You ever find out what happened there?" Of course I'd asked Gil after Maggie and Lizzy left for France. His black mood had been impossible to ignore for the rest of the summer. Then the whole goat incident happened in October with him and Ben in the gym. Luckily, no one could prove it had been either of them and the goat owner didn't pursue charges. In the spring, he acted almost normal after he started dating random girls when we returned from winter break.

"Maggie was bummed Gil didn't come over with us. I didn't really have an explanation for why, so I avoided the subject."

"I still think something went down. And by something going down, I mean blow job at the least."

"Quinn!"

"Okay, okay. He hoed her lady garden."

"That's worse!" She giggled. "Are you calling him a ho?"

"If the label fits."

Calming down from her laughing fit, she played with her long, silver chain. "In all honesty, something happened last summer. I'm a little nervous how it's going to be all living together this year. Aren't you?"

"I haven't thought about it. I think everyone will be fine as long as the Frenchie doesn't stay. What's French for awkward?" She lunged for my side and stole the cookies before scampering out of the kitchen.

TO CELEBRATE THE return of our traveling friend, Ben agreed to fire up the hibachi for a cookout the Friday following her triumphant return. It was a rare night when everyone had time off or didn't have other plans.

We lit the tiki torches in the yard and threw an old Indian cotton bedspread over the table to fancy things up. However, I was on dish duty according to Mother Jo's chore chart. We set the table with paper plates, plastic forks, and plastic cups.

"If we burn everything, we're saving it from the landfills." I proudly declared from my lawn chair.

"I don't think you can burn plastic. It gives off some sort of toxic fumes or something." Gil stabbed a bite of macaroni salad.

I took away Gil's fork and staked it into the ground. "Then you can use your fingers, Mr. Smartass."

He could manage macaroni salad with his fingers. Luckily, the rest of the menu included finger friendly burgers and corn.

Glancing toward the table, I watched as Julien sniffed the bowl of macaroni salad. He bent over and gave it a big inhale.

I silently asked Selah a question with my eyes. *Who sniffs their food? How rude.* Her expression replied.

"It hasn't gone bad. Try it." Maggie took the spoon and dumped some on her plate. "It's delicious. A classic American cookout food."

Julien frowned at her large serving and scooped two noodles, a slice of pickle, and a sliver of hard boiled egg on his plate.

"Maybe he thinks we're trying to poison him?" Gil kicked my shin. "Death by mayonnaise?"

"Ouch." I rubbed my leg. "Isn't mayonnaise French?" I whispered to Lizzy on my other side.

She shrugged. "He's very picky about food. Whatever you do, don't mention cheese."

"What are his thoughts about Velveeta?" I stage-whispered back at her.

Her hand pinched my bicep hard enough I knew it would leave a mark.

"Stop! The two of you are going to leave bruises." In defense, I made a kung fu gesture with my arms. "Fine, no one said it was real cheese."

Frenchie shot me a look from the corner of his eye. Lizzy hadn't been kidding about him. So serious. So stern.

Nothing like Gerard Depardieu.

Which, in all honesty, was a huge relief.

I'd worried he wanted a green card more than he wanted an American girlfriend. But from all the love eyes he kept giving Maggie, and the not-so-quiet love sounds coming from her room earlier today, this was definitely more *Last Tango in Paris* than *Green Card*.

If true, we should probably hide the margarine. I'd have to talk to Maggie about the love that dare not speak its name. I could recommend some water based lubricants.

So much for the night not being awkward.

Immediately after eating, Gil excused himself to go to rehearsal. I wanted to point out the band never rehearsed on Fridays because Mark worked. However, I figured from his sour expression all night, he needed an excuse to escape.

I couldn't blame him. The Frenchman had stolen his puppy. It hurt to watch him around Maggie.

For the past nine months, I'd optimistically hoped once they were back in the same space, they'd fall into their old platonic, barely suppressed sexual tension selves. For once, I was wrong. Very, very wrong.

The Berlin Wall may have come down, but a new wall had been built between the two of them. Sure, they were polite and even gave each other a hello hug, but a cloud of awkwardness hung over them like Pigpen's dust cloud.

I didn't know if Julien picked up on it, but the rest of us did. So many silent conversations had taken place in the last twenty-four hours using only our facial expressions and hand gestures, we could've all become a troupe of mimes. Ironic, oui?

TWO WEEKS AFTER the dinner, Maggie returned from SeaTac, red-nosed and puffy-eyed after saying au revoir to Frenchie. Later in the afternoon, the girls took over the living room with multiple pints of ice cream and sad movies from Blockbuster.

"Do you really think *Beaches* is the best thing to watch right now?" I walked through the living room on my way to the kitchen for snacks. A box of Cheez-Its called my name.

Four tear-stained faces greeted me. I flinched at the emotional messes sprawled on the couch and floor.

"It's cathartic." Maggie resembled a lab rat with her beady pink eyes swollen from hours of crying.

"You're all insane." I took another step closer to the safe zone of the kitchen.

Lizzy blew her nose. "We're watching *Steel Magnolias* next."

I paused. "I do love a snappy Dolly Parton quote." I squeezed next to Selah on the couch and picked up Jo's pint of Cherry Garcia.

"You can stay, but you cannot mock, and you have to get your own spoon." Jo snatched her spoon away from me.

By the time the funeral scene came on, they were all laughing through their tears, promising they'd always be friends. Girls.

I'd been distracted by Tom Skerritt's mustache every scene he appeared in. I liked his uptight demeanor and snarky banter with Ouiser. She reminded me of what I imagined Selah to be when she got old.

No way I'd ever tell her. Although, which would be worse? Mrs. Roper? Or Ouiser?

"Enough of the emo girl time. We should go out and listen to some live music. Dance away your blues." I threw Lizzy's old afghan over Maggie's head.

"Are Inflammable Flannel playing this week?" Selah asked, always the instigator.

"I could use some angry rock music." Maggie poked her head out from the tangled pile of pink and purple yarn.

"Speaking of music, Nirvana is playing the Paramount on Halloween. We should get tickets," Selah suggested.

"With the cute new drummer?" Lizzy's interest in most bands fell in direct relationship to the level of her crushes.

"Mmm . . . he's very cute." Selah's *sleeping with musicians* phase had been in full force since last summer. First, Mark, and then two guys from a four piece out of Seattle. Not at the same time. Or maybe she had. After I accused her of being a groupie and she stopped speaking to me for a week, I didn't ask. She didn't share.

"What about San Francisco and Castro?" I'd talked about this for three years, ever since the road trip freshman year.

Seeing my pout, Lizzy crawled over to me. "I'll go with you, Q. Maybe we can get cheap tickets and fly."

"You're the Wendy to my Peter." I kissed the top of her head.

FORTY

"Freedom! '90"
George Michael

LIZZY STUMBLED OFF the curb next to me.

"Are you okay?"

"I tripped over my flames."

For her Joan of Arc costume, I'd sewn lamé and starch-stiffened cotton flames to her shoes. If she stood still, she looked like a woman in a white dress. When she walked, she appeared to be on fire. It was brilliant, if I said so myself.

Next to her, my costume was a cliché.

"Nice Wendy and Peter Pan," a drunk girl shouted at us. "Where's the pixie dust?"

The man next to her threw glitter into the air. "I've got it right here!"

"I'm not Wendy." Lizzy pouted. "Everyone thinks I'm Wendy."

"Martyrs and saints aren't the typical San Francisco costumes, my dear." I pointed at the two girls standing next to us with shaved heads. "Sinead O'Conner, yes. Patron saint, no."

As soon as we got closer to Market Street, crowds filled the road and sidewalks. The heart of Castro sat a few blocks to the west, but the Halloween festivities spiraled out from there. Everyone dressed in costume, including several massive groups. We passed through an entire deck of cards and the cast of Wizard of Oz, including dozens of flying monkeys.

I'd stumbled into another world. Sure, I'd gone to clubs and gay bars in Seattle, but San Francisco was the mothership, gay heaven. I could have been on the planet of Transexual Transylvania with all the Dr. Frakenfurters from *Rocky Horror* parading around.

I wanted to stand still, absorbing everything around me. I wanted to run through the streets. I didn't want to miss a single thing. I barely resisted clapping my hands in glee.

I couldn't believe the rest of my friends weren't here with me. They'd stayed in Seattle to go to the Nirvana show at the Paramount.

I could've gone with them, but I'd dreamed of coming here for Halloween for years. Probably since high school. I'd imagined Castro like a rainbow Oz at the end of a multi-colored brick road.

Lizzy had been a good sport and ditched her dream of seducing the long-haired drummer to join me. She would always be up for an adventure.

I think the club we went to sophomore year really opened her mind to the fun of hanging with the gay boys. She made a fabulous hag—a high compliment.

Everywhere I looked were half-dressed men. October in San Francisco wasn't exactly warm, but they didn't seem to mind. Apparently, leather—even ass-less leather chaps—really held in the body heat. I wondered if body paint and glitter had similar insulating properties.

"So many leather boys." Lizzy spun in a circle as she took in the crowd around us.

"So little time."

"They don't seem your type. I thought you liked preppy guys." She pointed out a guy dressed as a nerd, complete with thick black frames and a cardigan. He was adorable.

"Now we're talking." Unfortunately, he held hands with another guy dressed as a nerd, too.

My fantasy of locking eyes with someone across a crowded space, the world falling silent around us as we recognized each other as soulmates began to fade.

Music pulsed from the doorways of bars and clubs along Market and Castro as we wandered the streets. The crowd surged around us, continually erupting into whoops and blowing whistles while dancing.

Hands grabbed my waist and spun me around. Before I could register the face, someone's tongue thrust into my mouth. The hands moved from my torso down to my ass and squeezed.

Well, howdy.

My kissing stranger's fingers stopped squeezing and his tongue slipped from my mouth. Opening my lids, a shocked expression in a pair of unfamiliar brown eyes greeted me.

He jumped back. I could see he'd dressed like Captain Hook, complete with wig and a very large hook.

You know what they say about pirates with large hooks, right?

He was cute. Very cute. Not much older than me.

"You're not Darren."

I licked my bottom lip where the tingle of his breath spray still lingered. "Not even close."

"I could die." He blushed despite his makeup. I could see the red slide down his neck to his exposed chest. "You're in the same costume."

"I won't tell Darren if you don't."

"I—" The crowd pushed us apart and he yelled the rest of his sentence, "I'm sorry. You're a great kisser."

"Did you just make out with a complete stranger?" Lizzy sounded awed beside me. "That's the coolest thing I've ever seen."

Strange and completely random, but totally cool. A man kissing another man in the middle of the street, and no one cared. I'd never kissed a stranger before.

At least I usually got a name first. By usually, I meant the two other times I'd kissed random guys at clubs.

"The night certainly has become more interesting. Come on, Peter, let's go have an adventure." Lizzy tucked her arm under mine and pulled me up the hill, dancing her way through the crowd.

AFTER TOO FEW hours of sleep, we decided to revisit the Castro for a late morning Bloody Mary before catching our flight back to Seattle. Like Stonewall in the Village in New York City, Twin Peaks was a must visit stop on the gay pilgrimage route. Inside the funky old bar, a group of even funkier old queens sat at several tables shoved together.

They welcomed us with a cheer and a shot of whiskey. "We're toasting to Aaron. Everyone who comes in has to have a shot."

"Which one of you is Aaron?" I raised the shot glass to toast to our generous host.

An older, very thin man pointed to the beautiful wooden box on the table.

"Oh." I gulped down the burning liquid. I nudged Lizzy to drink hers. "I'm so sorry."

"You have no idea. He's our sixth friend to die since summer." Tears spilled down his face and the guy next to him slung his arm over his shoulder in a hug. I immediately recognized the dark spots on the exposed skin.

Lizzy took an empty seat and hugged one of the strangers. "Oh my gosh, that's terrible. AIDS is heartbreaking, horrible." She patted one of his arms. "My uncle's neighbor has it. In Miami."

Her uncle's neighbor. Aaron. Keith Haring. Rock Hudson. Freddie Mercury. Little Ryan White. An endless list of names and nameless faces of the dead or infected ran through my head.

"To our friends who are no longer here, but still with us." She poured another shot and raised her glass.

The motley group clinked glasses with her.

Two shots of whiskey were enough to give us a buzz. We skipped the other cocktails. Instead, we sat at the table and listened to old stories of the glory days of bath houses and wild Quaalude fueled parties.

I had to cover Lizzy's ears a couple of times. I didn't want her to think all gay men were complete sexual deviants. Some of us wanted the husband, two-point-five kids, and a pure bred lab like anyone else.

By the time we left, I felt I'd inherited seven gay uncles. They were like Snow White's dwarves, including Carl in his powder blue cardigan, who kept falling asleep at the far end of the table.

Lawrence, the skinny one who first spoke to us, gave me a somber warning about reckless behavior. "At your age, you think you'll live forever. But we all die someday. Don't make it sooner because you were stupid, arrogant, and young."

I gave him a salute and my word.

Outside, Lizzy snapped a picture of the neon sign. "Forget a fairy godmother, I want godfather fairies."

I loved her acceptance of everyone she met. It had always been one of my favorite qualities about her. "I'll be your fairy godfather, Lizzy."

"Promise?" She clapped her hands.

"On one condition."

"If I ever fall in love—"

She interrupted to correct me, "When, not if."

"Okay, when I fall in love, and if—"

"When."

"Fine, when I fall in love and when we have a commitment ceremony, you'll be there standing beside me."

"Of course! You couldn't keep me away from it. I'll wear a pretty vintage dress and toss birdseed like a pro. Or we could release butterflies. Oh! We could throw glitter." Her favorite charm bracelet jingled when she tossed imaginary glitter.

"No glitter." I hugged her and kissed her forehead.

"Who knows? You could be a dad someday, too. Then I'll come over and babysit for you. Auntie Mame will have nothing on Auntie Lizzy."

I laughed at her optimism. "Are you going to carry the baby, too?"

"For you? Anything, Q."

I completely believed her. When we were together, she convinced me I could do anything. Me having a family? Crazy, but at least one of us believed in the impossible.

FORTY-ONE

"Finally"
CeCe Peniston

POST HOLIDAYS, I bribed Moping Maggie to get out of the apartment with the promise of French coffee and pastries at the Heron Bakery. I figured maybe something French in her mouth would help. First, I'd made her shower and change out of her pajamas.

All last year I'd dealt with Grumpy Gil. Magpie was home, and he'd become David Copperfield. Poof! Gone. Disappeared. I barely saw him.

Every once in a while, he'd hang out with the group at Lucky's, but ever since last summer, things had changed. No more sleepovers with Maggie. In fact, they never spent time together at all unless it was the entire group.

Hell, none of us really spent much time with him. He claimed a lack of time with a heavy class load and studying for the GREs, plus work and band rehearsal.

He could say all those things were the reason, but he lied like a rug. He avoided Maggie. Spent a year pining, then he couldn't get away from her fast enough.

It was the worst non-break up break up ever.

Nothing could be done.

Maggie fell in love with love. Gil was determined to be "fine."

If my heart wasn't cold and black, it would have hurt for them both.

I could only meddle so much in the love affairs of my friends. A few weeks ago a random postcard from London arrived for Lizzy. She'd clutched it to her chest and refused to talk about it despite my finest attempts to wiggle the truth out of her.

Not that I had my own love life to fret over. The most action I'd seen had been the random street kiss at Halloween. Three months ago.

Sad, sad, sad.

Inside the Heron, Maggie saved us a table while I waited at the counter to order drinks from the very cute blond guy behind the counter

"A cafe au lait for my friend the francophile and the biggest, blackest cup of joe for me."

"No one here is named Joe." The cute barista winked at me.

He. Winked. At. Me.

Flustered, I stumbled over my words. "I'll . . . have you. I mean . . . take you . . . have whatever you're having." I glanced at his name tag. "Warren."

Charming and handsome chuckled and leaned his elbows on the top of the pastry case. His biceps stretched the cotton of his black T-shirt. "I'm having a break in about twenty minutes. If you're interested."

I stumbled to our table in a daze of bulging muscles and winks.

"Where are the coffees?" Maggie stared at my empty hands.

"They're right here." Warren placed a beautiful bowl of cafe au lait in front of her. In front of me, he set a very tall mug of black coffee. "Can I get you anything else? You have the coffee. Tea? Pastry? Me?" He stared down at me.

Unsettled.

He unsettled me. His blond hair was darker than mine, but also pulled back into a ponytail. Rich, chocolate brown eyes. Taller than me, but similar lanky build.

Maggie giggled, her focus bouncing to Warren's sexy smirk and back to my stunned expression. "I think if you keep it up, Quinn's going to need a cold shower."

"Margaret!"

"What?" She had the nerve to bat her eyelashes at me. "I'm merely pointing out you look a little overheated."

The bell above the door jingled, calling Warren back to duty at the counter.

I fanned my face. "It is warm in here, isn't it?"

"No. It's really not." She sipped from her bowl. "Since when do you take your coffee black?"

I stared at the dark liquid. "I got a little flustered back there."

"I'd say. Your cheeks are pink like a little school girl."

I tried to drink the bitter liquid and almost spat it out. "This is terrible."

"Get some milk and sugar added to it."

"I can't go back up there and ask him."

Maggie leaned over to peer around me. "I think he'd be more than happy to give you some sugar."

"You think he was flirting with me?"

She snickered and tried to hide it behind her coffee. "Flirting? No. Definitely not run of the mill flirting. He had you stripped and naked in his mind."

"He did not!" I accidentally hit my hand on the table, causing my coffee to tip and spill.

"Oh, he did. He's coming back over here. Pull yourself together."

"Looks like you got a little excited." Warren appeared next to our table with a white bar towel. "Let me clean you up."

"Warren?" Maggie focused all her attention on him. "What brings you to be working in this fine establishment?"

"I studied glass blowing at Pilchuck but started working in a studio down here."

My jaw dropped. "With Chihuly? The glass genius?"

Warren grinned. "The one-eyed pirate of the glass world himself."

"You're a blower?" Maggie's eye twitched. It might have been an attempt at a wink. I would have to remind her to never do it again in public.

"I prefer glass artist, but I can blow with the best of them."

I groaned. This was too much.

Warren looked concerned.

Maggie poked me under the table with her foot, waggling her eyebrows like some silent movie actor. A really bad one.

"Don't like your coffee?" He pointed at my completely full cup.

"He likes his sweet and full of cream," Maggie murmured.

"Let me add some cream for you." He whisked away my cup.

I returned Maggie's poke with a kick to her shin. Not hard enough to bruise, but enough she got my point. "What are you doing?"

"I'm playing you if the situation were reversed."

"Huh?"

"He's very cute. He's a glassblower, which means he's artistic. Like you."

"Not all artists are gay, Magpie."

"True. But he's also flirting with you. Why would he be flirting if he were straight?"

I didn't have an answer to her question. It had been too long since I'd personally engaged in flirting as a means to an end. I went through my days flirting with everyone as a default.

This was different.

This flirting had a not so subtle undercurrent of sexual chemistry.

Undercurrent didn't cover it.

Tsunami of sexual chemistry.

Synapses fired in my brain I swore had gone dormant.

Things zinged.

Warren returned with a fresh cup of caramel-colored coffee. I took a sip and the sweetness erased the horrible taste from the unadulterated muck I'd first sipped.

"Better?"

"Perfect."

"Great. Ten minutes." He tossed his towel over his shoulder and returned to his post.

"What's ten minutes?" she asked me.

"His break."

"Oooh, are you going to go make out behind the dumpster?" Delight shone in her meddling expression.

"Classy, Magpie. Very classy."

"It's kind of hot."

"I'm not that kind of boy."

"Maybe not, but maybe he is." She drank from her cup, then smiled at me with a foamy mustache.

FORTY-TWO

"Real Love"
Mary J. Blige

WARREN AND I did not make out behind the dumpster during his break.

I wasn't kidding when I told Maggie I wasn't that kind of boy.

We did, however, sit outside on a bench and talk. Then he gave me his number and I gave him mine.

How old fashioned.

"WHO'S WARREN?" SELAH asked, holding out a message scrawled on a Hello Kitty pad of paper.

I reached for the note and she held it behind her back.

"Not until you tell me who he is."

"He's a guy."

"A guy who called here for you. He sounded eager. And cute."

"How do you sound cute on the phone?"

"He admitted he didn't know your last name. Fumbled over it, actually. Then told me he wasn't a random creep." Her expression softened and I could see her romantic side come out. "Someone you picked up in San Francisco?"

"No, he's local."

Her eyebrows rose toward her bangs. "It's about time."

"I'm not a virgin-hermit."

She handed me the note. "No, but Olympia isn't exactly a cornucopia of cute gay boys. Present company the exception, of course."

"Of course." I read Warren's message and smiled.

"He is cute." Selah grinned. "I can tell by your face."

"He's not bad. Now excuse me, I need to make a phone call." In the kitchen I punched his number into the phone on the wall, then pulled the long cord with me into the pantry closet.

I literally was in the closet calling a cute guy.

The irony wasn't lost on me.

He picked up on the third ring.

I would've hung up after the fourth.

We made plans to meet at the diner for dinner.

I wondered if we'd order one milkshake and two straws.

Probably not.

AT THE DINER, we sat in a booth near the windows.

Warren wore jeans and a long sleeve rainbow tie-dyed T-shirt. Out of his ponytail, his hair barely brushed his shoulders. His foot bumped against mine a couple of times while we studied our menus.

He ordered pancakes for dinner. How rebellious.

I had a burger and fries. And a chocolate milkshake—with one straw.

After the waitress left us, an awkward silence fell over the table. I tried to think of something to say not completely cliché and trite.

"You're an art major?" he asked.

"I am."

"What kind?"

"3D."

So far, I came across as interesting as the bowl of mini non-dairy creamers sitting on the table—bland, boring, and completely artificial.

The waitress returned with our orders. At least we'd have something to do with our hands and mouths now.

"What about you?" I asked.

"Studio art undergrad at RISD, now glass blowing."

"Are you afraid of getting burned?"

"Getting burned is part of the process. You learn the hard way immediately when you work with hot stuff, burns are inevitable."

"The same could be said about my dating life."

"Mine too." His laughter rumbled in his chest and I could feel it echo in my own.

"Could you teach me to blow glass?"

"You want access to my glory hole?" He sucked syrup off his fork

I choked on my milkshake.

"You okay?" His deep laugh filled the space while I sputtered and tried not to die on a mouthful of dairy.

I nodded, trying to replace chocolate milk with air.

"I'm not being rude. That's what it's called. For real. We have three furnaces and the middle one is the glory hole."

Finally able to breathe again, I looked around, wondering who else heard him say glory hole repeatedly. Two young guys with long hair and funky clothes were already out of the norm for this town. I didn't want to end up getting thrown out and called faggots.

"No one heard me."

"What?"

"No one is paying attention to us. You looked worried we're going to be jumped as soon as we walk out the door."

I rolled my shoulders back and pushed the sleeves of my black shirt up to my elbows. "I wasn't worried."

He toyed with the piercing in his eyebrow. I hadn't noticed it before. "Two men talking about glory holes might not be typical, even for here."

"Can you stop saying glory hole?" I stabbed a fry into the tartar sauce I'd ordered on the side.

He chuckled. "Only if you agree to come to the studio and let me show you mine."

I swore my cheeks heated. "Okay. Deal."

"Let's talk about things that can't possibly be turned into embarrassing sexual innuendo." Spearing one of the sausage links on his plate, he slowly lifted it to his lips.

I paused with my burger an inch from my mouth to watch him. He never broke eye contact as he bit down on the tip.

I closed my eyes. "You don't play fair."

When I reopened them, his warm brown eyes stared into mine.

"Who wants to play fair? You're too easy to fluster."

I took a bite of my burger. Flirting was second nature to me. I did it with everyone—men, women, dogs, cats, and sometimes inanimate objects. My default mode of communication equaled flirting.

I had nothing on Warren. He was a master.

What was the word I'd used when we met?

Unsettled.

I couldn't tell if this were his natural mode or if he really liked me.

I loved attention, but he was different. He fed off of walking on a thin edge of flirting and sexual harassment. He balanced between charm and spectacle, the kind to attract the wrong kind of people. We weren't in San Francisco or New York. Locals here were less forgiving about openly in your face gays.

I wanted not to care about fitting in. Most of my life I played the clown to get people to like me.

Warren acted like he assumed people liked him.

I liked him.

I finished my burger and listened to him talk about how he got into glassblowing.

Unlike Warren, I did care if people liked me.

I wanted him to like me.

"Let's get out of here." He threw his napkin on his plate and made the international sign for the check.

Outside he lit up a cigarette, cupping the flame of the lighter against the breeze. He offered me the lit cigarette and I took it. Inhaling the warm smoke, I squinted against the burn.

"Now what?" I exhaled and made smoke rings.

"Let's have some fun. I'll drive."

He led me across the gravel away from the lights of the diner to his small pickup truck

When he pulled out his keys and opened my door, I decided to be bold.

FORTY-THREE

"Whatta Man"
Salt-N-Pepa

I SURPRISED HIM when I grabbed his hips and spun him around to face me.

He blinked at me for a few seconds before he clued into my intentions. He dropped his cigarette to the ground, then took mine and crushed both under his boot.

I lunged toward him, thinking I'd go straight for the kiss.

Instead he held me back by placing his hands on my shoulders. Now I stared at him. Was he rejecting me?

Before I could process why he held me back, he yanked me closer by the front of my leather jacket until our bodies almost touched. One hand released its grip and moved over my chest. I wondered if he could feel my heart racing under my T-shirt.

His lips brushed against the scruff on my cheek, followed by the drag of his teeth along my jaw.

I focused on breathing and steadying my flying pulse. My own hands rested on the semi-neutral territory of his jean-covered hips.

He teased me. Close enough I could feel heat flowing off of him, but he hadn't kissed me yet.

I lifted my hand to his smooth jaw and stilled his movements. I felt his cheeks lift in a smile against my fingers.

"Quit teasing," I whispered.

"Do something about it."

I did.

My mouth crashed into his.

I tilted my head and kissed him. Sweeping my tongue across his bottom lip, I silently warned him before I kissed him harder, deeper. My tongue found his.

He spun us. My back rested against his truck. No longer were his hands still on my torso. He moved one to the back of my head and angled me how he wanted. My fingers sought warm skin above his jeans, underneath his shirt. His back was smooth and tight with muscle.

My moan echoed his. I wanted to touch more of his smooth back, shoving my hands under the cotton, lifting it out of the way.

I barely registered the sound of tires on the gravel or the car doors opening behind us.

"We should take this someplace else," he whispered against my lips.

I froze as footsteps, heavy boots, crunched on the gravel. Shoving my hands into my pockets, I stepped away.

"Faggots," a voice yelled across the parking area.

We both cringed at the slur. He leaned against the car next to his and lit up another cigarette before flipping the bird at the asshole's back.

The futility of the gesture made me laugh. Not exactly running scared, but also not fighting back. We waited until the guy went inside before we left.

"Let's get out of here." I opened his passenger door. Once inside, I reached over and unlocked his door.

He joined me and started the engine. When we drove past the asshole's truck, he rolled down his window and flicked his lit cigarette out. It sailed over the side of the bed.

In terms of retaliation for the slur, it was pretty lame, but we high-fived each other in solidarity.

Driving in silence, he headed east through town. After a series of right turns, I realized we were going in circles, and suggested Lucky's. Chances were I'd know someone there, but it wasn't a gay bar. I didn't know how out Warren was. Or wanted to be.

INSIDE MY FAVORITE dive bar most of the tables were full, but a couple of familiar faces occupied our regular booth.

Before I could suggest joining my friends, Warren walked over to them. "Hey, Ben."

"Hey, bro." Ben did a weird white guy high five-hand clasp with Warren.

"You two know each other?" I took a seat across from Ben and gestured for Warren to sit next to me.

"Warren makes the most beautiful bongs and pipes."

Warren beamed. "They're not much."

"Dude, I don't know a lot about art, but those things are beautiful." Ever since he saw *Point Break*, Ben's accent had gone from vague Northeastern to Keanu Reeve's surfer. Everything he said ended with dude and bro.

"Wait, you made Gandalf? Ben's right. That bong was gorgeous." Gil poured us both beers from the pitcher.

"Was?" Warren frowned. "Did it break?"

"I gave it away." He looked sad at the thought. "Jo wasn't really into it."

"I've heard that before, man. You get with a chick and she trades access to her body for your balls." Warren nodded.

"That's not happening." Ben took a long swig of beer.

Warren snorted. "Sure. Of course not."

"I think Ben happily handed over his balls to Jo. Probably served them up on a sterling silver platter with a specially designed spoon." I laughed at the thought of such a thing.

Instead of getting pissed, Ben surprised me by shrugging off Warren's insults. He must have really loved Jo not to get mad. Or his lack of balls had gelded him, removing all testosterone and the urge to fight. Poor guy.

Warren's arm stretched behind me along the booth. Noticing our position, Gil lifted an eyebrow while nodding in approval.

Ben prattled on about *Point Break* and the epic Halloween costumes we wore to a campus party before Castro. "Quinn found us a source for the president masks. I had enough blazers and ties for everyone already. The whole thing was a piece of cake." He snapped his fingers like some sort of Rat Pack cool guy.

"Genius." Warren gave him a high-five.

Really? Suits and masks were genius? Clearly the man had never been to the Castro.

"Man, I love that movie. Swayze going out in the monster wave was the bomb. He did life his own way."

The three of them fell into a discussion about robbing banks and the FBI.

I interrupted their animated conversation. "Listen, Johnny Utahs, we're out of beer."

"Okay. I'll come with you." Warren stood up to let me out.

While we stood in line for the bartender, his hand crept into my back pocket. I flinched at first then tried to cover it up by pressing back against him.

I wasn't used to PDA in front of my friends. I didn't have anything to hide. Hell, freshman year I'd practically run around screaming I was queer from the sheer joy of coming out and the weight it lifted off of my shoulders.

People waiting to order crowded the bar area. Warren leaned closer, pressing his front against my back. I felt his breath on my neck before he spoke. "I like your friends."

I turned to reply and realized his mouth, the lips which had been on mine an hour ago, was only a couple of inches from mine. He could kiss me with the tiniest movement.

Panicking, I backed away with a jolt.

I didn't know if he wanted to go in for a kiss. From his expression, my reaction surprised him. He quickly recovered and stepped to my side. When I reached for his hand, he avoided me by placing it on the bar.

We returned with a full pitcher and resumed our seats in the booth.

Warren played with his glass, no more arm resting on the booth. I pressed my leg against his and knocked twice with my knee. A small smile appeared on his lips, and he returned the pressure with his own leg.

I hoped it meant he understood my reaction at the bar and everything was okay between us.

Ben and Gil offered to bring me back to the house with them, politely saving Warren the extra trip and essentially cockblocking me. Thanks, friends.

Outside Lucky's, Warren and I awkwardly stared at each other while the guys shuffled around.

"I'm driving up to Pilchuck for a weekend session. You should come with me." Warren brushed the back of his hand against mine.

I grinned at him. "Are you inviting me to see your glory hole?"

"That's exactly what I'm doing."

"I thought you'd never ask." I stepped toward him and he coughed, his focus over my shoulder.

Right.

Our audience.

Something about kissing Warren in front of Ben felt incredibly awkward. I didn't think Ben would freak out, but he acted pretty conservative about most things. Two guys kissing in front of him might have been the thing to push him over into full Anita Bryant mode. I told myself I respected him too much to throw my sexuality in his face. The truth was, I didn't want to see his judgment.

"I'll call you tomorrow to get your address." Warren took a step away.

I waved as I walked backward to Ben's car.

No goodnight kiss for us.

FORTY-FOUR

"How Will I Know"
Whitney Houston

"I FEEL LIKE we're reenacting the clay scene in *Ghost*." My hands were wrapped around a hard blow-pipe. The heat from the furnace sizzled my exposed skin.

Warren chuckled behind me, his hands holding the end of the rod and helping me to spin it in the furnace as we gathered the molten glass onto the tip.

Just the tip. I chuckled as the glowing liquid clung to the end of the rod.

"Okay, pullout, and we'll start shaping this bad boy." He placed his gloved hand on my hip.

I carefully lifted the molten liquid-covered rod out of the furnace and slowly carried it over to the steel table.

The open air space held multiple furnaces and work benches filled with other students, but I felt like Warren and I were alone.

He showed me how to roll the ball on the cool steel to form a skin over the molten glass.

"Now put your lips together and blow." He demonstrated the action.

I licked my lips and mirrored him

"Now do it to the pipe." His smirk told me his mind had gone to the same place mine had.

As I blew, the blob expanded. "That's amazing."

"Do it again."

I did and a bubble formed at the end of the pipe.

Other than a fear of being scalded and deformed for life by million degree glass, the whole experience of glassblowing had been pretty amazing.

At the end of the day, my slightly off-kilter vase sat on a rack with other novice blowers similarly wonky pieces.

I assisted Warren as he took over and created his own work—a beautifully swirled bowl. The man had talent. He reacted fearlessly and the glass responded as an extension of his breath.

I was in awe.

I wanted to make out with him and didn't care who saw.

The things he could do with a pipe in his mouth and his hands on a rod may have had something to do with it.

I SPENT WEEKS of near sleepless nights finalizing my senior project. Warren helped by continuing to teach me simple glass blowing techniques. Good enough I could make the glass eyes for my Sammy Davis, Jr. collectible.

Everything in my senior show had a pop culture reference, but had been crafted out of classic materials. Puffy-heart-shaped gilt wood jewelry boxes contained tiny, spinning Liza Minellis inside instead of ballerinas. Porcelain doll heads resembled Cabbage Patch Kids. Thankfully, Gil's job had a huge screen-printing set-up for my Warhol inspired dead celebrity posters, and I cut a deal with the owner.

Maggie, Lizzy, and Selah brought me food in the evenings, even hanging out in the cluttered space of my studio studying as I worked. We listened to random cassettes we found at the thrift store or old eight-tracks I played on the ancient stereo from the seventies Gil dragged up here with me.

One Wednesday night, it stormed outside while we had a dance party to Donny & Marie.

An idea burned bright in my mind. "Do either of you knit?"

"No, but my grandmother does." Maggie flopped in the old armchair covered with a drop cloth.

"Can she make socks?"

"Are your feet cold?"

"I want to do Donny's purple socks. My sister had the doll and it came with little purple socks."

"I bet she can, but are you allowed to outsource?"

I pursed my lips. "Probably. I'll post something in the CAB or the Art Annex. Somewhere around here someone must know how to work a needle not involving heroin."

"You should work that upbeat image into a project, Q." Selah moved a pile of screens from my workbench and jumped up.

I scratched my goatee. "I do have the whole section on tragic deaths."

"Everything is so bright and cheerful, but utterly morbid and depressing." Selah pointed at the poster of Jean Michel Basquiat on the wall.

"Too soon?" He'd been dead for a couple of years. The latest member of the twenty-seven club, morbid but the coolest. In addition to Jean Michel, my posters included members Jim Morrison, Janis Joplin, and Jimi Hendrix. Apparently, your name also had to begin with the letter "J" to join.

"Maybe." Selah kicked her legs against the cabinets, her boots leaving behind more scuff marks.

"It's all kind of like celebrity and life?" I wanted feedback from them. This show would be the biggest thing I'd ever done and I felt nervous.

"You're an evil genius, Q." Maggie beamed at me, always my biggest supporter.

"Do you think it's too late for me to join a punk band?" Selah said out of nowhere. "I think I should be in an all-girl punk band."

"Do you play any instruments?" Lizzy asked.

"No, but I think I'd be great at screaming angry lyrics." Selah tapped an uncapped marker against her lips, unintentionally giving herself semi-permanent black lipstick.

"You'd be perfect as an angry front girl. Do it." I glanced at the clock. "I'm late to meet Warren."

Giggling and teasing me about a date, the girls gathered their things.

"When are Lizzy and I going to meet this alleged boyfriend of yours?" Selah paused by the door, waiting for my answer.

Boyfriend? "Who said I had a boyfriend?"

"Oh, please. We're not going into the whole 'he's a boy and a friend explanation' again, are we?" Lizzy crossed her arms and puckered her lips.

I kissed her cheek.

"We haven't really declared anything."

Sure Warren and I kissed, and "hung out" a few times. But it had never really gone any further. He spent most weekends up at Pilchuck or at the bakery. I could barely remember to stuff Ramen in my mouth most nights when I finally crawled home from my studio.

"Invite him to your opening. It's only a few weeks away." Maggie pulled her Blossom-style hat over her hair. I wasn't a fan. At least hers didn't have the big flower on it.

"Splendid idea," Lizzy said.

"Sounds good to me." Selah pushed the others ahead of her out the door. "No excuses this time, Dayton!"

I assumed Warren would come to the opening, but it hadn't occurred to me to invite him as my official date. Felt like a serious step.

FORTY-FIVE

"Say Hello, Wave Goodbye"
Soft Cell

MY SHOULDER ACHED from all the slapping and patting people felt I deserved for a show well done. The chicest of Olympia's chic and the cool people of Evergreen filled the white gallery space. Professors asked where I planned to study for my MFA and if I wanted gallery representation. Red dots spotted the walls and objects like a beautiful rash. Almost everything had sold.

I should've been on top of the world. Instead, my head kept turning to the glass doors.

Warren was a no show.

He'd left a message on my answering machine promising he'd come tonight.

I hated how his absence clouded the glory of the spotlight tonight.

I'd worked for four years for this moment.

Everything had led up to this night.

Every stupid prank and stunt like the lettuce boycott sophomore year had taught me something about making a statement.

This was my moment to shine.

Instead, I kept an eye on the entrance, and listened for his voice over the din of chatter.

Talk around me included references to Warhol, Haring, and other Pop Art icons. An older couple dressed all in black cornered me. His mustache reminded me of Burt Reynolds and her hair had been dyed so black it looked blue.

"What are you doing next? Will you do a commission? Have you thought about studying in Los Angeles?" Their questions hit me like a barrage of BBs.

"Grad school. I don't know. I've never done one before. I'm set on New York." I sounded like a well-rehearsed toddler, providing the right words, but not really listening to the questions because I studied the doors, willing them to open.

When they did open, an unfamiliar group of people walked through them. Not Warren.

Exhaling in frustration, I excused myself from the Edward Gorey couple, and headed to the crowd lining up at the bar.

"Quinn!" The girls greeted me with open arms and mostly empty plastic glasses of the cheap white wine, a must for a legitimate art opening.

"We're very proud of you." Maggie kissed both my cheeks. So French.

"I bought the heart thing with the spikes." Selah pointed to my Be Still, My Beetlejuice Heart.

"I would have gifted you one, Selah."

"I know, but I want everything to have a red dot. I think I sold one of Sammy's eyeballs, too."

"You need wine." Lizzy handed me her glass. "Drink up, buttercup. You're a star!"

"Where are Ben and Jo?" I didn't bother asking about Gil. I'd already spoken to him before he left with some woman who looked like Maggie's dark haired twin. Not as pretty as our Magpie, but if you can't be with the one you love, date her doppelganger.

Lizzy pointed over my shoulder. "Ben's talking to some long haired guy over by the beanbags."

I recognized Ben's shoes and legs, but couldn't see the rest of him or the other guy. Hope took flight in my chest.

"Be right back."

"You stole my wine," Lizzy huffed.

"You're already in line for the bar. Get us both another one." I lifted the glass above my head as I shuffled through the crowd.

It took me ten minutes to cross the room. People stopped me, touching my arms and shoulders, praising the show. As much of an ego stroke as it was, the rest of me wanted the night to be over. Or at least this part of it. A few rounds and hanging out with the gang at Lucky's sounded like heaven after hours of schmoozing.

When I finally reached the beanbags I'd requested for lounging, two girls sat in them. Ben was nowhere to be seen.

I sank down into an empty chair and drank my wine as I observed people looking at my creations. The girls next to me chatted about nothing related to the art. There seemed to be some guy named Roger who had apparently dated both of them. At the same time, they'd figured out, during junior year. They gossiped about his enormous talent while I eavesdropped.

The crowd thinned around us. My view no longer consisted of legs and shoes with glimpses of bright colors on the walls and pedestals.

Staring at the 27 Club posters, I stroked the goatee I'd grown in the past few weeks. Gil had one and I liked the musketeer look it gave him. I wasn't convinced about the look for me. As much as I loved the nickname Aslan, with the goatee I looked more like the Cowardly Lion than ever.

The girls helped each other out of their chairs and wandered away. Clumps of people gathered near the glass doors, putting on coats and making plans for later.

Tilting my glass, I realized it was empty. The bar sat far, far away across the room. It might as well be a galaxy away. I sighed and rested my head back on the faux yellow fur. I visualized someone bringing over a bottle of wine. Didn't matter who.

Squeaking from rubber soles and the clicking of heels came closer to me.

Selah and Maggie towered above me, a wine bottle held by each of them.

"My angels!"

Maggie shuffled the other beanbags closer to mine and plopped down in one.

"Boys suck." She held her bottle closer to me.

I took it and instead of refilling my glass, drank directly from the bottle.

"Very rock star of you, Q." Selah lifted her bottle and did the same thing. "I'd clink with you, but I'm trapped in this godforsaken chair and can't reach you."

She resembled a turtle on its back, legs wide open and her feet several inches from the ground.

"Shift yourself forward before you flash everyone." Maggie pulled on Selah's boot, dragging her lower to the ground.

"Nothing most of these people haven't seen before. If they've made it through college without seeing a vagina, then I don't even know what to say." Selah took another swig of wine.

"I've never seen your Bea Arthur, Selah. Can we keep it that way?" I covered my eyes with my hand. The whole truth was I'd seen more than enough accidentally last summer. Long story and I didn't want to relive it. Ever again.

She choked and spit out wine in a beautiful arc of spray. "My what?"

"Bea Arthur. That's what I imagine is down there. Maybe wearing a long sweater coat."

"What?" Lizzy stared at me.

"My mother called her," I gestured to my crotch, "lady business Maude. I always assumed she really meant the actress who played Maude, and I started calling them Bea Arthur."

Selah's head fell back as she cackled and kicked her feet, threatening us with a full view. Again. Such a lady. "That's the best thing I've ever heard. Who names their body parts? It's not like they have their own personalities or minds."

"Speak for yourself. Men have named their penises for millennium. And they do often have a mind of their own."

Lizzy blinked at me in doubt.

"I'm serious. Every guy in here probably has a name for his dick and an embarrassing story about some time or other when he got an erection at exactly the wrong moment. Ask them. Ask every single guy, then tell me the penis is just another body part. I've never been embarrassed by my shins or elbow going rogue."

"You have very nice calves." Maggie complimented me. "I'd kill for those shapely muscles."

"Why thank you, Magpie." The wine began to work its way through my body, giving me a warm, relaxed feeling.

"Speaking of names, if I'm going to start my all-girl punk band, we need a name. Something which screams girl power and badass."

"Sandra Day O'Connor?" Lizzy suggested.

"Not bad. Not bad. Hit me with more." Selah drank from her bottle.

"Bikini Razor?" Maggie frowned at her own suggestion. "Sounds sexy, but dangerous."

"Something with dolls in it." Lizzy twisted her mouth in thought. "Scary dolls or something."

"Aren't all dolls scary?" Selah snorted. "Dolls have been done."

"I know!" I set down my bottle and clapped my hands.

Three sets of eyes stared at me. "Maude!"

The gallery had emptied out while we talked about ridiculous things and laughed ourselves silly. I realized I'd forgotten about Warren completely. I gave the doors one last glare.

My mind went to all the horrible things that could have happened to keep him away. Car accident. Mugging. Kidnapped by Big Foot. Poking his eye out with a hot blow-pipe. Losing his hand and having to get a hook.

Okay, maybe some of them were revenge for standing me up tonight.

"Shall we adjourn to Lucky's?" Selah caught my attention and redirected my focus from the doors. "Toast to our amazing awesome selves?"

"Who says awesome anymore?" Lizzy wrinkled her nose. "It's so valley girl, circa '85."

"Totally." Maggie stuck her tongue out. "Let's go."

Selah held up her hands for me to lift her. When upright, she leaned close and whispered, "We'll toast to all the assholes we've loved over the years."

I choked on the last of the wine in my bottle.

"I mean figuratively, not literally. Of course." She kissed my cheek, tucking her arm under mine.

FORTY-SIX

"Enjoy the Silence"
Depeche Mode

"SORRY I COULDN'T make your opening tonight. I'm sure it was amazing and you sold everything. I really wanted to come, planned to come, but I couldn't. I got there and saw all the people."

Warren had been there.

"I couldn't go inside. I stood outside and saw everyone surrounding you . . ."

He paused for long enough on the message I checked to see if the machine still played.

" . . . I guess I'm not really ready to be someone's date for something big. You know. Like a boyfriend. I mean . . ."

Another long pause.

" . . . I really like hanging out with you and doing stuff. That's been fun. A lot of fun. You're really cool."

I hit pause.

If he wanted to break up with me, doing it on the answering machine I shared with a house of people had to be the lowest. He'd picked me up. He came on strong, made all the moves. When he needed to step up and support me, he bailed. Not cool.

I erased the rest of his message.

FORTY-SEVEN

"All Apologies"
Nirvana

I WOULDN'T SAY I was heartbroken over Warren, but my crushing disappointment stung. To get over him, I needed a change of scenery and a great diversion.

"We should go to Graceland after graduation. Make it the ultimate road trip. Follow Route 66 and get our kicks," I suggested to the group as we all sat in our booth at Lucky's.

"I'll go if we all go," Gil said.

"We can't."

"I'm sorry . . . what is this can't you speak of, Josephine?"

"Ben's going to Harvard and I'm going to Boston College." Once Jo had a plan, nothing deviated. Sure, they'd sweated applications and waiting like anyone else, but I knew deep down Jo had made up her mind. If she said he was going to Harvard and she would study law, then that's what would happen.

Jo's superpower was determination. When I first met Ben, he could have been playing any of the spoiled boys in a John Hughes movie. Under Jo's influence, he'd turned out okay. Still cocky and too uptight for me, but he'd been pretty cool about not being a jerk about Warren. Jo even offered to play matchmaker with some guy named Kyle.

I pushed forward with my argument. "Unless they do things completely differently in Boston, then your excuse is invalid because classes wouldn't start for months."

"We need to find a place to live and drive all our stuff back there."

"Boston is on the other side of Tennessee. You can keep driving north from Memphis. In fact, you can drop Lizzy and I off in New York on your way. Next." I wouldn't accept their lame excuse.

"I can't." Maggie picked at her napkin, shredding it into confetti.

"And why not, Magpie? You love fat Elvis as much as I do. We could finally eat those bacon, banana, and peanut butter sandwiches we've dreamed about for years."

The confetti got shredded into paper glitter. "I'm leaving for France right after graduation."

Silence fell around the table.

Lizzy spoke what we all were thinking. "Then I guess the affair with Julien wasn't a case of too much cheap wine and cheese addling your brain."

Maggie shook her head. "He's asked me to move over there. With him."

"I'd hope with him," Selah scoffed. "Asking you to move to the other side of the planet from your family and friends better mean a serious commitment."

Selah wasn't a fan of the Frenchman, whom she referred to as the French Incident in front of everyone but Maggie. Lizzy continued to call him Le Fromage, but from the face she often made when saying the word, she thought he was one very stinky cheese.

"If we don't take one last epic road trip together, at least we can have a party. The last hurrah before we're ejected from the womb of college."

Ben and Gil gagged on my words.

"Womb? Really?" Gil set down his beer.

"The cold, harsh world awaits. No more seeing each other daily or hourly. It could be years before we're all together again, you know. I'm merely pointing out the truth."

"Have you heard of Prozac?" Selah raised her hands like a television preacher channeling the good stuff. "Because maybe you need a little happy pill pick-me-up to combat your premature mid-life crisis."

"It's the truth," I mumbled.

"Then let's have this party. Maybe it'll cheer you up." Selah poked my shoulder.

"It will. Last time we had a huge party, Maggie and Gil—" Maggie covered Lizzy's mouth to shut her up.

"They what? Go on . . ."

I let it drop when Maggie shot me a death look and Gil frowned.

"I say we have a big bonfire." The thought of burning things did make me feel better.

"What are you going to burn?" Ben asked.

"First thing, the damn chore wheel Jo made. Cursed thing has been an albatross, a dodo bird, and the stone to my Sisyphus for far too long."

Jo gasped. "It's served a very important purpose!"

"What?" I asked.

"Separating men from the apes?" Ben joked.

"Dirty, dirty apes." Jo kissed his cheek. I sensed a really disturbing role play thing between them, but even I didn't want to know.

"Okay." Gil leaned back and pushed his glass away. "Tell me when to show up and I'll be there. If you want us to play, I'll call the guys." He stood up and grabbed his jacket from the rack near the door.

Lizzy and Jo pulled out their day-planners and started discussing dates, making plans for the party. Jo looked up and smiled. "I can invite Kyle. He's cute and definitely on your team."

Kyle would be a nice addition. Out with the old, in with the new.

"Don't forget to add lighter fluid for the chore wheel. It's going to burn like a ring of fire." I tapped the table in front of them and began singing Johnny Cash.

IT COULD HAVE been the indelible markers Jo used, or the copious amounts of lighter fluid, but the chore wheel burned in a rainbow hue of satisfaction. I tossed paper plates like frisbees into the fiery pyre. The wheel wasn't the only thing I burned. I threw Warren's number in the flames, too. I had it memorized, but I focused on the symbology.

We all watched the quick lifecycle of burning paper and cardboard. The sense of fulfilling a long term goal faded. I felt less smug than I'd hoped. The rest of the party guests had trickled away ages ago, leaving the seven of us around a dwindling bonfire.

Selah raised her cup. "To the end of an era."

The others toasted her. Ben poured a little of his booze onto the ground for the homies a la Ice Cube's song.

"A few more weeks and this will all be a memory." Lizzy sighed.

"Where did the past four years go?" Jo snuggled into Ben's side.

Gil strummed a sad procession of notes in a minor key on his bass.

Maggie wrapped a blanket around her and Selah on the picnic bench. "Next time we see each other will probably be Ben and Jo's wedding."

"Or yours." Lizzy attempted to look happy about Franco-American nuptials.

Gil's finger slipped and hit a wrong note.

"I hope we see each other on a more regular basis than weddings and funerals. That's depressing." Selah pulled out her cigarettes, lit one, and then handed them to Maggie.

"At least some things never change." Maggie held up the pack and pointed out the man with the erection hidden in the camel.

Even Gil cracked a smile over the old joke from freshman year.

Unlike the rest of my life, I knew one thing for certain.

When I grew up, I wanted to still be friends with these people.

More than friends.

We were family.

Epilogue

Lizzy

THE CREDITS RUN at the end of Owen's documentary and the theater lights brighten. Applause incites a round of awkward bowing from Owen, who invites everyone to the after party. We sit in our row as others around us get up and file out to the lobby. I have chills, but it could be the overzealous air conditioning in the old theater.

"Wow." Gil breaks our stunned silence.

"Were we ever that young and stupid?" Selah removes her boots from the seat in front of her and sits up.

"Did I really say those things? Sheesh, could I have been more of a Pollyanna Sunshine?" Maggie rolls her eyes.

"No, you really couldn't have." Quinn tosses a piece of leftover popcorn at her. "I forgot about your schoolmarm outfit."

"I think it's sweet." Jo gazes at Ben.

"I agree." Ben holds her hand.

"You would." I lean forward next to Ben to make eye contact with Jo on his other side. "You two were the happily ever after of the whole film."

"Unlike me, who according to this masterpiece of cinéma vérité, am a sexless virgin." Quinn gives me a devilish grin.

"The entire thing is a work of creative fiction, not historical fact." Gil brushes popcorn off his jeans and stands.

"Says the history major." Quinn tosses another kernel at him, which Gil catches in his mouth.

"How do you even have popcorn left in your bucket?" Selah pulls it closer to herself.

He yanks the tub away, scattering more popcorn. "Let's go to the after party. Maybe convince Owen to make a director's cut with all the footage from the editing room floor."

Everyone else groans, then starts complaining about finals and being busy.

"No, nuh-uh," I protest. "First, there will be free drinks. What college students turn down free anything? Second, this is it. Next week is graduation and the end. Finito. We go our separate ways."

"Doesn't mean we won't all still be friends. Half of you will be within a few hours of New York or in the city." Gil sweeps his arm in front of the group.

Maggie sighs. "Not me. I'll be an ocean away. An ocean and a continent from home."

"Living in France, mind you. The suffering will be unbearable, I'm sure." Quinn finally gets up and popcorn rains down on the floor.

"We have our whole lives ahead of us. We need to rally ourselves out of this funk."

"After grad school for most of us." Gil's tone holds no excitement despite getting into the program of his choice.

"Grad school will be different." Ben smiles at Jo. Quinn and I have a bet they'll become a Mr. and Mrs. as soon as he becomes a MBA

"You'll all make new friends and forget about me." Maggie seems on the verge of tears.

Quinn squints at her. "Hello, crazy French lady in the raspberry beret, you look vaguely like someone I used to know."

"It's not funny, Q." Maggie walks to the end of the aisle.

"We won't forget you, Maggie May."

Maggie's step falters at Gil's use of her old nickname, something he hasn't used since two summers ago. He shrugs and his mouth forms a half-smile. For a brief moment, they stare at each other in silence. We hold our collective breath, waiting to see what happens next. A small, sad smile flashes briefly on her lips before she composes herself again.

Quinn flaps his arms around like he's trying to calm a group of toddlers. "Everyone settle down. We're going to stay friends. We're like geoducks. Forever in the same holes. Or a hundred years. Whichever comes first."

"I don't want to be a penis clam." I frown.

"You're stuck with me. I'm like gay glue." Quinn pulls me up out of my seat.

A guy with a broom and dustpan walks down the left aisle. "There isn't a second showing. You need to leave."

"Charming," Selah mumbles.

We shuffle out of the row and up the aisle.

"If you're the gay glue of this friendship, what am I?" Selah asks.

"The heart. You act like it's a cold, black, shriveled thing, but you probably have the biggest heart of all of us."

"Do me next!" Maggie strolls backward in front of him.

"The memory. If not for you, we probably wouldn't have all met."

"And Gil?" Selah stomps past me, heading for the exit.

"The brain."

"Isn't memory part of the brain?" I ask.

"Exactly my point." Quinn looks smug.

"And Ben and Jo?"

"They're the body, strength and stamina."

"I do love your stamina," Jo whispers loudly to Ben. The rest of us grumble, all too familiar with their stamina after living together.

"And me?"

"You're the soul, sweet Lizzy."

"Perfect."

We arrive in the bright lobby, glance around the crowd, and meet each others' eyes.

"Free booze or not, I vote we go back to Lucky's." Ben stares at us expectantly.

"Their pitchers are practically free." Quinn meanders in the direction of the glass entrance.

We follow him, exiting the open doors together with arms interlinked or thrown over shoulders.

Doesn't matter what the future holds for us.

For now we're here.

In the moment.

Together.

TUNES FOR MY MAGGIE MAY

America –This is Spinal Tap (11) Cracklin Rosie–Mr. Neil Diamond
More than This – Roxy Music *La vie en rose – Edith Piaf*
⚡All of My Love– Led Zepplin ★Lorelei –Cocteau Twins *
Veronica– Elvis Costello *and Betty...You can Call me Al– Paul Simon*
★Bonnie + Clyde– Serge Gainsbourg (He's French, oui, oui!) ✳
Nearly Lost You🌳Screaming Trees🌳Then She Did –Jane's Addiction
Romeo Had Juliette – Lou Reed *Downtown Train – Tom Waits
Angel – Rock God, Jimi Hendrix * C'est Si Bon – Eartha Kitt (meow🐱
Going, Going, Gone –The Posies * Suck You Dry – Mudhoney ♦♦
Rhinoceros ~ The Smashing Pumpkins * Black –Pearl Jam *
Thank Heavens for Little Girls– M. Chevalier (très creepy)
oh, L'amour – Erasure * It Ain't over til it's over –Lenny Kravitz

Hope you have an AWESOME year in Paris.

I'll miss you.

Gil

A NOTE FROM DAISY PRESCOTT

I HOPE YOU enjoyed *We Were Here*. If you're curious to find out what happens to these characters in the future, please read *Geoducks Are for Lovers*. Spoiler alert: *Geoducks* is a second chance love story.

Evergreen State College, and Speedy the geoduck, aka the best college mascot ever, were inspiration for my characters' alma mater in *Geoducks Are for Lovers*. In *We Were Here,* my characters attend a fictional version of Evergreen. If you're a Greener, you probably recognize some things and could point out dozens of details I got wrong. When I sat down to write *We Were Here*, I deliberately fictionalized some aspects of Evergreen and Olympia to fit these characters and their stories. I hope the spirit of the real Evergreen shines through in these stories. *Omnia Extares*!

ACKNOWLEDGMENTS

I'M MOST THANKFUL for the people who buy and read my books. That's you, dear reader.

With deepest gratitude and love to my husband for being my alpha reader and my greatest supporter. He kindly and generously lets me borrow some of his charm and wit for my male characters. Another special thank you for never asking how long I've been wearing the same leggings when I'm on deadline.

I'm forever grateful to my beloved friends and family. Thank you for continuing to champion my writing. Special thanks to the Lost Girls for your love and support—may our list of adventures continue to grow!

I'm indebted to my beta readers on this book, Helena and Julia. Your feedback is invaluable, as is your friendship. I'm blessed to be part of an amazing community of fellow authors and readers. Shout out to Ashley Pullo for early conversations about how to structure this story. Big thanks to Erika, Dianne, Traci, and Kelly for reading early drafts and loving these characters the same way I do. To all my readers in Daisyland, thank you for sharing part of your days with me. To the bloggers and reviewers, who tirelessly promote authors and books because they love reading, thank you for all of your hard work and support.

Gratitude to my editor Melissa Ringsted for correcting grammatical sins, and to Marla Esposito for her eagle-eye proofing. Any remaining errors are my own. Sarah Hansen at Okay Creations, thank you for another gorgeous cover. CA Borgford at Perfectly Publishable, you make the inside of my books so beautiful.

I'm blessed to have Stephanie Lapensee and KP Simmon at Inkslinger PR on my team, along with my agents, Flavia Viotti and Meire Dias at Bookcase Literary Agency, who continue to promote my work around the world.

I appreciate everyone who takes the time to read my books—it means the world to me.

Thank you for leaving a review or telling a friend about my books.

Hearing from my readers is the best part of publishing. I can be reached on social media or at *daisyauthor@gmail.com*.

~*Daisy*

About Daisy

USA TODAY BESTSELLING author Daisy Prescott has published five novels and five Modern Love Story Shorts. Her lucky number also happens to be five. She lives in a real life Stars Hollow in the Boston suburbs with her husband and their imaginary house goat. When not in her writing cave, she can be found traveling, gardening, baking, and talking about herself in the third person.

ALSO BY DAISY PRESCOTT

Modern Love Stories:
We Were Here
Geoducks Are for Lovers
Missionary Position
Happily Ever Now (Winter 2017)

Wingmen:
Ready to Fall
Confessions of a Reformed Tom Cat
Wingman #3 (Summer 2016)

Modern Love Story Shorts:
Take Two
Take the Cake
Take for Granted
Take it Easy
Give and Take